Praise

***Spellbound*–**

"The story is a mixture of history and present day, fantasy and real life, and is really well done. I especially liked the biting humor that pops up occasionally. The characters are vibrant and likable (except the bad guys, who are really nasty). There is a good deal of angst with both romances, but a lot of 'aww' moments as well."
—*Rainbow Reflections*

"*Spellbound* is a very exciting read, fast-paced, thrilling, funny too…The authors mix politics and the fight against patriarchy with time travel and witch fights with brilliant results."—*Jude in the Stars*

"[T]he themes and contextual events in this book were very poignant in relation to the current political climate in the United States. The fashion in which existing prejudices related to race, socioeconomic status, and gender were manipulated to cause discord were staggering, but also a reflection of the current state of things here in the USA. I really enjoyed this aspect of the book and I am so glad that I read it when I did."—*Mermaid Reviews*

The Ashford Place

"[A] charming story that I can recommend to anyone who likes a well-written mystery with a good dose of romance."—*Rainbow Reflections*

"Another enjoyable story from Jean Copeland with a bit of a difference. I think this book is definitely one to enjoy with a glass of wine near the warm fire."—*Les Rêveur*

The Revelation of Beatrice Darby

"*The Revelation of Beatrice Darby* at its epicentre is a story…of discovering oneself and learning to not only live with it but to also love it. This book is definitely worth a read."—*Lesbian Review*

"Debut author Jean Copeland has come out with a novel that is abnormally superb. The pace whirls like a hula-hoop; the plot is as textured as the fabric in a touch-and-feel board book. And, with more dimension than a stereoscopic flick, the girls in 3-D incite much pulp friction as they defy the torrid, florid, horrid outcomes to which they were formerly fated."—*Curve*

"This story of Bea and her struggle to accept her homosexuality and find a place in the world is absolutely wonderful…Bea was such an interesting character and her life was that of many gay people of the time—hiding, shame, rejection. In the end though it was uplifting and an amazing first novel for Jean Copeland."—*Inked Rainbow Reads*

The Second Wave

"This is a must-read for anyone who enjoys romances and for those who like stories with a bit of a nostalgic or historic theme." —*Lesbian Review*

"Copeland shines a light on characters rarely depicted in romance, or in pop culture in general."—*The Lesbrary*

"The characters felt so real and I just couldn't stop reading. This is one of those books that will stay with me a long time."—*2017 Rainbow Awards Honorable Mention*

Summer Fling

"The love story between Kate and Jordan was one they make movies about, it was complex but you knew from the beginning these women had found their soul mates in each other."—*Les Rêveur*

By the Author

The Revelation of Beatrice Darby

The Second Wave

Summer Fling

The Ashford Place

Spellbound

One Woman's Treasure

Swift Vengeance

Poison Pen

POISON PEN

To Sue -
Thanks so much for your support! So great to see you again! All my best -

by

Jean Copeland

BOLD STROKES BOOKS

2021

POISON PEN

ISBN 13: 978-1-63555-849-4

This Trade Paperback Original Is Published By
Bold Strokes Books, Inc.
P.O. Box 249
Valley Falls, NY 12185

First Edition: July 2021

Credits
Editor: Shelley Thrasher
Production Design: Stacia Seaman
Cover Design by Tammy Seidick

Acknowledgments

Thank you to Sandy Lowe and the entire crew at Bold Strokes Books for their continued indulgence in every one of my ideas.

Shelley Thrasher, my editor, you are awesome.

Thank you to my friend Alison for insisting that I name a main character after her. I quite like how cheeky she turned out.

And Erin Zak, thank you for the cover art brainstorming sesh.

And last but never least, thank you to all my readers! You are why my stories end up in print! So thank you, thank you!

In memory of my beloved father and greatest supporter.
Thank you for making me a dreamer just like you.

James P. Copeland
1932–2020

Chapter One

Kendra Blake smiled broadly after making the last change to the page proofs for her debut novel. She leaned back in her chair, sipped her cucumber water, and stroked Sergio, the office cat who'd been keeping her lap warm. What a euphoric feeling to see her own pseudonym under a manuscript title for a change. After the hundreds of other names that had passed her eyes during her long editing career at Labrys Publishing, seeing her own staring back was more than a bit surreal. She closed her eyes and tried to imagine what it would feel like once an actual copy of the book was in her hands.

"Kendra?" MJ called out from the reception area. "Yo, Kendra?" Apparently, she'd needed to call twice to snap Kendra out of her reverie.

"In here," she replied, still staring at *The End* on her computer screen.

MJ Del Vecchio, Kendra's best friend and owner of the small, boutique publishing house they ran together, sauntered in her office with her jacket draped on her forearm and her leather laptop bag slung over her shoulder. "What are you still doing here?"

"Having a moment." Kendra grinned. "At long last, the manuscript for *The Winding Road* is polished and complete."

MJ shifted her weight to one hip and stared at her like a mother witnessing her baby's first steps. "After all these years of being a copy editor and proofreader, you can finally call yourself an author." She moved toward her and raised her hand for a high five, which Kendra gladly returned. "I think I'm gonna cry."

"Please don't," Kendra said. "I heard you sniffling in there earlier over that corny Cheerios commercial."

MJ's lips scrunched into a pout. "But it was so cute how one minute that little girl was feeding her daddy Cheerios, and the next, she was driving off to college with a big box of it in her passenger seat."

Kendra smirked. MJ was a smooth butch anchored with a tough exterior and a resting bitch face that, on her, was utterly captivating. They well concealed the fact that, on the inside, she was the kindest, most sentimental person she'd ever known.

"I'll walk out with you." Kendra grabbed her purse, put Sergio in his carry bag, and opened the door.

MJ looked at her watch. "I'm heading out for what's left of happy hour. Want to join?"

"No, thanks. I'm kind of tired."

"It's six fifteen on a Friday," MJ said. "Come for one drink. We have to toast to your accomplishment."

"We will," Kendra said as they walked to their cars in the strip-mall parking lot. "Isn't next weekend that women's dance?"

"Yes…" MJ's eyes grew wide with cautious delight. "Are you gonna come?"

"Why not?" Kendra shrugged amiably. "It'll be fun being showered with free congratulatory drinks. I'll dust off my dancin' shoes for the occasion."

"A lot of hot women have RSVP'd to the invite." She gave Kendra a quick once-over from head to toe. "You better dust off more than your dancin' shoes."

"You act like it's been a hundred years since I've had a girlfriend."

"It has…in lesbian years."

Kendra narrowed her eyes. "Two years. That's all it's been." She paused. "Or three? I think it's three. Whatever. It's not a problem. I don't need a significant other to feel happy. Or complete."

"You're preaching to the choir. I love a strong, independent woman. But I also love sex, and it's much better with—"

"I know, I know," Kendra said. "Someone you love."

"No. I was going to say with someone *else*."

Kendra gifted MJ with a chuckle. "Well, don't knock self-love. The sex-toy industry has been very good to us single gals."

"Whatever floats your boat, girl." With a dismissive wave, she headed to her car. "Have a good weekend. Text me."

Kendra nodded and got into her car, careful to balance the cat in her passenger seat. "We don't need anybody else, do we, Senior Sergio?" she said as she drove out of the parking lot. "You're the boss of the office, and I'm a novelist now."

She smiled hearing herself say it out loud, even if it was only to the cat. Why had she waited so long to embark on fulfilling her dream? Now that the journey of crafting her first novel manuscript was over, it seemed silly that she'd made so many excuses in the past.

She sighed, a tad rueful that she hadn't found the confidence sooner, but she'd finally made it happen at forty-five. Yeah. Forty-five.

She looked at the cat through the mesh side of the bag. "Well, better late in the game than never at all. Right, Sergio?"

She drove on to a drive-through and picked up a sandwich for her and chicken nuggets for the cat. Who needed to go out to celebrate?

Alison Chatterley had come to America from the UK over a year ago. She'd worked as a live-in au pair for a wealthy American executive in London, and when he offered to bring her back to America with the family, she leapt at the opportunity. She'd intended to use her work visa with him as a stepping-stone to finding a job as a journalist here and eventual citizenship. As of yet, though, her plan hadn't panned out. She was growing more frustrated with her situation, especially since she'd indulged in what she thought would be a one-time sexual tryst with Mr. Dillford's wife, Vanessa. Sadly, as was often the case, her impetuous, ill-conceived plan had gone awry.

Once Mrs. Dillford had dabbled in the delights of woman-on-woman sex, Alison had become to her the proverbial Lay's potato chip. It was a problem.

"Is it though?" Alison's friend, Danni, asked as they chatted at a winery. "You have a blazing hot MILF chasing you out of the shower when her husband's off at work, and you're getting paid for it. Can we please trade problems?"

"You do realize you've just called me a prostitute."

"Did I?"

"Well, what else do you call a person who's paid to shag someone?"

Danni sighed. "After meeting Vanessa? Lucky."

"You're incorrigible." Alison laughed and flung her blond, wind-whipped tendrils away from her face. "I suppose I'm playing to the wrong audience. Any potentials on your dating site?"

Danni frowned, then sipped her wine and glanced out toward the vast expanse of grapevines.

"I dunno why you're so eager to cuff yourself into another relationship. You just got out of one."

Danni frowned again. "A six-month relationship, the longest I've ever had."

"All right, but you still get credit for time served."

"Alison." Danni sounded frustrated. "We're both thirtyish. I don't know about you, but I want to settle down and nest with someone, adopt some dogs I can put rain booties on, and spoon somebody when I go to sleep at night."

Alison tried to prevent her expression from revealing her true feelings about nesting. "You can spoon with the dog then, can't you?"

"You're getting laid. It's easy for you to be flip about my situation."

"Well, yes, I was getting laid, but it wasn't without complication. Do you know what would've happened if her husband had caught us? That wanker. I'd be deported, and so would my dream of becoming a respected journalist in America. That's why I cut her off weeks ago."

"How did this mess ever get started?"

"At first it was just some harmless flirting out of boredom. The husband is so caught up in his job he's hardly ever there. One night after the kids went to sleep, and I'd had a glass or two of chardonnay, I kissed her."

"What audacity," Danni said, grinning. "No wonder you guys ruled the world for centuries. And then what happened?"

"Well, I pulled her over to the sofa, and we started making out. All of a sudden, she began writhing beneath me, moaning like a woman possessed. I figured I'd started it, so I had to finish her. I didn't want to be rude."

"That's so British of you," Danni said.

"Afterward, it became a regular thing. Even now, she'll come up on me, and I can't shake her off. She's like a booger on one of her kid's fingers. Anyway, you know this story. Why are you asking me about it again?"

"Because I like it."

Alison stared at Danni's weird smile.

"You really should get out of there," Danni said. "Put in your notice. Sounds like you're being 'me-too-ed' in a major way."

"I'm working on it." Alison looked around and added in a soft, confessional tone, "Part of me likes it. She's a bit of a freak in bed, and it's a huge turn-on."

Danni shook her head. "You need to do something that will get you noticed in the news world. Freelance for magazines, apply to local newspapers."

"I've had three freelance articles published, but nothing's come of it. As for the newspapers, when I submit my resume, all I receive back are 'thank you, but it's not what we're currently looking for' emails."

"At least you have your blogs," Danni said.

"Right. Well, they're certainly getting seen, but I can't earn a living off the advertisers alone. It's expensive here in Connecticut, and so is a citizenship attorney, so if I'm to leave the Dillfords, it has to be for a well-paying position."

"Why don't you find a nice American woman, fall in love, and get married? Then your work visa won't be an issue. And you won't have to play Mrs. Dillford's whore anymore."

Alison shrieked with laughter. "Mrs. Dillford's whore? What a brilliantly clever name for a romance novel."

Danni laughed, too. "There you go. Forget journalism. Start writing romance novels. Look at Danielle Steel. She's a bah-jillionaire."

"I'd have to be rounded up by ICE before I'd consider churning out that rubbish."

"With your blond hair and blue eyes, you could host your own ICE raiding party, and they still wouldn't deport you."

"I suppose that's true, but my visa's expiring in a few months. I have to be employed to renew it."

"I know you'll land on your feet no matter what you decide." Danni nodded with confidence. "And don't tell me you're not into lesbian romance. I read your blog."

"Of course I'm into it. I'd just never want to be associated with writing it." Alison gave her a wink, and they enjoyed the rest of their bottle of red.

CHAPTER TWO

Kendra's friends had been pestering her to take her out for a pre-release celebration of her debut novel. Not only had they eagerly anticipated it, but they were also rejoicing that they'd be able to see her a little more often now that she'd finally finished it. Although she'd always been the classic, introverted book nerd, she was excited about going out with them. She had been neglecting them, her head buried in her manuscript for months, but they'd understood how much the process meant to her, and she loved them for it.

They parlayed the lesbian spring dance at the venue overlooking Long Island Sound into a soiree for Kendra. As MJ had noted, based on social-media responses, it would be well-attended, and Kendra's appearance there would satisfy her extrovert friends at least until early summer.

"I got your cover, Kendra," MJ said as she whipped out cash from her leather pants.

"Thanks. I'll buy your first drink," she replied, knowing that after the first round, MJ would disappear into the arms of some young… well, any attractive woman who couldn't resist her deep tan and sexy boi mojo.

"I'm so ready to get my groove on," said Violet. Their lanky blond friend was already grooving in place, ready to hit the dance floor and stay there all night.

Kendra scanned the crowd as they waited in the drink line. She recognized a lot of the women her own age and marveled at how much larger the baby-dyke crowd had gotten since she'd last gone to a dance.

"Nice turnout," MJ said. "You should've brought some of your bookmarks—do a little early direct marketing."

"That's not why I'm here," Kendra said. "We're here for a girls' night out, so try not to disappear on us."

MJ's eyes narrowed. "Look. You can't bring a sugar addict to a candy store and expect her not to get a little lost in the merchandise."

"I think I see Tanisha out on the dance floor," Violet said. "Bring my drink out to me?" She jetted off, and the gyrating crowd swallowed her up.

"You can't take off yet, MJ. Someone has to help me carry the drinks."

MJ winked, apparently limbering up her flirt game for the evening. "I got you, girl."

After dispensing the drinks, Kendra found a table near the dance floor and sat keeping an eye on everyone's jackets and cell phones as she people-watched. She admired her friends—Violet for her blissful obliviousness in the throes of rhythm and MJ for her ability to connect with women so naturally—too naturally, sometimes. Would MJ ever find a woman who'd inspire her to settle down again?

As Kendra sipped her old-fashioned, she also wondered if she'd ever stop being ambivalent about relationships of her own. She'd had a couple of long-term ones that met traditional demises, and now in her mid-forties, she could take them or leave them. Although she wasn't too jaded, she'd always been plagued by trust issues, whether conscious of that tendency or not. If she ever were to take that leap again, the woman was going to have to be pretty special.

When Alison wandered into the elegant banquet facility, the house music's thrumming bass reached her out in the lobby as she waited to pay the cover. Danni hadn't answered her texts about meeting her there, but Alison wasn't concerned about going alone. She was bound to run into women she knew from the lesbian activity group she'd joined soon after arriving in the States. The group kept her informed of local happenings, which enabled her get out of the Dillford house in the evenings once she was off duty. She'd put her phone on Do Not Disturb to avoid any temptation to reply to Mrs. Dillford. Lately, Vanessa had taken to faking a domestic crisis or two to get her home early on her nights out.

After a couple of hours of mixing and mingling, dancing and drinking, she was ready for a dose of fresh air. As she walked toward the patio exit, she spotted a middle-aged woman sitting by herself at a table piled with other people's belongings. She obviously wasn't there alone, but why was a woman that hot sitting by herself? Of course. Her wife must be on the dance floor with some of their mates.

Without further thought, she stepped out onto the deck into the chill of a spring night and watched the waves undulate under a full moon. Now it made sense why she felt off, a bit restless in both her private and professional lives. That crafty moon. After inhaling the crisp night air, she went back inside, making it a point to pass by the hot woman's table. By then she was standing with a short, butch brunette. The elusive girlfriend? But their body language and proximity suggested they were merely friends. She strode by slowly enough to catch the other woman's eye, and when she had it, Alison smiled with a lingering glance that lasted several paces. The woman smiled back, then did a double take. Hmm. Was that a double take of interest or a double take of *what's this mutant creature staring at*? Alison smiled to herself as she headed to the bar. Whoever this woman was, she would have to get to the bottom of that mystery by last call.

❖

MJ nudged Kendra in the arm. "Did you catch that young blond chick checking you out?"

"I'm not blind." She tried to act cool, but inside it tickled her that she'd attracted the attention of a much-younger woman.

"Move your ass and go talk to her, ask her to dance."

"Simmer down," Kendra said. "Just because someone smiles at me I'm gonna go chase after her? Seems kind of desperate."

MJ elbowed her playfully. "I said ask her to dance, not smother her with a chloroform rag. Jesus."

"She's too young anyway."

"No, she's not. And who cares about age? She's hot."

"I care when the woman is in her twenties."

"No way. She has to be in her mid-thirties if she's a day."

"Get out of here. Not even close." Kendra stifled a yawn. "Are you ready to go yet?"

MJ consulted her watch. "No, Cinderella. And neither is Violet." She bobbed her head toward the dance floor.

Violet was clearly feeling her cocktails along with the beat of the music. Kendra slumped down in her chair.

"If you wanna go, we can get a car home."

"I can't leave you guys," Kendra said. "Violet would never forgive me."

MJ glanced toward the dance floor. "Trust me. She's not going to remember much, so do as you will."

Kendra grinned. "I'll get a soda, then hit the road. Keep an eye on her." She flicked her head toward Violet.

"Aye, aye, Captain," MJ replied.

As Kendra made her way to the bar, she covertly scanned the crowd for the young blonde who was entirely unfamiliar with the subtle approach. The bartender slid a Diet Coke toward her, but when she tried to pay, the bartender said her drink was already covered.

"By who?" Kendra asked.

"Some pretty femme. Blonde in a blue jacket."

"Thanks." Kendra left a couple of singles on the bar and embarked on a mission to find the kid and thank her for her generosity.

She stepped to the edge of the dance floor and noticed her dancing with Violet. That was fast. A twinge of regret crawled under her skin. Had she missed a chance at something she hadn't known she wanted? As she watched the girl grind against her friend, she thought how they would've made an attractive pair—fair-haired look-alikes about a decade apart. Good for Violet.

Kendra turned and headed toward the exit, placing her empty glass on a nearby table. Before she'd reached the foyer area, someone tapped her shoulder. When she turned around, she was dazzled by the young woman's smile.

"You weren't going to pull an Irish good-bye then, were you?"

Whaaat? Was that a British accent? No way! Kendra fell immediately in love with the young woman's voice.

"My friends knew I was on my way out," Kendra said in a half giggle. "I wanted to thank you for the drink, but I didn't want to cut in on you and Violet."

"That's your friend? She's quite a good dancer."

"Yes. She is."

"I bet you've got some moves yourself then, haven't you?"

Kendra tried not to swoon over the accent, but she was failing. "How old are you?"

The woman seemed to wince at the terse question. "Old enough to be here."

"I know that," Kendra said. "I was just curious."

"And why might you be curious about that?" Alison was so making use of those long, mascaraed eyelashes.

Kendra pretended to survey the crowd. "Just making conversation."

"Well, then let's start with names. I'm Alison." She extended a hand.

"Kendra," she replied as she slipped her hand into Alison's.

"Pleasure to meet you, Kendra." She cocked her head to the side. "I noticed you were here with others but are leaving alone. Is it because you have someone waiting at home?"

"If I did, I wouldn't be letting you flirt with me." Kendra surprised herself with her retort. That definitely wasn't like her. She might have been done with her novel, but her love of creating flirty character dialogue seemed to be on autopilot.

"Okay. You got me. I was flirting," Alison said. "A little."

"Fine job," Kendra replied and avoided eye contact by glancing around again. Apparently, she was good for only one quality comeback per scene.

"Any chance you might stay on for one more drink?"

Kendra shrugged. Actually, she suddenly wasn't in such a rush to leave. But she wasn't going to let Alison to know that.

"Oh, come on. Maybe I can help you meet someone. See anyone you like?"

"I don't know," Kendra said shyly. She couldn't help grinning at the quirky approach.

Alison studied her, almost boring into her soul with her eyes. "The place is mobbed. Isn't there anyone here you fancy?"

Kendra shook her head, willing her face to appear indifferent.

"You can't be serious. There's nobody here that you fancy?"

Under pressure, Kendra pointed to a middle-age brunette who happened to be walking away from the bar. "Maybe her?"

"Her?" Alison seemed aghast. "She looks just like you. What are you, some sort of narcissist?"

Kendra took a step back. This conversation was getting away from her. "I, uh, no, but um, I'm not looking for anyone at the moment."

Alison's frown screamed pity. "Oh. Just out of a horrid affair then?"

"No, actually. My last relationship ended pretty amicably a few years ago." Kendra was usually good at reading people's expressions, but Alison appeared thoroughly perplexed.

"So it just ended?" Alison's eyebrows crinkled as she seemed to puzzle it out. "You decided it wasn't working anymore and then off you went?"

"No. We made the decision together, and she moved out."

"Fascinating," Alison said. "I wasn't aware relationships could end without heaps of drama."

Intrigued, Kendra attempted to do the mental math on Alison. "Where did you say you're from?"

"I didn't say, but I'm from the UK. Milton Keynes to be precise."

"Cool. So, yeah. I try to do everything in my life drama-free. I'm too old for games and insincere people. To be honest, I kind of always have been."

"I'd say you're not too old for anything, but it's refreshing to meet someone who's anti-drama. I'd rather like to text you sometime, if that'd be all right." Alison's face melted into a warm smile.

"Uh." Kendra stared at her as though this direct in-person, face-to-face interaction was something out of a sci-fi novel.

Alison stared back expectantly. "It's a yes-or-no question, but please don't feel obligated. It was lovely to meet you."

"No. Wait," Kendra said as Alison turned to leave. "I'm, uh, yeah, sure, you can have my number." Feeling awkward, she offered a faint smile.

"I promise I won't post it on the bathroom wall." Alison added a sly grin.

Kendra glanced at her in amusement as she entered her digits into Alison's phone.

"Good night, Ms. Kendra." Alison's hand lingered on hers as she took her phone back.

"Good night, Ms. Alison."

They stood for an extended moment, neither seeming willing to break eye contact first. When Kendra's teeth started going dry from smiling so long, she snapped out of it and headed out.

Walking to her car, she thought about that random encounter. Alison was obviously too young for her, but she certainly was intriguing. Her self-assured, no-nonsense approach was refreshing and a perfect match to Kendra's natural social reticence. She seemed to draw out a flirtation and self-confidence in Kendra she'd forgotten she had. Or maybe never knew she'd had.

Meh. Don't go getting too jubilant, she warned herself. She probably wouldn't even contact her. But if she did, she'd try to reserve judgment and see what came of it.

She studied her eyes in her rearview mirror before driving off. Things were changing in her professional life. Why not in her romantic world, too?

CHAPTER THREE

The next morning Alison awoke with a sense of relief. Mr. Dillford was actually gracing his family with his presence, so that left her the entire Sunday to enjoy for herself. She was meeting Danni for breakfast, and then they were going on a hike near the falls. Among their conversation topics, she was most eager to regale her about the older woman she'd met at the dance the night before.

"Sounds like a fab time. I should've gone," Danni said, more focused on the smiley face she was tracing in her plate with the ketchup squeeze bottle.

"I told you it would be a fab time," Alison said in a huff. "I don't know why you never listen to me."

"I wanted to go," Danni said in a nasal voice, "but I was with my nieces, and the day just got away from me."

"How does any entire day get away from you? I'd only texted you three times yesterday. Why don't you pick up your phone once in a while?"

"What did I miss?"

"The DJ was fantastic, and the place was brimming with lovelies of all ages. In fact, I met one quite attractive older woman called Kendra and got her number. I might just ring her up."

"How old?"

"I dunno. Forty maybe. Should it make a difference?"

Danni shrugged. "You should stick to your own age. Older women are far less likely to let you get away with your usual shenanigans."

"What do you mean? I'm not looking for shenanigans. If anything,

I'm looking to avoid shenanigans. I just thought she was beautiful, and she seemed pleasant enough."

"How would you explain Mrs. Dillford to her?"

"I'm bloody well not going to. That's how."

"You'd just lie to this poor, unsuspecting older lady?"

"What do you say it like that for? She's not a grandmama whose life savings I'm looking to nick. For fuck's sake. She's like forty. Anyway, I've cut Vanessa off. I think she's finally gotten the hint."

"Finally. If she likes women so much, let her get out there and put in the work to find one like the rest of us."

"I don't think she likes them enough to disrupt her situation. But that's not my problem anymore."

"Good. So did you stalk this woman on Facebook yet? Do you have a picture of her?"

Alison frowned. "I didn't think to ask her last name, just her first—Kendra. What a splendid name," she added, dreamily. "I suppose I'll have to do this one the old-fashioned way and find out details about her from her on an actual date."

"You can't do that," Danni said. "Nobody does that here. You have to skulk through her social-media pages and find out who her friends are and what celebs she follows. Find an unflattering picture or two to prove she's human. How are you even going to know if she has a sense of humor if you don't see what kinds of memes she posts?"

"If you find out all that beforehand, what are you supposed to talk about on the date?"

"I don't know," Danni said somberly. "I usually don't get that far."

"Well, that's brilliant." Alison lamented the last five minutes of her life wasted on discussing dating with Danni. She loved her American friend dearly, but the girl was definitely orbiting in her own galaxy. "Are we going on this hike or not?"

"Yes." Danni signaled for their waitress. "While we're walking, maybe you can give me some of your secret tips on how to attract women."

Oh, dear. Where would she even begin? She immediately noted Danni's bushy eyebrows and unkempt hair stuffed under a Yale baseball cap. A makeover and quite possibly a personality transplant were in order if she wanted to start living her best post-graduate life beyond the research lab.

She decided to keep it simple. "It's no secret, really. You might start by getting out of your gym clothes once in a while."

"They're not gym clothes." Danni's voice was tinged with indignation. "This is called leisure wear."

Alison surveyed her outfit as they stood to leave. "That's a little bit too leisure for me, but you could at least match your socks, then, couldn't you?"

"Fashion coordination takes time. My work as a color creator for cosmetics takes up a lot of my mental energy."

Alison noticed the dark circles under Danni's eyes. "Does Revlon let you take home any samples, then?"

Danni's jaw hung. "Now my face isn't good enough either?"

"I didn't say that. But you asked me for advice, didn't you? Your face is fine, adorable, but a little mascara and lip gloss with a dash of color to it wouldn't kill you."

"I don't do mascara and lipstick," Danni said primly. "I prefer the natural look. I'm a ChapStick lesbian."

"Well, you're not any type of lesbian if you never go out with women. It's like keeping a Ferrari locked up in your garage and calling yourself a race-car driver."

"Now you're just being cruel. I suddenly get why your blog is so popular." Danni turned her nose up in the air and left the diner.

Alison chased her to the car and gently turned her around. "Danni, I don't know why you ask me questions like that in the first place. You're perfect just the way you are. Frankly, I'm surprised I haven't fallen in love with you yet."

Danni demurred from the compliment, and Alison knew by the blush on her cheeks she'd patched up their row before it had gone too far.

"All right?" Alison asked in her sweetest tone.

Danni nodded with an endearing smile.

"Brilliant. Off we go, then," Alison said.

As they drove away, Alison wondered if sometimes she wasn't a little too honest for her own good.

❖

After completing her Saturday morning chores, including tending to Sergio and her own pets, two Iguanas named Lois and Harriet, Kendra took a ride to visit her younger brother, Ryan, at the animal shelter. Between his responsibilities as animal-control officer and the dad of two young athletes, she hardly got any quality sibling bonding time with him.

They sat around his desk drinking the coffees she'd picked up on the way. As he gabbed away, she studied his rugged face and broad shoulders in his uniform, his long legs poking out sideways from his desk. Behind it all, she still saw the twelve-year-old boy who needed the emotional shelter of his big sister after their mother's illness had finally taken her away from them.

"Are you listening to me?" he asked, scratching at his goatee.

"Yes." She tried to head him off. "You said Hayden wants to try out for the state traveling league."

"I said he did. We're waiting to hear back so we can figure out the logistics."

"That's exciting. I'm sure he'll make it. He's a great ball player."

Ryan beamed with pride as he crossed his fingers. "And Alyssa's team is looking strong this season. They definitely have a shot at going all the way."

"I know. She was breathless telling me about it on the phone."

"I love her enthusiasm," he said. "She's convinced she can do anything her older brother can."

"That's because you encourage that in her, as any great dad would."

He seemed to revel in his sister's approval. "So when is the book coming out?"

"Its official release is in two and half months, but when I get my author copies, I'll give you the first one."

"No freebies," he said. "I want to order my sister's book online like every other fan."

"Just don't forget it's under Meredith Hodges."

"Yeah. I don't get that. You wait your whole life to make this happen, and then you don't even put your own name on it? Nobody's gonna know it's you."

"The important people will. Anyway, I've wanted to honor Mom this way as long as I've dreamed of writing a novel."

"She sure did love to read," Ryan said, sounding pensive. "She'd find it really cool that you chose to use her maiden name."

"Thanks," Kendra said, warmed by her brother's validation. "I always thought she had the kind of name that belonged on a theater marquee or something. *Meredith Hodges*," she added dreamily.

He agreed. "Does Dad know about your pen name?"

She shrugged. "Who even says more than hello or good-bye to him?"

"I do, because he likes to come to the kids' games."

She arched an eyebrow. "Hard to believe the second Mrs. Blake allows it."

"By this stage in their marriage I think she encourages it," he said as he tapped a pencil on a notepad.

"Great. Well, I don't have any little jocks to win him over with, and since I don't see either one of them reading lesbian fiction any time soon, I guess we'll be keeping it status quo."

"I don't think you need to perform any great act of heroism to impress him these days. He's mellowed out. They both have."

She finished her coffee and tossed the cup in the trash. "Why are you telling me this?"

"The season starts soon," Ryan said casually as he stood and stretched. "Why don't you come by and actually sit with the family for a change?"

Kendra felt her feathers ruffle. It had been decades since she had anything that would qualify as a relationship with her father. A lot of time had passed, and a lot of trauma still lay buried. He was not a subject she enjoyed talking about. How could Ryan be so nonchalant about him coming back into his and his kids' lives as if nothing went down between them in the years after their mom died?

"Send me the schedule," she said, totally unenthused. "I'll have to check my availability."

"Why? Are you going on some world book tour that'll keep you away all summer?"

"I wish," she muttered. "Do you want my help hosing down the kennels or not?"

"Yes, I do. You're my most reliable volunteer."

"Fine," she said sternly, her emotional guard firmly in place. "Let's get to it."

"Yes, ma'am," he replied with a salute.

She smiled when he turned away and followed him into the kennel area. What a great guy he'd turned out to be. Her debut novel would always be her second greatest achievement.

❖

It had been a week since meeting Kendra, but Alison hadn't yet texted her. She'd picked up the phone several times with the intention. She'd even composed two practice texts. But the actual one that would make the connection was still rattling around in her brain. To her, Kendra was a unique find. Alison had come to know many women in her short time in the US—pretty ones, sexy, older, intelligent, charismatic—but never were all of those qualities packaged up quite so nicely in the same woman.

She looked at the clock. Soon she had to leave to pick up the children from school, and then Vanessa, er, Mrs. Dillford, would be home from her "work" at some charitable foundation she was elected to head after several sizable donations. If she wanted to send the text with a clear head, she'd better get on it.

When she picked up her phone, her damp palms surprised her. Blimey. What was she so nervous about? It's not like this was her first time asking a woman for a date. She'd texted women she'd just met numerous times. But this one was different. She knew that from the moment they'd locked eyes.

She started pacing the family room with phone in hand, rehearsing out loud what to write. "Hey, Kendra. It's Alison from the dance…" No. That's lame, she thought. "Hello, Kendra. It's me, Alison. How'd you like to…" *That's awful, too.*

She looked down, surprised to see her hands shaking. What was happening? She was acting like a teenage bloke asking his first girl to a dance. Besides, the woman was miles away, not standing directly in front of her. What's the worst that could happen sending a "hello, how are you" text anyway?

Oh, hell. What if Kendra hadn't even given her the correct number? Now that she thought about it, she had handed it over without much of a fuss. Well then, she might as well end the suspense by texting her and getting it over with.

❖

Kendra was at her desk at work staring at her large desktop monitor, reading the same dull paragraph for the third time. She couldn't seem to keep her mind on her task, for a variety of reasons.

MJ knocked on her slightly open door and came in. "You're quiet in here. Plotting out your next great work of fiction?"

"I wish." Kendra reclined in her ergonomic chair. "It's funny how boring a technical brochure is to write and edit after composing an all-consuming fictional romance."

MJ nodded. "That's a big part of how we earn a living, so hopefully you'll regain your passion for it soon."

"Don't worry. It's still important to me. The nice part is that I don't get all sentimental and weepy writing about how effective an industrial lubricant is in cutting down on heat during the grinding process."

"Are you referring to lesbian romance or machining operations?"

Kendra giggled. "Touché."

"Here." MJ handed her phone to her. "You left this on the coffee table out there, and it sounds like you're getting texts."

Kendra pressed the home button and saw that she had indeed received some texts: one from her niece, one from the pharmacy, and one from an unknown number. She opened that one first. "What do you know? It's from that girl, Alison, from the dance." She looked up at MJ with what had to be the goofiest grin.

"Really?" MJ narrowed her eyes. "The one you were all blasé about because she's too young?"

"I never said her attention wasn't flattering." She struggled to keep a huge smile from swallowing up her face. "And the fact that she actually followed through is kind of impressive."

MJ stared at her expectantly. "Are you going to tell me what she said?"

"Oh, yeah. She wants to know if I want to chat sometime." She glanced at the message again. "Either through text or in person."

"She's brazen," MJ said with a lascivious grin. "I like her already. Meet her somewhere," she added as she plopped in the chair by Kendra's desk.

Kendra absently fiddled with her phone. "I don't know. I don't think I'd want to let it go that far."

MJ rolled her eyes. "You know I say this out of love, but you don't have anything else to do. What have you got to lose?"

Kendra tried to remain patient with her friend. "I have plenty of things to do, you ass face. And of course, I say that out of love."

After a giggle, MJ persisted. "She's a beautiful woman. Why aren't you open to even a coffee date? Those are super low-risk."

"I don't want to lead her on. I've never dated a younger woman before, and I don't think it's for me." Her response was reflexive, but even she wasn't entirely convinced.

"Kendra." MJ sat forward and stared at her gravely. "Have you really given up like this? Don't you have one last fight in you? Christ, we're only in our mid-forties. We're not ancient."

"I'll bet you she's thirty at the most. What could we possibly have in common?"

"You could have a ton of things. But you won't know that unless you sit and have a conversation with her. That's not leading her on."

"No?"

MJ scoffed. "Not even close. Maybe you two will hit it off, or maybe you won't. Either way, meeting her for coffee for an hour is a no-brainer."

Kendra exhaled. She couldn't refute MJ's logic. A tug-of-war raged inside her, but she couldn't decide which side she should root for.

"Look," MJ said as she stood. "I know you're fine being single and that maybe this girl won't be your cup of tea, but the universe basically dropped an opportunity in your lap. Shouldn't you show your gratitude to the goddesses by seeing it through with one cup of a caffeinated beverage?"

"No fair invoking the goddesses," Kendra said.

"Desperate times, my friend." MJ winked and breezed out of her office.

Kendra reread Alison's text, then added her name and number to her contacts, a move that surely would've won MJ's approval. After listening to make sure MJ wasn't lurking outside in the common area, she replied to Alison's text.

CHAPTER FOUR

At around eleven p.m. Kendra finally climbed into bed. She should've been deep into REM sleep by then, but thoughts of Alison kept dancing around in her head. After she'd returned her initial text the other day, they'd been regularly exchanging playful banter. It felt nice to be a focus of someone's attention again, even if it was just through texts.

She took Lois and Harriet out of their tank to crawl around on the covers with her for a while and giggled as Harriet crawled over Lois and sat on her head. "Hey, you." She picked up the iguana and stared into its golden eyes. "We'll have none of that on my watch."

The sudden sound of the FaceTime ring startled her. Alison was FaceTiming her. Should she answer? She looked horrible. Her makeup was off, and her hair hadn't been touched since that morning. She couldn't *not* answer, but was she ready to have Alison see her in her natural state before seeing her at her best?

Her curiosity was piqued.

"Hello there," she said in an almost whisper. The greeting came out sounding mysterious as she kept the phone up and away from a full face shot.

"Hello yourself. Hope you don't mind, but I wanted to say good night." Alison came across sexier than ever, all sleepy-eyed with her voice soft and raspy.

"How could I mind that? It's sweet."

"I'm glad you think so. Any chance I can talk to you and not just your forehead? Although it is a handsome forehead."

Kendra laughed. Alison's sense of humor had revealed itself throughout the week, making her seem far more approachable than at the dance. "I'm not suitable for FaceTiming right now. I'm in bed."

"Oh. I didn't wake you, did I?"

"No, no. I was just giving my iguanas some exercise." Ugh. While she couldn't tell Alison she was wide-awake thinking of her, did she have to go right to the iguanas? She gathered them up and put them in their tank for the night.

"And how do you do that? Put them on leashes and take them for a jog?"

"That's not a bad idea. But it would probably be too hard to keep up."

"I dunno know about that. They can probably scamper along quite quickly on those little legs."

"I was talking about me."

Alison broke into a high-pitched giggle reminiscent of a character in one of the British sitcoms Kendra enjoyed watching. "That's brilliant. But something tells me your legs could get the job done as well."

Kendra tilted the phone up when she felt a blush break out on her cheeks. How had someone so young cultivated that level of confidence? "So I know I've asked this before, but I don't believe you ever answered me. How old are you?"

"That depends."

"On what?"

"Whether or not you're interested in younger women."

"I guess that depends," Kendra replied with a flirty lilt.

"Oh? On what?"

"How young."

"Cheeky. You're very cheeky," Alison said. "All right. I'm thirty-two, well beyond the cradle-robbing years."

"Yes, thankfully," Kendra said. "So, what did you mean by am I 'interested' in younger women?"

"Oh, em, I just meant I was wondering if you'd be interested in meeting me for coffee some night. Remember? That's why I texted you the other day."

"Yes. I remember."

"So can I pencil you in for this week? Like tomorrow night?"

Kendra's stomach fluttered. This was actually happening. No

more hiding behind the calculated wordplay texting afforded. They'd be sitting across from each other, unable to control things with thoughtfully chosen words or a carefully angled phone camera. Oh, how she'd always dreaded first dates—those and job interviews. The idea of serving herself up on a platter for inspection and then judgment…She shuddered.

"Sure. Coffee sounds great," she said, forcing herself to sound cool. "You know that coffeehouse in the center of Branford?"

"Yes. I love it there."

"Perfect. I'll see you tomorrow, then."

"How about around seven?"

"Great. Looking forward to it."

"Me, too." Kendra cringed. Why was she feeling so awkward about arranging a simple coffee date?

Alison stared at her screen quietly, smiling slightly. But there was definitely something more in that smile—something inviting, something absolutely enticing.

Oh, no. Was this the "who's gonna hang up first" dance? She couldn't bear the intensity in Alison's gorgeous eyes any longer. "Well, good night."

"It certainly ended up being one. Sweet dreams," Alison said and ended the call.

Kendra stared across her dimly lit bedroom at nothing in particular, clutching her warm phone. Despite her dread for first dates, the idea of meeting Alison in the relaxed atmosphere of her favorite coffeehouse filled her with positivity about the date. Whatever this was or would lead to, she certainly wanted to know more about Alison.

The next evening, Alison had the phone on her bathroom vanity as she applied the finishing touches to her makeup. She'd hoped Vanessa wouldn't notice the extra pizzazz she gave her eyes and hair for her date with Kendra. One of the things she'd hated most was having to explain herself to others. First, she could never figure out why people required others to explain themselves, and secondly, she wasn't very good at it. Growing up, her mum and dad had been strict on her and her siblings, her dad an officer in the British Navy, and her mum, a harried housewife left to raise three children while her husband was at sea for months at a time.

"You're such a willful child," her mum would bark at her whenever she'd refused to comply with her in-home martial law. Alison was a free spirit by nature and resented ever since she could remember her mother's attempts to cage her.

After years of tearful threats to her mother that she would run away from home, she'd made good on them at eighteen when she'd left for university, eventually becoming an au pair as a means to avoid returning to parental oppression.

Ironically, she currently found herself under an oppression of a different kind with her sex-crazed employer.

"I can't believe Kendra agreed to go out with you," Danni said on speaker.

Alison grabbed the phone and turned down the volume. "Let's not discuss this now. I don't want our conversation overheard. And what do you mean, you can't believe it? What's wrong with me?"

"Nothing's wrong with you, but I checked out her Facebook page, and she seems pretty buttoned-up. Not much happening there. Does she know you have a wild side?"

"I used to have a wild side, and no, that's not something we delved into in our conversations up to now."

"I don't know if you can say you 'used to' so soon," Danni said. "It's only been, what, a week since you actually stopped sleeping with Vanessa?"

"No way," Alison said. "I broke it off with her over a month ago." She then stopped applying her mascara to reflect. "Of course, then we had breakup sex. Then the week after that, we had 'are you sure we're truly broken up' sex. Then the week after that it was the official 'one last time, but we can never do this again' sex."

"So then a week."

"Two weeks, but I suppose you can spin it any way you want…" Alison grimaced at her, then finished her eyes.

"I guarantee you that's how Vanessa sees it."

"I told her I'm meeting you. That's all she needs to know." She was about to apply a light lipstick but decided she'd do it in the car. No need to set off any alarms with Vanessa. "I'm off. Wish me luck."

"Good luck," Danni said. "You're gonna need it."

"Pish posh," Alison replied. "Talk to you later." She stuffed her makeup back in the vanity drawer and headed out of her bedroom. She tiptoed down the staircase toward the front door.

"Oh. I thought you'd left already."

Alison swung around to see Vanessa standing in the great hallway with a hand on her hip. "Nope. I'm leaving now, as you can see."

"You look gorgeous. Got yourself all dolled up for Danni?" Vanessa moved toward her with the stealth of a lioness approaching a gazelle that had wandered off from the herd.

"This is hardly dolled up. Just going out for coffee. No biggie."

"You're not going for coffee with Danni." She and Alison were now nose to nose.

Alison sighed. "Fine. I'm meeting Kendra, the woman I met at the dance."

"I knew it." Vanessa pursed her lips as jealousy roared in her eyes like flames. "Your bed sheets haven't even gotten cold yet."

"What have my bed sheets got to do with anything? I'm having coffee. That's all." Alison disliked having to play down her feelings about the evening. She was quite hopeful the encounter would lead to something much more. But since Vanessa had revealed her emotional volatility several weeks earlier, this was the most expedient way to deal with it until she was ready to move out.

"Okay." Vanessa eyed her with suspicion and a fake smile. "Let me know how it goes—friend to friend, of course."

Alison returned the suspicion through narrowed eyes. This seemed way too easy. "Right then. Have a great evening."

"Mmm-hmm. You, too."

After Alison shut the door, she exhaled. That went better than she'd anticipated, but she had a feeling it wouldn't be the end of it. Damn it. The ambush had dampened her armpits. She hurried to her car flapping her arms like a bird, then applied her lip gloss as she drove.

❖

Kendra sat at a small table in the coffeehouse, her posture perfect, as she waited for Alison. She'd arrived a few minutes early, and after downing a nip of Jim Beam Honey in her car, she wanted to get started on a hazelnut latte to kill any lingering aroma of alcohol on her breath.

The shot was to calm nerves that were agitating all day in anticipation of their get-together. It's not that she expected anything to come of it, but even low-to-no expectations didn't exempt her from the classic first-date jitters.

Was it an actual date? The word was never uttered, so…Whatever it was, Kendra looked forward to listening to Alison's accent, which sounded sort of like Ringo Starr rounded a corner and smashed into Julie Andrews.

When she finally walked through the door, Kendra did a double take. She'd forgotten how striking Alison was in person. Or maybe at the dance, in the flashing, flickering lights, she hadn't been able to take in the full picture.

As Alison approached the table, her wispy blond hair danced just above her shoulders, and her smile grew a bit wider with each forward step.

"Nice to see you in 3D again," she said as she gave Kendra a light hug. She placed her bedazzled wristlet on the table as she sat. "I hope I haven't kept you waiting long."

"Not at all. I got here a little early." Kendra stood there thinking definitely more Julie than Ringo. "What can I get you?"

Alison peeked into her large, half-full mug. "What you're having looks good. I'll take one of those."

After lingering on Alison's dazzling smile for an extra second, Kendra went up to the counter. When she realized she'd been holding back a smile of her own, she sent off a quick text to MJ saying the "family emergency" phone call was not going to be necessary.

Initially, Kendra had prepared herself for a one-and-done event. The age difference was pretty hefty, so the odds were that they would enjoy a light conversation, then be on their separate ways, each with a new friend for their collections.

To her surprise, the night had flown by as they chatted. They'd moved to a comfy, well-worn leather sofa and continued talking long after the residue on their second round of lattes had hardened inside the cups.

"I think we have time for one more before they close," Kendra said.

"I'll have to switch to decaf," Alison said. "I've got a long day with the sproggies tomorrow, and if I have another of these, I'll never nod off."

Kendra laughed. "Sproggies? Are those kids or dogs?"

"I suppose it could go either way in that house, but I was referring to the children."

"How old are they?"

"The boy is twelve and the little girl is nine. Even though they can be rather rambunctious, they're actually quite polite in spite of their privilege and their mum and dad's hands-off parenting style."

"They should be polite. They have their own personal Nanny McPhee to keep them in line." Kendra giggled at what she thought was a witty reference.

Alison stared at her blankly.

"I mean without the tooth and the hairy mole," she said. She then went in for the save. "Emma Thompson is very attractive."

"Em, yes, she is," Alison replied. "I just hadn't seen the film."

"Oh. Well, it was more than one…never mind." Kendra cringed. The one time she attempted a perfectly timed joke, she ended up bombing. She was already back to hating first dates.

"I've gone on about myself long enough," Alison said. "I want to know more about you, Kendra."

When Alison spoke, she looked directly in Kendra's eyes, as if hearing her responses was vital to national security or something. It was a tad unsettling, maybe because no one that she could recall had ever seemed so genuinely interested in her.

"Well, as I mentioned earlier, I work as an editor and technical writer for my friend MJ's small publishing firm, and I also help her run the day-to-day aspects of it."

"Have you been an editor long?" Alison asked with the finesse of James Lipton.

"Since I graduated college back in ninety-something. What else was I supposed to do with a BA in English? My advisor said I should go into teaching, but the thought terrified me. Standing in front of a room full of kids every day?" She quivered as if a nor-easterly wind blew through the coffeehouse. "But I love my job. I get to read and write by myself each day."

"You sound like a true introvert."

"I guess so." Kendra paused in thought. "And then when you add that I live with my two pet iguanas and have a cat as a part-time roommate, my life sounds even sadder."

Alison laughed loudly. "Why is the cat only a part-time roommate?"

"He's the office cat, a stray we found in the strip-mall parking lot when he was a kitten. I take him home on the weekends so he's not lonely. Do you like animals?"

"Yes. I love them. But in my current living situation, there are two testy Pomeranians that I try to avoid at all cost. Dreadful, yappy little creatures." Alison seemed to drift off momentarily, muttering, "I suppose it's true what they say about dogs taking on the traits of their owners."

"Your job must be interesting," Kendra said. "If you like kids."

"The kids are fine. It's the bloody parents who drive me bonkers. Hopefully, it won't be for much longer. I'm long overdue to start on my next career. I've got a few prospects I'm pursuing."

"What kind of writing do you want to do?"

"General news reporting and pop culture have always been my interest, but I have to say, your American politics are utterly fascinating. I've written a couple of freelance articles, but I want to establish myself with a news outlet so I can build a professional reputation."

"You certainly have your work cut out for you if you're trying to make sense of our politics."

"I love that about writing, the challenge of trying to make sense of everything, even the senseless."

Kendra smiled at their kindred connection. "Other than MJ, I've never met anyone who shared my love for the written word."

"Yes, I thought of that straight away when you said you're in publishing." Alison's round eyes sparkled. "I suppose it was fate that I crossed your path at the dance."

The flirtation in her voice chased Kendra's gaze down into her lap. "I suppose it was," she said, striving against her shyness.

"Then if I ever need help editing my copy, I can hire your services?"

"Of course," Kendra said, playing along. "I'll even give you a discount."

"Ooh, that's lovely, but I'd insist on compensating you properly. Wouldn't want to create an international incident."

Kendra's stomach fluttered with delight. Whatever Alison was stirring in her was way bigger than butterflies. "We can negotiate."

She contemplated giving Alison a preview of her soon-to-be-released debut novel, but she was firmly rooted in her superstitions. If she went around bragging about it before it was actually on the virtual shelves, something could go terribly wrong. No need to tempt fate so close to the debut just to impress a pretty woman.

"Well, I should be getting on now," Alison said as she stood. "If you wouldn't mind, perhaps we can discuss negotiations over dinner sometime."

"Sure," Kendra said as they walked toward the exit. "Text me when you're free."

Alison stopped on the sidewalk. "I'm free this Wednesday. Would that work?"

"Uh, yeah. That's fine."

"I'm over here on the street," Alison said as they continued walking.

"I'm right here." Kendra stopped at her car and prepared to receive the same quick, casual hug Alison gave her when she'd arrived.

Instead, she seemed to study Kendra's eyes, as if weighing the odds of her hand in a high-stakes poker game. Then she moved in, not for the hug but for a warm, mocha-tinged kiss that landed somewhere between her cheek and the corner of her mouth. Kendra's body tingled at Alison's sweet command.

This was a woman who went for what she wanted.

Kendra demurred as she opened her car door. "Looking forward to dinner."

"Me, too." Alison slowly headed down the sidewalk backward toward her car as if she didn't want to leave, a move that turned Kendra's legs to noodles.

All the way home, Kendra flitted from one moment of their date to another. By far her favorite was how Alison's lips felt against the corner of her mouth and the floral smell of her hair as she kissed her. If only Kendra had turned just a smidge…

❖

About 11:45 Alison skulked around the back of the house and entered through the kitchen as stealthily as possible. It was late enough that Vanessa had probably nodded off watching Real Housewives of Somewhere in her California-king bed flanked by snoring dogs. Could she be lucky enough that Mr. Dillford had come home and was asleep beside her?

After taking off her shoes, she crept up the stairs and slowly padded toward her bedroom. Just as she was turning the doorknob, she heard her name whispered. What she wouldn't have given for the voice to belong to some disembodied demonic spirit come to snatch her soul away to the underworld.

No such luck. When she turned, Vanessa was posed in her bedroom doorway in a flowing, silky nightgown with one strap fallen off her shoulder. Damn, she was sexy. Outrageously.

"Aren't you going to tell me about your date?" Vanessa's voice rolled out like velvet.

"Sure. In the morning," Alison said, forcing herself to look away.

"Since we're both awake, why don't you come to my room now and tell me."

That was always how it started. Some transparent excuse Vanessa fabricated to get her alone that she fell for every single time. Frankly, Vanessa was nearly impossible to resist—a curvy, bronzed, Fifth Avenue–salon redhead who'd sold her soul long ago to be a multimillionaire's trophy wife. But like so many multimillionaires before him, Brandon Dillford's interest in her as a woman waned after the birth of their two children. Rumor was he'd been working his way through some of the college-age daughters of business associates, unbeknown to them. Alison actually felt sorry for Vanessa. She could be rather shallow about most things, but she was a human being after all, and a very lost one.

"Em, if you don't mind, I'd like to get to bed now. It's late and I'm knackered." She faked a yawn for emphasis.

"Have it your way. I'll come to you." Vanessa rushed down the hall and squeezed into the room before Alison could shut the door.

She leaned against the door with her hands behind her back, jutting out her ample breasts barely concealed under the sheer nightie. "So? How was the old lady?"

"Well, she's forty-five, so she's not—"

"She's ancient," Vanessa snapped.

"She's only a few years older than you."

"Seven years. I'm not even forty yet. Do I even look thirty-eight?"

Before she could answer, Vanessa lunged at her, threw her arms up around Alison's neck, and kissed her aggressively. Despite the lure of her buttery soft skin and musky perfume, Alison peeled her arms off and gently nudged her back.

"You're as stunning and youthful as ever, Vanessa. But can't we talk about this in the—"

"Why are you pushing me away? Are you in love with her already?" She stomped her bare foot on the wood floor as her eyes flashed with anger.

"No. I'm not in love with her. We've just met. Let's keep our voices down so—"

"Kiss me then," she said, moving toward her. "If you're not in love with her, you'll kiss me." She moved closer.

Alison stepped back. "Vanessa, I've already explained to you that I've—"

"You're doing it again. You're rejecting me." Suddenly, Vanessa's eyes started to pool.

"Vanessa, I'm not rejecting you. Now if you'll stop bloody interrupting me…" She sighed in frustration. "I've told you before I even met Kendra that we're not doing this anymore. You're not going to leave Brandon, and I'm tired of playing your mistress."

"You're just like a man. You have your fun with a fresh piece of ass, and then when you get bored, you move on to the next one without any remorse. You're cold, Alison."

"But I'm not, Vanessa. I didn't tire of you. I was starting to have feelings for you, and since I know it wouldn't have led anywhere, I had to put a stop to it."

"I didn't say I'd never leave Brandon. I said I can't leave him now, not while the children are still minors. There's some sketchy language in our pre-nup concerning custody if I divorced him, and I can't take that chance."

"He made you sign a pre-nup? And you agreed?"

"Don't judge me," Vanessa said. "I was young, and his family was, is very wealthy and powerful. What did I care back then? I thought we were going to live happily ever after."

In a rare moment, Vanessa looked so sad and defenseless that Alison almost forgot about her enchanting date with Kendra. She hadn't lied when she told Vanessa she'd had feelings for her. But it was time for her to exit this reality show that Vanessa had created for herself to fill the emptiness in her life.

Still, she couldn't help but walk over and wrap her in a hug. Vanessa clung to her and sniffled against her shoulder. Maybe she was finally ready to let go.

"Good night." Vanessa headed toward the door, then swung around. "You'll be back. I know you will."

Or not.

Alison hadn't known where things with Kendra would go, but she was sure she was interested in finding out. Even if she never saw her again after their dinner date, she couldn't keep allowing Vanessa to suck her back in.

CHAPTER FIVE

Monday morning Kendra strolled into the office balancing a tray of coffees and Sergio in his travel bag. A beautiful bouquet of roses on the coffee table stopped her before she reached a place to free her full hands.

Assuming MJ was in her office, she called out, "What are these?"

She appeared at the door and smirked. "Red roses, a sign of love."

"Who sent them to you?"

"They're not for me," MJ said and took the coffees from her.

Kendra put Sergio's carrier down and let him out, then grabbed the card. These had to be from Alison, but she didn't want to be presumptuous. She held the card to her chest before opening it. "These aren't from you, are they?"

"Why would I have roses delivered to you here?"

"I don't know. Maybe you want to congratulate me on my upcoming debut novel."

MJ stared at her. "Congratulations."

Kendra tore open the card, and indeed, the flowers were from Alison. She read the card aloud. "Thanks a *latte* for a great night. Can't wait for Wednesday."

"She didn't write 'thanks a latte,' did she?" MJ made a face.

"I think it's adorable." She inserted the card into the plastic holder and carried the vase into her office.

MJ followed her. "What did she say when you said you have a novel coming out?"

"I didn't tell her." As soon as she sat down, Sergio jumped into her lap.

"You didn't tell her? What the hell? That's something you lead with on a first date."

"That's something *you* would lead with. I'm a little more low-key about self-promotion. Of any kind."

"No kidding," MJ said. "I've told you before you're not going to jinx something by talking about it before it happens. What are you, twelve?"

"No. And, yes, that's exactly what will happen. I learned that during my teenage years."

"Give me a break, Kendra. You cannot still believe that Gary Fletcher didn't ask you to the prom because you told us all you were sure he would."

Kendra looked at her in disbelief. "You think I still give a shit about Gary Fletcher? I'm talking about my mother. My parents told me her last round of treatment was going to cure her. I was so excited, I told everyone I knew. And then, poof, she's dead in less than a year."

MJ sat in the chair next to her, looking duly reproachful.

"Look. I know it doesn't make sense," Kendra said. "The logical part of my brain knows it's superstition. But it just makes me feel better to celebrate things *after* they happen. That's all."

"I get it. I'm sorry." MJ stood to leave. "But roses? Roses are a clear sign of things to come."

Kendra smiled. "Don't be sorry for being excited for me. You're a good friend. The best, in fact."

"And don't forget it." MJ stopped at the door. "I know one thing—you don't need to talk about writing a novel to impress someone. That's for sure."

Kendra blew her a kiss, then picked up the manuscript she was editing. She hoped she'd impressed Alison a little. Alison certainly left an impression on her.

❖

After dropping the children off at school, Alison sat cross-legged on her bed and stared at the blank screen of the laptop cradled on her thighs. She'd chosen an ARC from NetGalley for a novel called *The Winding Road* because the title alone sounded cheesy enough to make it easy to trash on her blog. But the title and the short-and-sweet synopsis didn't give the story anywhere near the justice it deserved. It was amazing—a psycho-sexual romantic thriller about a gorgeous young widow accused of murdering her business-tycoon husband and the dysfunctional lawyer who defends, then falls in love with her. Sometime after the acquittal, the lawyer receives a message from an anonymous albeit unreliable third-party suggesting that her lover was in fact the murderer. It was so riveting Alison had finished it in two sittings.

Now she struggled to whip up her usual witty hatchet job for the novel that her readers had come to expect. Her advertisers expected it, too, as they paid to place ads on her highly trafficked blog site, *The Poison Pen.* Since she'd arrived in America with the Dillfords, she'd been blogging LGBTQ film and book reviews and even reviews for various health and beauty products she'd used. She'd started the blog intending to write honest, helpful reviews, but after trashing the first subpar lesbian film and a couple of novels, her biting wit and delicious sarcasm had soon attracted a cult-like following. It seemed that readers wanted to be entertained as much by Alison's writing style as they looked to be informed about whatever she was reviewing.

Even when she'd liked something, she usually had no trouble trashing it in a playful way. But this time, something about this book blocked her flow. Her nerves were still vibrating from the sexy, dynamic characters, the surprising plot twist, and the seamless dénouement, so much so that she simply couldn't organize her thoughts into a hit piece worthy of her Poison Pen readership.

Her phone chirped with a riff from Tom Petty's "American Girl," a custom text tone she'd assigned to Kendra's number. She dived across the bed to grab the phone from her nightstand. She must've received the roses.

After Kendra bombarded her with effusive thank-yous for the flowers, she asked what an au pair does once her charges are off at school.

Enjoy the peace and quiet.

Is the mistress of the manor off at her high-pressure job?

LOL! Not hardly. Mrs. Dillford's shopping in the City with her girlfriends. I'm just hanging about.

Definitely not a bad gig.

She thought about telling Kendra the truth—that she wasn't just lying about doing nothing but rather was deeply engaged as her alter ego, the Poison Pen. But she decided against it. It was too early in their relationship to begin revealing things that might be perceived as less than tasteful. Kendra and her best friend, MJ, were in the publishing biz and might not appreciate the nuances of her unique way of supplementing her income until they'd truly gotten to know her personality.

Besides, she wanted Kendra to know her first as Alison Chatterley, journalist. If she read her blogs now, she'd likely take them out of context, which would sully Alison's credibility as a serious writer, something she was still working hard to establish.

It's a great gig until three o'clock, when they come bounding through the door already shouting at each other. Wink emoji. *They're good kids, tho.*

They're lucky to have such a patient nanny. BTW I'm looking forward to dinner Wednesday, too. Blushing-smile emoji. *Any place in particular you'd like to go, or would you prefer I choose?*

Assertive. Alison liked that in a woman. It sometimes foretold of assertiveness in other areas, which was one of Alison's biggest turn-ons. *Yes, please choose. I love surprises.*

You're a brave woman. I'm not a fan of them myself, but it's fun that you are.

Alison couldn't determine if Kendra was trying to be flirtatious or if she was just reading into things. She fancied it the former because she loved the way it felt.

How about you choose this time, I'll choose the next?

Hmm. Don't you want to make sure you enjoy dinner #1 before committing to dinner #2?

Alison's heart beat faster. How could a woman do that to her merely through texting? *I'm quite certain I will enjoy it. But if you're not, we can split the check.* Laugh emoji.

I'm sure that won't be necessary. Smiley face.

She smiled at Kendra's formality in speaking, even in texts. She gave off this wildly sexy vibe of sophistication and aloofness with just enough flirtation to keep her wanting more. She shivered as she envisioned what it would be like to melt away some of that reserved veneer with a passionate kiss…the slow unbuttoning of her blouse…a stroke of her…

Are you still there?

The swoop noise from the incoming text jarred her back to reality. *Ha ha. Yes. I was just thinking how tragic it is that I have to wait till Wednesday to see your face. How about sending me a selfie?*

I'll think about it...

What a tease.

After they ended their conversation, Alison was keyed up enough to buckle down and start writing her review. The money she earned from advertisers wasn't the Queen's ransom, but it certainly was helping her build a nest egg so she could get her own apartment and be free of her complicated situation with Vanessa.

The sooner the better.

❖

Kendra sat at her dining room table simmering in resentment as she watched MJ and Violet polish off the bottle of her favorite Bordeaux she'd been saving for a special occasion.

Violet spoke with her mouth full, her set of chopsticks still hanging in the air. "What could be more special than your two best friends showing up at your house with sushi from your favorite restaurant?"

"Maybe if they called first?" Kendra said.

"Ha! And give you the chance to say no?" MJ said. "No, sir. Ambushing you is the only way we can get you to hang out during the week."

"Too bad you didn't pick tomorrow night," Kendra said as she sucked out the beans from an edamame pouch. "I wouldn't be home."

"Duh," MJ said. "Why do you think we came tonight?"

"You must be so jazzed about your date," Violet said. "Alison's so cool. Did you read that article she wrote for *Modern Women* magazine? It's a satirical piece on body image. She wrote it as if it were men who are always the target of criticism. It was awesome."

Kendra felt a twinge of jealousy. "No. How did you see it?"

"We're friends on Instagram," Violet said. "Aren't you?"

"I'm constantly on her case to get active on social media," MJ said. "It's like talking to a wall." She then glared at Kendra. "Your book is coming out in five weeks. You have to have a presence on the major platforms to promote yourself."

"I thought that's your job as my publisher," Kendra said.

MJ topped off her glass with more of Kendra's expensive wine. "When you make the best-seller list it'll be my job. Until then, I have to devote my time to all the projects, especially the ones that pay the overhead."

"I'll help you, Kendra," Violet said. "I'm on all the time."

Kendra turned to MJ with a prim smirk. "You see that? I now have my own media consultant."

"I'd love to have your job where I can be on social media all day."

"No, you wouldn't," Violet said with a frown. "Account data analysis and management sounded so stimulating when I interviewed for the job. Ten years ago."

"It did?" Kendra said with a mouth full of salmon roll.

MJ pointed at Kendra with a chopstick. "Well, when she sells her millionth copy, I'll put you on my payroll. In the meantime, have her join all the LGBTQ reading groups I'm part of." She turned to Kendra, all her fierce business savvy sparkling in her deep-set brown eyes. "It's time to get the ball rolling. You're up on NetGalley now, so we can start looking out for reviews."

Ugh. This was getting real. "I can't imagine people writing about what they think of my writing. It's usually just readers reviewing in literature groups, right?"

"Uh, no," MJ said. "A lot of times a book will get picked up by LGBTQ sites and outlets that have thousands of followers. You get noticed by the right one, and your name and title will spread like herpes."

"Eww. That's charming," Violet said.

"I'm so glad I chose a pseudonym, then," Kendra said.

MJ took on the posture of a boss at a board meeting. "The important thing now is to get you out there, so women will want to read and talk about your debut novel. That's how we afford to publish more in the genre."

A prickly nervous sweat spread across Kendra's upper back. "You're not pinning the future financial hopes of your business on my book, are you?"

MJ emptied the rest of the special-occasion wine into their glasses. "No, but I've always wanted LGBTQ fiction to be a main facet of my publishing business. If any novel can help set that in motion, it's yours." She clutched the top of Kendra's hand. "I know I've said this to you before, but it really is a gripping, well-written story."

"Aww." Kendra batted her eyelashes. "I thought you were just saying that to keep me from having a mental breakdown before I finished it."

"That was part of it," MJ replied, "but the sentiment was nonetheless true."

"She's not blowing smoke up your ass," Violet said. "I've read it twice."

"You guys." Kendra fought back some eye-watering as she stretched across the table and grabbed their hands. "I have the best friends in the universe."

"After thirty years, you better say that," MJ said.

"Well, I've known you guys for only ten, but I feel the same way." Violet leaned against Kendra.

"I'm a lucky woman," Kendra said.

"Does that mean we're forgiven for drinking your special-occasion wine?" Violet asked.

"No. That's what I was planning to serve Alison if I decided to invite her back here after dinner tomorrow night."

"If you invite her here, you better not waste time drinking wine," MJ said. "Do that at the restaurant."

"I'm not gonna sleep with her tomorrow night."

"If dinner goes well, why not?" MJ asked.

"She's not a hoe like you," Violet said.

"Thank you, Violet." Kendra's nerves kicked into motion at the question. "I mean I guess it could happen. I don't know. I'm not planning the grand seduction or anything."

"If it happens, it happens," MJ said.

"But it's been so long." Kendra reached for a bottle of red blend from her wine rack. "I know you don't forget how to have sex, but I'm so out of practice."

Violet took the bottle and opener from Kendra's trembling hands. "Ken, you met her a few weeks ago. If you feel you need more time getting to know each other, just put it out there. She'll understand if she truly likes you."

Kendra glanced at MJ for reassurance.

"Take it from this hoe," MJ said with a thumb pointed at herself. "Sometimes going at it too quickly isn't the best way to start a new relationship."

"That's why she always winds up single," Violet said.

"Oh, really?" MJ cocked an eyebrow. "What's your excuse?"

"I go for quality, not quantity," Violet replied.

"Now, now, ladies." Kendra gave the time-out hand signal. "Let's not turn this into a competition. I have you both beat on duration when it comes to being single."

"Yeah, but your streak is about to end," Violet said. "You're so lucky. I wish I could meet a stable woman who's looking to build a life together."

"Don't be maudlin," MJ said. "You'll find someone eventually."

"When? I just turned forty. It only gets harder the older you get."

"You don't say?" MJ said. "We have five years on you."

"Look. It's all relative," Kendra said. "I wasn't even looking, and I met Alison. She seems awesome, but who knows if we'll make it beyond a few dates, let alone build something permanent together. You never know what's waiting around the corner for you. In the meantime, just enjoy and appreciate the life you have in the present."

MJ studied her for a moment. "You watch a lot of *Iyanla: Fix My Life*, don't you?"

"How do you know?" Kendra searched her eyes for signs of sorcery.

"Nowadays the only way one gets that enlightened is through memes or watching OWN. And I know you don't read memes."

"That's how you pronounce it? I always thought it was 'meh-mees.'"

After MJ and Violet exchanged worried glances, MJ said to Violet, "You have your work cut out for you" as though Kendra wasn't sitting there with them.

"Well, I for one am inspired, Kendra," Violet said. "You've renewed my faith in life and love and the magical workings of the universe. Thank you."

"Don't thank me. Thank Iyanla."

"Anyway." MJ got up, gathered her dishes, and placed them in the sink. "I expect a full report at the office Thursday morning. Except if she sleeps over. Then I'll expect the report by noon."

"Ooh, I want to know, too," Violet said, fidgeting in her seat. "Let's do a Zoom meeting."

"I'm not doing a Zoom meeting about my date," Kendra said.

"Fine. FaceTime," Violet replied.

Kendra stared at them.

Violet's eyes grew glassy and sad. "Group text?"

Kendra stood to finish cleaning up. "All information about my date will be on a need-to-know basis. Now get out, both of you."

"We're helping you clean up," MJ said, seeming offended.

"I've got it. Thank you." Kendra was ushering them toward the door. "I'll see you tomorrow, and Violet, keep hope alive."

"But we—"

Kendra closed the door on them before Violet could complete her sentence. She leaned against the door, smiling and full of gratitude. No matter what the Fates had in store for her romantic life, she'd always have those two crazy, loving, trustworthy women by her side.

CHAPTER SIX

Kendra struggled all morning to keep focused on her work, but the anticipation of dinner with Alison that night kept intruding on her thoughts. She wanted to complete her work on this technical manual and get into her next editing project, a self-help book by a local guru that combined nutrition, mindfulness, and exercise—three things Kendra had been castigating herself for not being better about. This one promised to be infinitely more interesting than a manual about industrial-lubricant-product application and safety-use data.

By one o'clock she needed to cool her fried brain down, so she grabbed her keys and headed out for lunch. She picked up two enormous subs from a nearby Italian deli and popped in on her brother at work at the animal shelter.

"What's going on? Did you get fired or something?" Ryan said as he tore open a bag of chips.

"You think MJ would ever fire me? I practically run that business."

"Nah. I was just kidding. But you never show up here during the week in the middle of the day. Everything okay?"

"Yeah, yeah. I'm just a little restless. I'm meeting someone for dinner tonight."

"You have a date? Holy shit."

"You don't have to act that surprised. I still have some game left."

"Pffft. I know you do, sis. I didn't mean it like that. I just…I didn't even know you were looking."

"I wasn't, but the universe obviously had other plans when it sent this cute, young British woman my way at a dance. We've been talking ever since. We had coffee the other night, so I guess tonight is our first official date."

"That's great. I hope it goes well." His weird smile and penetrating stare unnerved her. "How young is young?" he finally asked.

"Early thirties."

"Nice."

"Stop smiling at me like that. It's creepy. So, how are the kids?"

"Everyone's great. By the way, I told Dad you'd be at the game Friday."

"Oh, really?" Kendra groaned as she chewed a bite of her chicken-cutlet sub. "Well, I hope he won't be terribly disappointed when I don't show up."

He dropped the end of his sandwich on the wrapper. "Alyssa will be. You remember her, don't you? Your amazing athlete niece who calls you her favorite cheerleader?"

"Ryan, come on. That's not fair." She balled up her napkin and threw it at him.

He wasn't catching on. "What's not fair is you taking out your hostility for Dad against her. She'd be devastated if you didn't come."

God, she hated being proved wrong so easily. "Fine. I'll just sit on the visitors' side, like I usually do."

"And run to your car immediately after the last out."

"Ry, what is your deal with trying to play mediator between me and Dad? Can you just leave it alone?"

"My deal is I'm tired of this stupid rift between you two. And being stuck in the middle of the tension and having to make up excuses for you to Hayden and Alyssa, who, by the way, are getting old enough to figure things out."

"Then tell them the truth. Tell them that their grandfather emotionally abandoned his kids at a time when they needed him the most."

Ryan brooded for a moment.

"Am I wrong?" she asked. "Don't even try to make excuses for him. And do not tell me I'm just overreacting."

"You weren't overreacting…then," he said. "He basically did that as soon as Joyce came around. But he still took care of us. At least he didn't dump us off on Aunt Gloria."

"Not permanently, but we spent a ton of weekends at her house until they got married. And then it wasn't much better living with them. She was controlling, and he just went along with whatever she said."

"You do realize that Mom's death was a huge loss to him, too? She was his life. He had his own grief to deal with."

"Could've fooled me. He didn't waste much time replacing her."

Ryan shook his head. "He didn't replace her. He needed to move on. He was too young to be a widower in mourning the rest of his life."

The heat of anger began rising in her. "We were too young to lose our mother. He was the surviving parent. He didn't have the luxury of worrying about only his needs."

"It was almost thirty years ago. When will you be ready to get over it?"

Kendra didn't answer him. If she continued this conversation she might say things to him she'd only regret later. Besides, she couldn't answer the actual question. After all this time of keeping her emotions buried, she had no clue what it would take for her to get past the pain of betrayal by the person she'd trusted the most as a teenager.

"I have to get back to work." She stood up, crumpled the lunch wrappers, and tossed them into the pail. "I brought you a sandwich because I knew you were working alone today and would probably forget to eat."

"I never forget to eat. I probably just wouldn't have found the time. Thanks." He gave her a warm smile.

"Anytime," she said as she reached for the door handle.

"Hey, Ken. I'm sorry if I said anything—"

She held up her hand. "No worries, little brother. It's all good."

His question still nagged at her as she strolled to her car. Does anyone ever "get over" childhood trauma? They at least learned to process it in a healthy way. But the how part of that seemed like a Sisyphean moment she wasn't ready to take on.

When she got in the car and checked her phone, she smiled at Alison's name and text on the message bar. "I'm looking forward to tonight, too," she said out loud.

❖

They left Kendra's favorite Italian restaurant after a long dinner in the glow of soft lighting, 1950s love songs, and engaging conversations about their families and friends. Heavy flirtation accentuated the entire night, as did some leg and feet brushing that might or might not have been intentional. Kendra was already musing about where they'd go on their next date—assuming Alison wanted another one.

As if peeping into Kendra's thoughts, Alison stopped short on the sidewalk and whirled around to her. "I hope our date isn't ending here. But if you have to get up for work in the morning…"

Kendra checked her watch. "It's only nine o'clock. I suppose I can have a nightcap."

"That's what I was hoping you'd say." Alison's smoldering gaze made it feel like that ordinary sidewalk in that ordinary town was the most romantic locale on earth.

"There's a wine bar not far from here. We'll have time for a glass before it closes."

"Let's take one car," Alison said. "I'll drop you back here afterward."

Kendra agreed to the sensible suggestion, but in the closeness of the car, she began feeling a bit anxious. During their long, casual dinner conversation, which seemed to fly by, she'd thought multiple times about kissing Alison, and not just a little peck either. Now, with their forearms touching as they shared the console armrest, she was drawn to Alison with a desire to feel more than just her arm pressed against her.

When they pulled into the parking lot, Kendra thought it strange that Alison drove to the back of the lot when she'd noticed several open spaces closer to the entrance. Then when Alison threw the gearshift into park and turned off the ignition but didn't move to get out of the car, it all started to make sense.

"Do you know what I've wanted to do all night?"

Alison's arresting blue eyes left Kendra speechless. She shook her head to indicate no, but inside she was dying. Alison apparently wanted the same thing she'd wanted all night. She licked her lips as her mouth watered with desire.

Then it happened.

Alison leaned in, and her soft, warm lips tantalized Kendra's. A thrill rippled through her from head to toe. She glided her hand across Alison's jawline to the base of her head and pulled her closer, countering the teasing with aggressive kisses. Alison groaned with approval and slid her tongue into Kendra's mouth.

They kissed each other deeply. Before Kendra knew what was happening, Alison had climbed over the console and straddled Kendra in her seat. She nearly smothered her with ravenous kisses, and everywhere Alison touched her pulsated with currents that all led to one central region. She squirmed beneath her at the tingling happening below as she reached up and unclasped Alison's bra.

"Oh, yes," Alison whispered when Kendra reached up and cupped her breasts. She began grinding in Kendra's lap.

And just as she was about to experience car sex for the first time, an SUV's bright headlights illuminated their entire sordid scene, prompting Alison to retreat clumsily into the driver's seat.

Kendra opened the car door to get some air as she wiped the sweat from her forehead and caught her breath. "Wow. That was…Um… Shall we go inside?"

Still flushed, Alison looked at her with a seductive grin. "I'd rather go and have the wine at your flat."

She was about to say yes, when Violet's and MJ's warnings sounded in her head. *Slow down there, girl. Jumping into bed after one and a half dates is not the ideal way to embark on a meaningful relationship.* Age difference notwithstanding, Kendra realized after only a couple of weeks of talking with her that Alison was someone she'd like to pursue something meaningful with. Whether they'd ever get there wasn't important. She'd at least like to try. So as difficult as it was…

"Uh, I have an early staff meeting tomorrow," she lied, hoping she hadn't ruined more than just the mood. "But we still have time for one more drink if you want." She motioned toward the bar.

"I'd like that. A lot." The dreamy gaze Alison sent her way proved Kendra hadn't ruined a thing.

So they went inside and continued their conversation, both knowing the best was yet to come.

❖

Upon returning home this time, Alison managed to sneak into the house without waking Vanessa. She'd anticipated her lying in wait somewhere, behind the kitchen island or a potted palm, ready to pounce. She'd already survived an inquisition before she went out since this was the first official date that came after the coffee prequel. She'd never pictured Vanessa as the jealous type, but the minute Alison had called off the affair, she'd morphed into a disagreeable child forced to share her favorite toy. Thankfully, Brandon was home, and would be for a while, as his usually excessive business-travel schedule began to slow as summer approached.

This was good. It would buy Alison more time to scrounge up enough money for a security deposit on a flat of her own. Imagine Kendra's face if she'd said to her, "Hey, how about coming over and hanging out in my nanny's quarters?" She couldn't trust Vanessa's reaction to meeting Kendra, especially if she knew how into her Alison was. The abrupt end to their affair had left her somewhat unpredictable.

She shook the images from her mind as she picked up her phone to send Kendra a good-night text. At the risk of seeming too eager, she wrote that she was already thinking about dinner again on Saturday. She went into the bathroom to brush and floss for bed, and as she was spitting out the toothpaste, her FaceTime ring went off.

"I didn't wake you, did I?" Kendra's gravelly voice and sleepy eyes were the best things Alison could experience before falling off to sleep.

"No. I'm about to climb into bed," she replied.

"I'm there now…I mean in my own bed, not yours." That would've sounded immensely sexy had Kendra said it with conviction rather than self-consciousness.

Alison giggled at her innocence. "I knew what you meant, but I do like the suggestion."

After a nervous laugh, Kendra sighed. "I hope I didn't offend you by not inviting you back to my place."

"No, no. Weekdays aren't great for late dates. I totally understand."

"I'm glad. I, uh, I just didn't want you to think the idea hadn't appealed to me."

"Not at all. And I'm happy to hear that it did."

In the brief silence, Alison studied Kendra's features: her round, hazel-brown eyes; chestnut, slicked-back 'do; and full, mouthwatering lips. Was she more beautiful with a light dusting of makeup or how she was right then, au naturel? What a deliciously difficult choice.

"So I was thinking," Kendra said. "If you wanted to have an after-dinner drink at my condo Saturday night…that would be cool."

Alison secretly gushed at how adorable and shy Kendra now seemed as she had invited her to her place. "I have an idea. How about I come over and make us dinner. I took a Japanese cooking course and learned how to make sushi. Do you like it?"

"Uh, it's only my favorite food," Kendra said, perking up. "But we can go out for it. I don't want you to go to the trouble—"

"Oh, it's no trouble at all. I love cooking, especially new and different cuisine. And for someone I fancy as well as you."

"You fancy me?" Kendra said in a bad British accent.

Alison giggled. "Quite."

"Well then, I will pick up a bottle of sake for the occasion."

"Brilliant. I'll bring over all the supplies, and we'll make ourselves a delicious dinner."

"We?"

"Yes. We'll prepare it together. I'm going to teach you."

"This is going to be an interesting night."

"I have no doubt."

When they finally said good night, Alison sank down in her pillow and snuggled the covers close to her chin. She could definitely see herself falling for Kendra in a big way. Big, fast, and hard.

But did Kendra share the feeling?

Kendra arrived to work early the next morning. She'd had trouble falling asleep last night after her date with Alison, and after hours of tossing and turning, experiencing only fragments of sleep every hour, she got up and headed out first for a coffee run. Although she was being productive, she kept an ear on the door, anticipating MJ's arrival between flashes of recollection from the night before.

When MJ finally had arrived, she made Kendra's office her first stop. "Well?"

Kendra giggled knowingly. "I had a great time."

"Then why are you here so early? Did you come here straight from a hotel or something? Are those the clothes you wore last night?"

"No. Calm yourself, woman. I didn't sleep well last night, so I got ready early and came in. And yes, I'll take that second cup of coffee you've got there."

MJ pulled a cup from the tray and handed it to her before having a seat. "Okay, so give me the highlights now. Then you can go into full naughty detail at lunch."

"We went to dinner, then to a wine bar, and had great conversation. I thought the age difference might be an issue, but it wasn't. She's intelligent, a devoted listener, and I just love that accent."

"And she's super easy on the eyes."

"That, too. But aside from the first-date jitters, it felt so easy. The conversation flowed, and I just adored her company."

"That's awesome. So I'm assuming there'll be a second date?"

Kendra nodded. "She's already locked me down for one. She wants to come over and make me sushi."

"Seriously? She knows how to make sushi?"

"She took a class. She's so worldly."

"How nice," MJ said. "You'll probably have sex after dinner."

A rush of exhilaration fluttered through her, but she kept a lid on it. "Noooo. You think?"

"Uh…why not?"

Kendra squirmed. "I guess you're right. It almost happened in the car last night."

"What?" MJ's eyes sprang wide open. "Man, Kendra. You really have to learn what to open with. What happened?"

"After dinner, we took the same car over to the wine bar, and as soon as she threw it in park, she climbed into my lap."

"That is so hot."

"It was about to be until a car pulled in slowly and shined its lights on us."

MJ slumped down, issuing her disappointment in a groan.

"It's all for the best. I'd rather it happen in the privacy of my own home anyway."

"Well, make sure you take care of your lady garden," MJ said as she stood. "'Cause it's happening after sushi. No doubt about it." She flashed the okay hand sign and left.

Kendra slipped off her reading glasses and sat back in her chair. She could play prim and proper all she wanted, debate with herself whether she was ready to take that next big step, but if their chemistry was as sizzling as it was in the car last night, they would absolutely go there.

CHAPTER SEVEN

Kendra glanced at the wall clock as she made a lap around her dining-room table. Alison was due to arrive in ten minutes, so she wanted to ensure everything was in its place. The dinner candles were set next to a small bouquet of miniature roses. It was such a romantic scene. She hoped she hadn't gone over the top too soon. But then Alison was the one who invited herself, so she was clearly comfortable with moving forward in an intimate setting.

Alison arrived precisely at six thirty, surprising Kendra with a bottle of her favorite wine.

"I can't believe you remembered. I barely recall talking about this."

"In fairness, we were on our fourth glasses by the time we hit the wine bar the other night."

"Or maybe I was distracted by your sparkling blue eyes."

"I like your excuse much better." Alison giggled shyly, then leaned in for a kiss. Had their hands not been full, who knew where that kiss would've led them.

"So, let's get this stuff on the counter." Kendra showed her into the kitchen. "Would you like a little sake before we get down to work?"

"Sounds fantastic," Alison said. "I'll set up some things for us."

As Alison unpacked her cloth bag full of food and supplies, Kendra glanced at her long legs wrapped in tight black jeans. While she was lean and sleek, she had just enough curve in all the right places. Kendra could only imagine how she would feel naked and wrapped around her body. Someday.

She blotted out the erotic imagery and focused on pouring two shots of sake in small porcelain cups especially purchased for the occasion. "Do you know what I learned when I stopped at the Asian store?"

Alison looked up from her task.

"That this is actually called nihonshu." Kendra held up the bottle. "Sake is just a generic term for alcohol, but what we're drinking is a Japanese alcohol made from rice."

"I'm impressed that you actually did homework for our date. That's quite romantic."

Kendra demurred. "I've always been a book nerd. Now I'm an internet nerd. I can't help wanting to investigate and learn new things."

"Nerd-chic," Alison said. "I like that. Intellectual curiosity is one of the first boxes I hope to check off when I meet an intriguing lady."

"I'm intriguing?" Kendra smirked. The word sounded like something you'd call a secret agent, not a reserved woman who was one step above a librarian in the reputation department. "And why is that?"

"When I met you at the dance, you were literally the only woman there not lamenting about being single and how hard it is to find someone. You couldn't care less. Or at least that's how you came off."

"That was pretty much true at the time. I mean the part where I wasn't looking. And then you showed up."

"I wasn't sure what, if anything, I was looking for that night, but I certainly wasn't going to let a prize like you go unclaimed."

Kendra smiled as she came around to her with their drinks. "I feel like all British people have a way with words. Maybe it's because of all the Shakespeare I read in high school."

"It's the accent."

"Whatever it is, it's working." Kendra raised her cup. "Cheers."

"Cheers," Alison said and moved in for a sensual, slow-burn kiss before downing her sake in one gulp.

Requiring a second to reclaim her wits, Kendra sipped her shot and bowed to Alison's alcohol prowess.

"All right then." Alison beamed. "Are you ready to get down to work?"

❖

After Kendra came around the island and stood next to her as directed, Alison took a good whiff of whatever was making Kendra smell so good. Was it perfume? Body lotion? The fruit of the gods? Whatever it was, she savored it for a moment as she gathered her thoughts.

"Okay. The trick to making sushi is it's all in the rolling."

"Is that right?"

"Definitely. Have a look. This is your sushi-rolling mat." She displayed, then flattened the bamboo square in front of Kendra. "Take a piece of plastic wrap and cover it for easy cleanup."

Kendra did exactly as instructed, her eyes gleaming like a child's during arts-and-crafts hour.

"Now place a seaweed sheet on the mat and spread a layer of sticky rice over it."

"How much should I use?" Kendra asked as she spooned rice out of the bowl.

"That depends on how thick you want your roll. I like a thin layer, but it's entirely up to you."

Kendra mashed the rice down with the spoon, but it wasn't cooperating.

"Here. Use your fingers."

"That's what she said," Kendra replied with mischief in her smile.

Alison broke into laughter. "You're the last person I'd expect that from."

"Me, too. I don't know where it came from."

"Good thing I love surprises. You're full of them." Alison paused, locked in a gaze with Kendra.

As she was about to lean in for another kiss, her cell phone chimed with a text. Damn it. She'd forgotten to put her phone on silent. She looked quickly, and when she'd confirmed her suspicion that it was Vanessa, she flicked on silent mode and shoved the phone into her back pocket.

"Everything okay?" Kendra asked.

"Yes, fine. It was just my boss." Alison reached over to grab the packages of salmon and crabmeat.

"Do you have to answer her?"

"Not when I'm off. She knows I'm on a date. She's just being her petulant twit self. She can wait."

"I suppose that's one of the drawbacks of living with your boss. Blurred boundaries."

Alison went on alert. Was that a note of suspicion she'd detected? She'd better start minding her demeanor. It wouldn't do to have Kendra figure out she'd been involved with her boss, who was now texting her in the middle of their date. "Yes, well, in her case, it's more self-centeredness than anything else. Now, where were we?"

"I think we're ready to add the stuffing." Kendra's focus seemed to have fully returned to her project.

"Okay. Here are all your toppings. Now flip it over and select away."

"Hmm. I think I'll go with the salmon, avocado, and…" She looked over the vegetable choices. "Is this grilled zucchini?"

"It is. That's a great combination. Now layer it all at the bottom, and then you can roll it up."

Kendra again did as instructed, pushing the bamboo mat over until the roll was formed. As she tried to pull the mat away, rice started coming with it.

"Oh, dear." Alison placed her hand on top of Kendra's to stop further destruction. "I forgot to mention the step of spraying the plastic wrap."

When Kendra looked at her, her hand still underneath, Alison again fell to the temptation of her allure. If she was reading the look in her eyes correctly, Kendra had wanted it to happen as badly as she did.

As their lips touched, Kendra released a whimper of pleasure. Or surprise. Or both. Alison surrendered to the sweetness of the kiss and the longing it communicated without a word exchanged. She'd be happy to stand at the counter and taste her lips all night long were the physical desires Kendra stirred in her not causing her to squirm.

Kendra pulled away before clothing items started coming off and looked at her with dreamy eyes. "How did I do?"

"You're the best damn kisser I've ever experienced," Alison blurted.

"I meant the sushi," Kendra said through laughter.

Alison envisioned her creamy white skin turning rosy with heat. "Well done on both counts."

Kendra put some space between them as she returned to the sushi. "You're pretty amazing yourself."

"Perhaps we'll need to do some further research to know for sure—after dinner, of course." Alison turned away to catch her breath. She'd had an older woman before. She'd had numerous women before, all varied in looks and personality and sexual appetites, but Kendra was a variety all her own in the way she made Alison feel.

She certainly didn't want to rush through dinner, but she was dying to get Kendra on her couch. Or whatever piece of furniture things might have drifted toward.

When they finally sat down to feast on the fruits of their labor, Kendra surprised her by mentioning the article Alison had written for an online women's magazine.

"It was spot-on," Kendra said. "I loved how you satirized society's expectations and objectification of women. Your point of view of a man obsessing over his body image was hilarious and so sharply focused."

"Thank you," Alison said. "I guess you've googled me."

Kendra smiled. "Guilty. My friend Violet raved about the piece, so I checked it out. Your essay on politics as pop culture was awesome, too. You're right about Americans. We're as obsessed with the players in political parties as we are with movie stars."

"We do that over in the UK with Parliament, although we're not usually as devoted to the false idols of the House of Lords or Commons as Americans are with your Republicans and Democrats."

Kendra stared at her in what seemed like awe. "I don't know how you haven't been picked up for more than just freelance work. You're obviously a genius."

"If you're trying to woo me with flattery, Ms. Blake, I must tell you…it's working beautifully."

Kendra laughed. "I am trying to woo you, but not with flattery. Your writing is good, no question about it. I love reading think pieces."

Alison felt herself blushing at the bombardment of compliments. She had thought it a good time to reveal that she was also the Poison Pen, known and feared for her wicked and witty book reviews, but after Kendra had gone on and on about how impressed she was with the intelligence and sophistication of her essays and articles, she was afraid she'd undermine herself by revealing that she'd supplemented her income trashing other people's intellectual property.

"Thank you for such a generous review," Alison said. "I'm hoping to land a permanent position soon so I can get out of child-rearing once and for all."

"I have a feeling it won't be long," Kendra said and raised her glass. "You have a voice the world needs to hear."

❖

All during dinner Kendra replayed their smoldering kiss at the counter. The homemade sushi was more flavorful than Kendra imagined it would be, probably because of that kiss. Now that they'd just settled down on her couch, she was feeling shy and a little nervous again. Even though their chemistry was palpable, they were still in the early stages of dating. She didn't want to move too quickly with Alison, no matter how wonderful it felt.

Alison emptied the bottle of white wine they'd opened during dinner into both of their glasses. "Those rolls you made were scrumptious. You've got the talent to become a sushi chef for sure."

"And you mix a mean seaweed salad," Kendra replied. "I doubt sushi chef is in my future, but I can definitely pick out dessert. I never would've guessed something called red-bean ice cream would taste so good."

"Yes. I love it and green-tea ice cream as well."

"I'll have to pick that up next time we do this." She embarrassed herself a little with her sudden presumptuousness. "I mean, you know… if you feel like hanging out again."

As if reading her mind, Alison shifted toward her, resting her knee on the sofa cushion. "Kendra, I think it's safe to assume I'll want to hang out again. I really like your company. To be honest, I think about you quite a lot when I'm not with you."

Okay. So much for being afraid of moving too quickly. She exhaled in the relief of knowing her feelings for Alison were mutual. Still, reason should prevail. Too much too soon was never good in any situation.

"I really like being with you, too." Kendra sipped her wine as she observed Alison's body language. The open stance toward her and her arm stretched across the top of the sofa signaled a lot more than "like" was happening between them.

Alison's lips parted as though she wanted to speak, but she just smiled.

"What?" Kendra prodded her with a barefooted nudge to her knee.

"Would you mind if I kissed you again?"

"I wouldn't mind at all," Kendra replied, a shiver running through her. She took Alison's glass and placed it with hers on the coffee table.

Alison scooted closer, luring Kendra into her aura of body heat. Her fingers traced Kendra's jawline as she kissed her.

Their tender, sensuous kisses grew stronger, and Kendra pulled her down on top of her. Alison's warm tongue undulated against hers, tingling every inch of her. To release some of the sexual tension about to boil over, Kendra squeezed the flesh on her back as Alison's tongue explored her mouth. Making out with her had been the most erotic experience she'd had in ages, maybe ever. She wanted it to last forever, but the ache between her legs was threatening to become an entity all its own.

She clutched Alison's silky V-neck tee and dragged it up and over her head. Alison unbuttoned Kendra's blouse and pressed her hot skin against hers. Kendra moaned as she massaged Alison's firm back and fingered the clasp of her bra.

Kendra knew this was the precise definition of moving too fast, but they were both at the point of no return, so she forced herself to stop overthinking and indulged in the physical experience of Alison with all her senses.

"I can't believe how sexy you are," Alison whispered. "I've never been so aroused."

"Me either," Kendra whispered back. "What did you put in that sushi?"

Alison giggled. "That's the one secret ingredient I'll never reveal."

She began massaging Kendra's breasts roughly through her bra as she ground against her. Once Alison had discovered it had a front clasp, that bra was history. Her mouth descended on Kendra's nipples, and the ache was as glorious as it was unbearable.

Kendra ripped open Alison's bra from behind and drew her back up to kiss her more. She let out a loud groan when Alison's fingers clawed at the button and zipper on her jeans. This was happening. It needed to happen. She couldn't take the throbbing any longer. "I need you to touch me," she said breathlessly.

When Alison's tongue plunged into her, she nearly shrieked. She could hardly control her breathing as Alison pleasured her slowly. She luxuriated in the ecstasy as she tried to thwart the extreme stimulation so it would last a little longer. But it was no use—Alison was just too skilled at what she was doing. After numerous intervals of teasing, Kendra grabbed Alison's head and kept her steady, resulting in an explosive climax that transported her.

"Sorry it happened so fast," Kendra whispered as she caught her breath. She was embarrassed at how quick and loud she was.

"No need to apologize. The night is young, and I'm nowhere near done with you." She dragged her fingers up the inside of Kendra's thigh.

"That's not fair. I haven't had my chance at you yet."

"Shall we wrestle for it?"

"I have a better idea." She swept Alison's hand from her thigh and kissed her fingers, daring to lick one or two of them.

When Alison closed her eyes and relaxed into her pillow, Kendra took it as a green light to continue. It had been so long since she'd been interested in sex that this seemed almost like her first time. She'd forgotten how much she'd missed giving and receiving such sensual pleasure. Alison's lack of inhibition had freed Kendra from the insecurity and self-judgment she'd been experiencing since they'd met.

She let her natural desires and instincts take over, and soon she was arched over Alison tasting every inch of her, from her soft pink lips, to her tangy neck, all the way down her pearly white chest and stomach.

The next morning Alison woke nestled against Kendra and, after a mild fit of panic, remembered it was her alternating Saturday off. Vanessa was going to have to be dealt with when she returned to the house. This she had surmised after she and Kendra woke up on the sofa around two thirty a.m. As she trailed Kendra to her bedroom, four text messages from Vanessa were waiting for her. This ugly reality was already overshadowing the magnificence of last night and the warmth of her morning afterglow.

"Good morning," Kendra said. "How did you sleep?"

"Not too bad, considering I had two reptiles ogling me from across the room."

Kendra's giggle sounded like she was still groggy. "Lois and Harriet are sweethearts, voyeurism notwithstanding."

Alison snuggled up against her and squeezed her torso. "You're a sweetheart, and your lizards can stare at me all they want if I get to spend the night with you."

Kendra propped herself up on her elbow. "I hope it's the first of many."

"So do I." Alison kissed her and nudged her back down.

"Are you looking for seconds already?" Kendra helped her slide on top of her.

"I think you mean thirds or fourths. But who's counting?" Alison began kissing her neck.

"I could stay in bed with you all day," Kendra whispered. She seemed to be enjoying the kisses but stopped her abruptly. "Unless you have plans for today. Don't feel obligated—"

She put a finger over Kendra's lips. "I don't have anything planned. I'd love to spend it in bed with you, or doing anything with you, really."

"Are you sure? I feel like we're powering ahead at lightning speed. I don't want you to think I expect you to change your life around."

Alison studied the look of concern in Kendra's eyes. It was true, they were moving fast, but she didn't care. She was infatuated with Kendra, but in a way that would blossom into full-blown love if she took the care to cultivate it.

"It does feel a bit hasty," Alison said. "But I'm not terribly concerned about it. I've had several relationships. Some developed slowly, whilst others took off like a shot. But none ever made me feel the way I do when I'm with you, Kendra."

"Really? You're not just saying that?"

Alison's heart fluttered at the vulnerability Kendra was exposing. "Why would I just say that? If this isn't what I wanted, I could've easily slipped out on you before you woke."

"That's true. I didn't snore, did I? Sometimes when I fall into a deep sleep it happens."

"I was sleeping so peacefully in your arms I doubt I would've heard it if you had."

"Let me make you breakfast," Kendra said. "I make a mean banana French toast."

"I suppose I should eat some actual food. I can't live on just you, can I?" Alison flashed a naughty grin.

"No, but I like how that sounds." Kendra got out of bed and walked naked to her dresser.

Alison couldn't resist the sexy view. She loved the wildness of Kendra's messy hair, the musculature of her upper back, and the way her waist curved in above her shapely rear end. She relished the view until Kendra put on a T-shirt and baggy pajama bottoms with coffee cups all over them.

She got up when Kendra tossed her a light robe to wear for breakfast and followed her into the kitchen.

"What can I do to help?"

Kendra turned around with a playful grin. "Hmm. Well, you can sit at the table and look pretty, or if you're brave enough, you can feed Lois and Harriet."

Alison's stomach flopped, but she didn't want to seem chicken. "Is there a chance I'll lose a hand if I do?"

"Only if you wrap it in kale."

"Well, all right. I wouldn't want the little ladies to go hungry while I'm about to be fed a feast."

"Atta girl," Kendra said. She pulled out a bag of mixed greens and stuffed them into two small bowls, then topped them off with shredded cantaloupe. "Here you go." She handed the bowls to her, then added, "And don't worry. I live close to an urgent-care center in case…" She looked down at Alison's hands. "You know."

"That's not funny," Alison replied. "It's two against one in there."

She took the food into the bedroom and carefully placed the bowls on either side of the tank. After watching the creatures scurry over to each bowl and chow on their breakfast, she glanced around the bedroom and stopped at the collection of framed photos on Kendra's dresser. She assumed they were of the family Kendra had told her all about during their last date: one of her and her brother, another of her adorable niece and nephew, and the third, a photo of her and her mother when Kendra was a young teen. They looked like they were so close, and she resembled her mum a lot. How tragic that Kendra had lost her at such a young age. No pictures of her father in the gallery.

Although he was still alive, Alison had gathered from the way Kendra had spoken of him that they hadn't much of a relationship.

"How's it going in there?" Kendra called from the kitchen. "They didn't pull you into their tank and eat you, did they?"

Alison giggled at Kendra's dark sense of humor as she returned to the kitchen. "No. In fact, once I told them that I'd been to a country where they'd be mixed into the soup of the day, their attitudes came online straight away."

Kendra whirled around with her spatula in hand. "You haven't eaten iguana before, have you?"

"God, no. But when I was in Nicaragua with Habitat for Humanity, it was on every menu."

"You volunteered for Habitat for Humanity?"

Alison sat down at the table with a cup of black coffee. "Yes. After I finished at university, I wasn't quite sure where to go next, so I took a year off to volunteer."

"Impressive. Is there any continent you haven't been on?"

Alison gave a modest giggle. "Of course. I haven't been to Antarctica or Australia."

"You haven't? Slacker." Kendra's dry tone made Alison think she was serious.

"Have you been to all seven?"

Kendra scoffed as she slid the second round of French toast onto a platter and brought it to the table. "Uh, no. Just North and South America. I believe I owe you an apology."

"What for?

"When we first met, I assumed someone fourteen years younger wouldn't be worldly enough for me, like we couldn't be on the same life-experience page. Turns out you have more life experience than I do."

"Only because I was avoiding going home after I graduated."

Kendra sat at the table, and they began to eat breakfast. "That's funny. I started college late because I couldn't persuade myself to leave home. Why didn't you want to go back after graduation?"

"My dad was an officer in the Royal British Navy, and I think my mum wanted to earn his respect by ruling over my sisters and me like we were cadets. After four years on my own at university, I couldn't possibly survive going back home to domestic martial law."

"I didn't finish my college degree until I was twenty-eight," Kendra said. "I had a hard time focusing."

"That's understandable. You'd lost your mum at a young age."

"Yeah," Kendra said, appreciating Alison's empathy. "It took a long time to spring back from that and find my worth and my purpose."

"The important thing is that you did. Now look at you—a successful editor living life on your own terms. That's all any of us want, really."

"So are you," Kendra said. "That's one of the things I find so attractive about you. You're a lot younger than me, but you seem to have it figured out."

"Hardly, but thank you." Alison finally dug into her French toast. "Maybe the two of us crossed paths so we can figure it out together."

"I like that," Kendra said. "Because I can't think of anyone I'd rather spend an afternoon contemplating life's mysteries with."

"Same here. Does that mean you're not going to kick me out after breakfast?" Alison's tone was playful, but her desire to stay with her was very real.

"On the contrary, I was hoping you could spend the day," Kendra said.

❖

"Where on earth are you taking me?" Alison watched the blur of vegetation going by as she gazed out the passenger window. Trees lining the narrow country road made a canopy over it that let in patches of sunlight. It was a pretty ride.

"The Prudence Crandall House," Kendra said. "She's an unsung hero of the early movement for racial equality in the early 1800s. Her story is fascinating."

Alison studied Kendra's profile as she drove. She loved the contrast of her strong jaw and supple lips that she loved to kiss. And her dark hair brushed back over her perfect ears adorned with three different earrings up her lobes. And the beauty mark on her cheek that—

Kendra whipped her head toward her. "What? What are you smiling at?"

"I didn't know I was," Alison replied. "But your gorgeous profile must've had something to do with it."

"I know what it was," Kendra said with a frown. "You're laughing at me for being a women's history nerd. This sounds boring, doesn't it? We can go somewhere else. It's not that big a museum."

Alison sprang up in her seat at Kendra's misconception. "No, no. It sounds amazing, really. I'd love to learn about old, em…"

"Prudence. Crandall."

"Right, yes. Lady Crandall."

"Are you sure? I mean you're not even from this country. Why would you care about tiny little Connecticut's official state heroine?"

"Based on your fervor for the woman, I simply must learn more about her. I'd feel positively treasonous if I didn't, especially since I'd like to earn citizenship."

Kendra's smile lit up her entire face, and Alison was enamored.

"Are you sure you won't find it boring?"

"Impossible, Kendra. I find you quite stimulating no matter what we do." Alison continued taking in the passing rustic scenery. "By the way, will cocktails be involved later?"

Kendra turned to her. "They're included. After the tour, we'll check out a local whiskey distillery in the area."

"Excellent," Alison replied and continued absorbing the scenery.

❖

As they walked around the museum, an eighteenth century, two-story colonial, Kendra watched Alison take everything in. It seemed that Kendra wasn't the only history geek.

She sidled up to Alison and leaned against her shoulder. "What do you think?"

"She's fascinating, all right. I can't believe that in the North, New England no less, the attitudes were as atrocious as in the South back then."

Kendra nodded. "I still can't believe this country hasn't moved past this color division yet. It makes me sad."

"We have our racial issues over in the UK, but here in the States, some of you honor the strife like a hallowed tradition."

Kendra laughed ironically. "I always wonder what other countries think of us whenever we make the news for stupid shit. Now I know."

"We Europeans have to deal with our own share of knob heads, so we realize that the lot of you are quite lovely people."

They continued walking through the house, viewing and reading the captions on the exhibits, and sharing what they found striking.

"Do you know what I like about you?" Kendra asked.

Alison whipped her head toward her. "That I love the smell of musty old colonial homes?"

Kendra laughed. "Uh, no, but now that you mention it, that one's right up there with gasoline and homemade cookies."

"Yes." Alison enthusiastically agreed.

"I was going to say that I love how no matter what topic I bring up, you always have something thoughtful to offer. I never run out of things to talk about with you."

"I thought you were about to say my legs or my boobs, but depth of conversation is nice as well."

"Oh, and you're not a picky eater," Kendra said. "My ex, the one I was with the longest, was the worst. She drove me so insane whenever we tried to decide on restaurants. It got to the point where we rarely went out to eat."

Alison grinned. "I'm still waiting to see if my boobs or arse make it into your top ten."

Kendra grabbed her around the waist and checked for the old woman selling the entrance tickets. "Your entire body makes the top ten, especially these." She pointed to Alison's lips, then glided hers over them.

"Mmm. How much longer is this tour?"

"It's self-guided." Kendra winked. "Should I guide us out of here?"

Alison nodded as she licked her lips.

"I have to confess, after the distillery tour, when you suggested we go back to your place for a bit of the bubbly, I honestly thought you were referring to champagne."

Kendra smiled and raised her flute of chilled prosecco from across the bathtub. "Bubble bath, champagne—it's all a means to the same end."

"I like this interpretation better." Alison clinked her glass against Kendra's, then submerged her hand into the bubble bath. Once she found Kendra's leg, she slid her hand up the inside of her thigh. Kendra chirped with surprise, jolting up and exposing a suds-covered, luscious breast.

"I have to say, I love how you're up for any suggestion," Kendra said. "Something tells me if I suggested hang-gliding nude over an active volcano, you'd probably say yes to that, too."

"Probably." She placed her glass on the floor next to the free-standing tub. "Do you know a place where we can actually do that?"

Kendra's eyes widened. "No. I was being facetious."

"Oh. Of course." Alison chuckled. "But yes, I'm up for anything. I'd say the naughtier the suggestion, the better, but I wouldn't want you to think less of me."

"I'd think more of you, even more than I already do." Kendra lifted a tuft of bubbles and blew it at her.

"It can't be more than me. You have no idea how often you're on my mind."

Kendra stubbornly folded her arms across her chest. "I totally win this competition."

Alison giggled and leaned forward over Kendra to kiss her. Kendra pulled her down with a splash, and their warm, soapy bodies melded together. Alison tingled as their kisses grew more intense, and suddenly she felt Kendra's fingers slide between her legs. And slide slowly back and forth. And then stop.

When Alison opened her eyes, Kendra tugged at her hips, indicating she wanted her to lift them. Alison hoisted herself by draping her arms on the sides of the tub and extended her legs over Kendra's shoulders onto the edge. Kendra did the rest, grabbing her under her butt and pulling her into her face. From there Kendra's magic tongue finished the job.

After climaxing, Alison slid back to her position at the opposite side of the tub, causing water to splash out onto the floor. "Oh, sorry. Let me mop that up."

"After," Kendra whispered as she climbed onto Alison's face.

❖

Later, in bed, Kendra and Alison ate from bowls of kettle corn and seedless grapes as they watched a serial-killer documentary. Sergio had already lost interest in their snacks and was asleep next to Kendra, but Lois and Harriet were all about the green grapes.

She watched Alison bite off a piece of grape and gingerly feed it to Lois, then do the same with Harriet, careful to quickly retract her hand.

"You're so funny," she said.

"I like having all my digits, thank you very much," Alison replied.

"I have to admit, you've made leaps of progress since this morning. You wouldn't even touch them, and now look at you. You're letting them crawl all over you."

"Well, I figured if you fancy them so much, I should give them a chance. Perhaps I'm missing something."

Kendra scooped up Lois, kissed her on the head, then held her out. "Your turn."

"Er, em, not tonight," Alison said, leaning away. "Let's save some fun for tomorrow."

"Okay, okay." Kendra got up and put the iguanas back into their tank. "I've tortured you enough for one day between a history museum and bloodthirsty iguanas."

Alison moved the bowls to the nightstand as Kendra got back into bed. "It wasn't too awful, especially dinner at that bistro in the country and a shag in a bubble bath. All in all, I'd call that a magnificent day."

When she cuddled into Kendra's arms, Kendra kissed her on the head. "Besides, you're paying me back by making me watch the biography of a killer clown."

"Oh, no. You won't have nightmares, will you?"

"Nah-ah," Kendra said. "I've already seen this one. Twice."

Alison giggled into Kendra's shoulder, and before long, she'd fallen asleep in her arms.

Chapter Eight

Kendra poured a second mimosa from a pitcher during Sunday brunch at their favorite Columbian restaurant. Although this was a monthly thing with MJ and Violet, she felt different this morning, almost disembodied as they casually discussed Violet's latest dating-site misfire. She watched them eat their breakfast selections, sipping her mimosa almost meditatively as thoughts of Alison and their smoldering thirty-six-hour date floated through her mind.

"Why aren't you eating?" MJ asked.

The question drew Kendra back to reality. "I am," she said and promptly picked up her fork.

"What do you think of Violet's situation?"

"I'd say give the dating sites a rest for a while. I've never been a fan of them, but after meeting Alison the old-fashioned way, it's unlikely I'll want to get on one again."

Violet raised her eyes from her huevos rancheros long enough to snarl. "Well, ain't it great to be you?"

"You're a little touchy this morning," Kendra replied, then deferred to MJ. "Was I being insensitive or is she being touchy?"

MJ looked up from her phone. "You're asking someone who doesn't care about meeting Ms. Right. But if I was, yeah, I'd get pissy about your comment, too."

"I'm sorry, Violet." Kendra patted the top of her hand. "You'll meet someone, too, someday. It has to happen. You're too fabulous to stay single forever."

"Thank you," Violet replied, still hovering over her breakfast dish.

Kendra studied her. "Did you eat at all yesterday?"

"Keep your hands away," MJ said. "She has food aggression."

Kendra laughed, and even Violet couldn't resist smiling.

"So did you two fuck yet?" MJ asked.

"Ugh. I hate when you blurt things out like that." Kendra crossed her arms over her chest. "Do you have to be so blunt?"

"I'll take that as a no." MJ returned her attention to her phone.

Kendra lowered MJ's phone with her index finger. "For your information, yes, we had relations, and it was exquisite."

"Relations?" Violet said. "My ninety-year-old grandparents have relations."

MJ put her fork down. "This is heading to a place I never wanted to go."

Kendra sighed as she recalled her night with Alison. "You know, you just don't realize how much you've missed the intimate connection and wild abandon of making love with someone until it finally happens again."

"Are you in love with her?" Violet asked.

Kendra felt her face blossom into a wide smile as she nodded.

MJ scoffed. "Fell in love after one fuck. Amateur."

"What do you mean?" Kendra snapped. "That's exactly how I hoped it would be. I don't know how you can have such intimate experiences with women you don't even know."

"Uh-oh," Violet said. "Slut-shaming. Shots fired." She leaned forward as though trying to secure her view of the imaginary brawl about to break out.

Kendra glowered at Violet in offense. "What about her prude-shaming me? That's not shots fired?"

"Prude-shaming?" MJ covered her eyes as she laughed.

"That's not a thing," Violet said.

"It is so," Kendra said. "I'm making it a thing. And I don't apologize for wanting to have sex only when it's meaningful. And by the way, it was way more than once."

At that, Violet froze with her lips still wrapped around her fork.

"Hey, you do you, boo," MJ said. "But after finding out Patty was cheating on me after twenty-three years together, 'meaningful' is now a relative term."

Kendra frowned. "You're not punishing Patty by refusing to let someone else in. You're closing yourself off from finding the right person to share your life with."

"Who says I need that? Or want it, for that matter. You were peachy keen for over three years before Alison came along. Now after three weeks, you're the love guru we all didn't know we needed?"

"Wow. I'm getting on everyone's bad side this morning. I'm sorry." Kendra bowed her head in shame.

"Don't be sorry," Violet said sincerely. "Deep down we're just pissed it was you who met the woman of your dreams and not us."

For verification, Kendra looked at MJ, who grudgingly gave the "half and half" hand tilt in response. At that moment, she didn't want to feel all bubbly with optimism every time she thought about Alison—not when poor Violet was feeling so down. But she couldn't stop it if she tried.

"Listen. What I said before about Violet goes for both of you. You guys are too amazing *not* to have someone special in your lives. It will happen."

"Thank you, honey," MJ said. She raised her flute glass to toast them. "But I still stand proud with all the single, middle-aged women who are tired of everyone's shit."

"Fair enough," Kendra said, and they all clinked glasses again.

Although Alison hadn't wanted to leave Kendra Sunday morning, she realized their extended date would have to end eventually. Who knew a Friday dinner plan would turn into a two-night sleepover that included lovemaking, a stroll along a lake, and dinner at a rustic New England restaurant, followed by wine and more lovemaking in a tandem bubble bath? She sighed as she pulled into the Dillfords' driveway, partly at the scent of Kendra still on her shirt from their good-bye hug, and partly because the Dillfords hadn't left yet for a Sunday excursion at their exclusive country club.

She stopped to say hello to the kids dressed in their Sunday best as they cavorted on the side of the house. When she went inside, Brandon and Vanessa were in the kitchen, and it appeared that Alison might have interrupted a tense conversation.

"Morning, Alison," he said with a friendly smile.

"Good morning, Brandon. Vanessa." She glanced between them, trying to decipher who was responsible for hardening Vanessa's expression to stone—Brandon or her.

"I'll be outside waiting for you," he said, then nodded at Alison.

As soon as he disappeared out the door, Vanessa wheeled around on her.

"Where were you?" She glared at her with a deportment about as stable as the lid on a pot about to boil over.

"I was with Kendra."

"Why didn't you answer my texts?"

"It was my day off, and when I saw it wasn't anything work-related, I just—"

"Blew me off," Vanessa said through clenched teeth. "That's priceless. You meet someone new, and suddenly I'm nothing more than a meaningless fling."

"Vanessa, you need to calm down. Your husband and kids are right outside the window."

"They can't hear. These are expensive windows."

"That's not really the point," Alison said. "And there's nothing sudden about this. I'd explained that you and I were through weeks before I'd even met Kendra."

Vanessa's eyes flashed with rage. "You used me. You took advantage of my vulnerable situation to satisfy your lustful needs."

"Now look, Vanessa. None of that's true, and you know it. Please be reasonable about this. You're my employer and—"

"I'm your lover," she replied and pushed Alison against the stove. Pure mania replaced the look of rage in her eyes. "Let's run away together. We'll go to Europe, live in an artist apartment in Paris. You can write your stories, and I'll learn to paint portraits of tourists, and we'll have tea at outdoor cafés and make love in—"

"Vanessa, please. Get hold of yourself." Alison extricated herself from her clutches just in time for Brandon to walk in the side door.

"Ready to go, dear?" He consulted his Rolex. "We don't want to be late. A potential investor I've been grooming will be there, and I want to get to him before the hyenas come around."

"Yes, darling," Vanessa said. "Let me fetch my purse." Her eyes were daggers piercing Alison before she marched off.

"So while we have a minute, I want to talk to you about something." Brandon's expression was serious, and were it not for his coral Bermuda shorts with little crabs on them and manicured toenails peeking out from designer sandals, she might've worried he suspected something was going on between her and Vanessa.

"Certainly," she said. "What about?"

"How's the job hunt going?"

"Not as well as I would hope, but I'm still plugging along."

"Oh. Sorry to hear that. Say, I know you have bigger career aspirations than this, but the kids love you, and I know Vanessa is fond of you as well. Any chance a handsome salary increase might convince you to stay on till Julianna starts prep school?"

"That's not for another five years," Alison said in surprise. No way in hell could she be in the same house with Vanessa for another five months, let alone years.

"True, but I'd make it financially worth your while." He leaned an elbow on the counter and smiled grandly.

What a wanker. It was just like a wealthy, straight, white man to think nothing of asking a working-class woman to postpone her dreams if he threw a little extra cash at her.

"If you don't mind, may I have some time to think about it?"

"Oh, sure, sure," he said as he shoved his hands in the pockets of his silly shorts. "When you're ready, give me a figure that works for you. And don't be shy."

"Right, then." She nodded and looked around, suddenly feeling awkward standing there. But she wasn't about to venture into the wilds of the second floor while Vanessa was still up there.

Thankfully, Vanessa breezed into the kitchen and out the door without so much as a glance in Alison's direction. Alison thought it quite rude, but in light of Vanessa's recent tantrum, she'd take rude.

And speaking of rude, Brandon's offer inspired her. She went upstairs, hopped on her laptop, and banged out a draft about white male privilege and the condescension those of a lesser echelon faced in their dealings with the men who tossed it about.

❖

Kendra was particularly eager about her biweekly Monday night get-together with her brother, Ryan, at the pool hall not far from his house. Their tradition that began years ago consisted of a family dinner at Ryan's house first, with his wife, Christy, and the kids, and then the two of them would head off for a couple of hours of sibling bonding over beer and billiards.

She chalked her pool cue as she moved around the table to line up her shot.

"Christy was serious about you bringing Alison over for dinner next time," he said.

"I know," she replied, partly distracted as she strategized. "Her enthusiasm is contagious, but I think it's still a little too soon."

"It doesn't seem too soon by the way you were talking about her all through dinner."

Kendra smirked, trying to suppress her titillation. "It doesn't *feel* it to me either, but practically speaking, it is. It's only been a month." She took her shot, and her ball flew into a corner pocket.

"Nice," he said.

"Thanks." She swept by him to align her second shot.

"Okay. No rush," he said. "Maybe when the time is right I can invite Dad and Joyce, and we can make it a whole family thing."

The timing of his suggestion knocked off her focus, causing her to miss. "Do you mind?" She scowled at him as she passed him for a sip of her beer.

"Sorry." He grabbed the chalk block. "I just know the kids would love to have all of us together for dinner some night."

"Your kids are fine no matter who shows up. They're very well-adjusted."

Ryan chuckled. "That's all Christy. I'm just the baseball coach and the ATM."

"That's nonsense. You're a great dad, which is no small feat, considering your mentor."

"Man, you are tough on that guy."

Kendra shrank inward at his observation. She was so used to making digs at their father's shit-poor parenting skills that they just seemed to dribble out of their own volition. Maybe she was tough on him, but not without valid reason.

"It must be nice to live with revisionist history," she replied as she made her next shot.

"I haven't revised anything," he said. "I just found it easier to let go than keep carrying it on my back. Besides, becoming a parent's also helped clean the lens."

"Another way I've let him down."

"What are you talking about?"

"Evidently, you don't remember how he reacted when I came out. That might've been his opportunity to redeem himself with me, but nope. Just scathing disapproval."

"Wasn't that like twenty years ago? No parent was approving of that back then. Besides, I know for a fact that he and Joyce are totally over any prejudice they once had."

Kendra whirled a finger around in the air. "I'll be sure to nominate them as grand marshals for the next Pride parade."

Ryan laughed and elbowed her in the arm. "Where's our waitress? We need a shot."

"Yeah, we do."

When the server brought over their shots of bourbon, Ryan did the honors. "To family."

As the warm liquid rolled down her throat, Kendra contemplated the idea of expanding "family" beyond just her brother and his brood.

She wasn't too keen on the idea of her father and Joyce, but maybe Alison was the place it could begin.

CHAPTER NINE

Kendra looked heavenly framed in the dusky light as they sat outdoors at a café overlooking the Hudson River. That weekend, the inviting late spring weather had inspired them to head off to New York City for the day. After taking in a matinee of a popular musical, they toured an outdoor art exhibit in Bryant Park before capping off their day with dinner. While their spontaneous jaunt into the City was loads of fun, it was also a strategic plan on Alison's part. Vanessa was becoming increasingly difficult as her relationship with Kendra became an established thing.

The day before, Vanessa had interrogated her with a barrage of casual questions about Kendra, including where she lived and worked. Alison grew concerned that perhaps she was plotting to do some reconnaissance work of her own, i.e., stalking. Making matters worse, Brandon was leaving for a weekend golf junket with his firm's associates that same day, which left Vanessa uninhibited in her pursuits. Alison understood this because their affair began on one of Brandon's said weekend golf junkets. And it was apparent when Vanessa had backed her against the refrigerator yesterday that she was under the mistaken notion that Alison would continue to honor that tradition.

Alison refocused her full attention on Kendra as she discussed her complicated relationship with her father over pre-dinner cocktails. She felt good that Kendra was already comfortable enough with her to go there, considering how reserved she sometimes came off.

"I'm sorry you experienced that after your mum passed," she said. "I suppose it would be rather difficult to move on from it as easily as your brother thinks."

"Right?" She leaned forward, apparently responding to Alison's support. "I mean, first of all, he's a guy, so you know how they are with feelings. Plus, being younger, he didn't have the pressure on him to look out for a younger sibling after it happened."

"And how long ago was this?"

"She passed when I was sixteen." Kendra suddenly became pensive. "Wow. Twenty-nine years already. That's kind of a long time to hold a grudge."

"I don't suppose that's something someone on the outside could judge," Alison replied. "It's about how you feel, not your brother or anyone else. Does your dad try to contact you?"

Kendra shook her head. "We had a big blowup about five years ago and haven't spoken since, other than hellos or goodbyes when we can't avoid each other."

"But now he wants to make amends?"

"To be honest, I have no idea if that's what he wants. All I know is my brother, for some reason, is trying to facilitate a family reunion. I think he believes when we're all together, we'll experience some epiphany and magically be a family again."

"That's a nice fairy-tale ending, isn't it?"

"Exactly." Kendra's posture stiffened as she leaned back in her chair and sipped her cosmo. "And I don't believe in fairy tales."

"I do. My favorite is the one where the two princesses fall in love and live happily ever after." Alison planted her chin in her palms and grinned.

Her shameless attempt to win Kendra over seemed a success, as a blossoming smile smoothed out the wrinkles in her forehead. "I have to admit that I've never read that one, but I do think I'd like it."

Alison sipped from her glass of white wine. "This river view, lovely wine, and even lovelier company is doing something to me."

"Something good, I hope."

"It's making me want to blurt out things I probably shouldn't at this point."

"Like what? You're a spy for British Intelligence? Or a member of the royal family who fled to America to escape an arranged marriage?"

Alison giggled. "You have quite the imagination. But no, nothing of that sort."

"Then what?"

"I…" A surprising wave of shyness swept over her, stealing the words from her mouth. She looked down to gather herself, then, after a deep breath, took Kendra's hand in hers. "I can absolutely see a fairy-tale ending with you."

"Alison." Kendra met her gaze, her eyes sparkling with happiness. "I thought it was just me. Thank you for being brave enough to say it."

Alison doubled down on Kendra's excitement. "I love you, Kendra. I've never met anyone quite like you."

"I love you, too." Kendra grabbed her other free hand, and they held on, basking in the shine of their mutual revelations.

They finally, reluctantly let go when the server brought their seafood dinners. Alison reached for her phone in her back pocket when it dug into her as she sat back to eat. Her heart jumped into her throat when she saw a series of missed calls and texts from Vanessa. That petulant little…

"Is everything okay?"

Alison snapped to attention. "Yes, fine, great. Just the mistress of the manor." She turned the phone facedown on the table and admonished herself for not taking a handbag to keep her things in.

"Does she ever let you have a day off without summoning you?"

"Oh, yes. Em, she just wanted to remind me of an appointment she has Monday morning so I didn't run off to Tahiti with you." Alison forced a laugh to defuse the guilt she felt lying to Kendra's face immediately after being so honest. That reaction could swiftly turn into a dangerous habit.

Kendra seemed satisfied with her answer. "Go ahead and reply. I won't be offended."

"Yes, right. I better do that." She seized the opportunity and texted Vanessa back.

We'll talk when I get home!!!!!! Now FUCK RIGHT OFF!!!!

"There. That should take care of it." With a dainty smile, she stuffed the phone back into her pocket. The physical discomfort of sitting on it was suddenly less discomforting than the idea of having to explain the truth about Vanessa on the night they exchanged *I love yous*.

❖

As they walked to Grand Central Station from the subway hand in hand, Kendra watched the illuminated billboards lighting up the night sky in Times Square. She'd had such a wonderful day with Alison exploring Manhattan, deciding on activities as they came upon them. Then the day culminated with that meaningful exchange she'd thought a lot about lately but felt it was too soon to share. And it probably was. MJ was sure to give her lots of shit for it, but not everything in life can be perfectly timed. One of the things she loved about Alison was her uncompromising desire to go after what she wanted. Every woman Kendra admired had that quality.

Hot and tired, she settled in for a nap on Alison's shoulder in the air-conditioned train car back to New Haven. "You don't mind, do you?"

"Of course not." Alison threw her arm around Kendra and pulled her in. "It'll hold me over until I'm cuddling beside you in your bed."

"I was hoping you had the day off and could stay," Kendra said.

"Vanessa wasn't too happy about it. Hence, all those urgent texts, but it's been settled."

"I thought she was texting about her Monday-morning appointment."

"Oh, well, yes. That, too."

"Jeez, it must stink to have such a demanding boss," Kendra said. "MJ has her moments, but at least I can tell her to chill out when she gets to be too much. That's the benefit of working for someone you have a close relationship with."

Alison suddenly started choking.

Kendra sprang up. "Are you are all right? Have some water." She watched in concern as Alison chugged the bottle, her eyes tearing from her cough. "Okay?"

Alison nodded. "Phew. Went down the wrong pipe."

"Maybe all this work talk got you choked up." Kendra giggled and nuzzled down against her again.

Alison began rubbing her shoulder, and Kendra closed her eyes to relax. Who could blame Alison for wanting to change the subject? It had to be such a pain to have the kind of job where you were that entrenched in the family. It was almost as though the woman felt entitled to keep tabs on her.

Kendra exhaled as she further relaxed, enjoying the feel of her cheek on Alison's breast. She must've dozed off without realizing it, because when she opened her eyes, they were already at the first stop in Connecticut. She glanced over at Alison's phone as she typed a response in what looked like a continued conversation. When she moved her head to read the name at the top of the screen, Alison quickly closed her phone without exiting the text first. Kendra swore she saw the name Dillford at the top. She couldn't tell whether it said Mr. or Mrs. before the name, but it was definitely Dillford. It had to be the wife again. Why on earth would she be communicating with Mr. Dillford after midnight?

For that matter, why would Mrs. Dillford be communicating with her?

She lifted her head and sat back, pretending she'd just woken up. She smiled and studied Alison's face as she smiled back. Something felt off. But was it really, or was Kendra just being paranoid? What if Alison was seeing someone else besides her? If she was, what a great cover to have the person's contact listed as her boss's last name.

Ugh. Come on, Kendra. Get a grip. Writing romantic intrigue must've gotten to you. She chastised herself for going there immediately. Yes, she'd been cheated on once by an ex, but that was years ago, and not everyone was a cheater.

Still riding the high of an amazing day, she convinced herself to let it go and laced her fingers through Alison's.

CHAPTER TEN

The next morning after they'd made love, Kendra lay in bed scanning through the photos she'd taken of Alison and the sights around New York City. With her phone battery about to die, she contemplated if she should join Alison in the shower. She was rather surprised at how her libido had changed since they'd started dating. The more of Alison she had, the more she wanted. And now the thought of Alison's tall, shapely body all naked and soapy in her shower had her revving up for another round.

She got out of bed and wanted to plug her phone into the charger before sneaking into the bathroom. When she unplugged Alison's phone, the screen lit, revealing five texts from Mrs. Dillford that had all come in that morning. This was crazy. No way should an employer harass her employee like that with constant texts and phone calls. It had to be some sort of labor violation. She moved toward the slightly ajar bathroom door and listened to make sure the water was still running. She then pressed the home button, but it was password protected.

Alison was hiding something. That was obvious. Her heart sank with a thud when she concluded it was likely her initial suspicions of another lover. Her blood began to boil, more with herself for placing so much trust in her emotions and in Alison's deceptive charm so soon. She was old enough to know better.

Pacing her room still clutching Alison's phone, she tried to calm down enough to decide her next move. What were her options? Throw Alison and her clothes out onto the front lawn? Wait. Maybe she should confront her first. Then when Alison concocted some ridiculous story, Kendra could toss her out, towel and all.

She heard the squeak of the faucet and the water stop. In a panic, she tossed the phone onto the unmade bed and froze in place. Alison came out with her hair in a turban, wrapped in a towel just barely covering her nipples.

"For future reference, I wouldn't mind if you joined me." Alison walked up and planted a sensual kiss on her. "It would conserve water." As Alison kissed her harder, Kendra almost forgot she was supposed to confront her.

"Wait. Wait a second." Kendra stopped her and tried to assemble her wits. "I need to talk to you about something."

"Okay." Alison tightened the towel knot and readjusted the one on her head. "What about?"

She took a deep breath as though ramping up to dive off a cliff. "Is there anything I should know about Mrs. Dillford?"

Alison's eyes darted to the side and back. "No…"

Kendra huffed. Why did she think this was going to be easy? "Let me rephrase that. Why the hell is Mrs. Dillford constantly texting you, and don't tell me it's work related."

"Well, uh, okay. Um, let me start at the beginning."

"Aha," Kendra shouted with satisfaction. "I knew it."

Alison appeared confused. "Okay, then. Shall I continue with my answer or not?"

Kendra cringed, realizing she'd shot off her Sherlock Holmes style "aha" too soon. "Yes, yes," she said, trying to remain impassive. "Just tell me who she is. Or he is. Or they. Whoever you're fooling around with behind my back and using 'Mrs. Dillford' as a code name."

"What? Kendra, darling, I'm not fooling around with anyone behind your back. I swear." Alison moved toward her as if to reassure her, but Kendra warded her off with outstretched hands.

"Don't you come at me with your old-timey movie talk. I'm not your 'darling,' especially if you're screwing someone else. I think you should leave."

"But Kendra, please." Alison scanned the room frantically. "Do you have a robe? I can't mount a proper defense standing in front of you completely starkers."

"This better be good." Kendra fumed as she went to her closet and yanked out a fuzzy winter robe.

Alison dropped her towel in front of Kendra and slipped into the robe. "As I was saying before, let me begin by assuring you that I am not seeing anyone but you. That honestly is Vanessa, er, Mrs. Dillford who keeps texting."

"Why does she keep blowing up your phone?" Kendra shouted.

"Because she's a huge pain in the arse," Alison shouted back.

"You're gaslighting me. Stop trying to convince me that one and one equal three because I know they don't. I want you to tell me the truth." Kendra dropped down on her bed and covered her face in her palms, exasperated.

Alison stared at Kendra, feeling entirely horrid about upsetting her. She wanted to sit down beside her and convince her that this was all a big misunderstanding—anything but the sordid truth.

"Kendra," she said quietly.

Kendra looked up.

"I promise you, since I met you there's been no other man, woman, or what have you in my life. I've not slept with anyone else, nor do I want to. Please believe me."

"I want to, but come on. Don't you see how this looks?"

Alison scrambled for a way to put out the fire. "Yes, yes. I can see how it might seem to you. But Vanessa is inordinately demanding. I only allow her to get away with it when it comes to the job, not on my time off."

Kendra stared up at her.

"I'm not seeing anyone but you," Alison said. "If I'm lying to you now, may God *not* save the Queen. Please. Say you believe me."

Kendra stood up and threw her arms around her. "I do believe you, honey." The words were muffled in the plush collar of the terry-cloth robe. She pulled back and faced Alison. "I'm sorry I got crazy and accused you of cheating. I think I'm a little overwhelmed by the pace of things and just got paranoid."

Alison faced a pivotal moment as she gazed into Kendra's vulnerable eyes. She was clearly spent and seemed likely to accept any semi-logical explanation for the unreasonable barrage of communication from Vanessa. She'd already told her that Vanessa was an entitled witch accustomed to getting her own way, but that was only the partial truth. If she didn't come clean about her previous sexual relationship with Vanessa, then that would be lying by omission. Now was her chance to clear the air and unburden herself of the stress of imagining how far Vanessa would go to get her attention.

However, what if Kendra couldn't handle the truth? Not many women would be amenable to dating a woman who was currently being harassed by an ex-lover with whom she still resided. That was a rather tall order for anyone, let alone an emotionally guarded woman already overwhelmed with her feelings.

Her heart was screaming, *Don't say anything, you twit. She'll dump you. Just go home and change your cell number!*

But her conscience overrode the screaming with a soft entreaty. *You love her. She deserves the truth. She's begging you for it.*

Alison sighed deeply and led Kendra to sit on the edge of the bed. "You're not paranoid, not entirely."

"What do you mean?" The sweet vulnerability vanished from Kendra's eyes, replaced with something that looked like death lasers about to shoot from her eye sockets.

"Well..." She paused and rubbed her forehead. "This is so hard to say."

Kendra leapt up from the bed. "It's her? You're fucking Vanessa?"

"No, no, no." Alison sprang up in a panic, then added sheepishly, "Not anymore."

"Not anymore? Well, thank God I'm not losing my mind," Kendra said calmly.

Alison smiled, thinking the worst of it was over.

"And fuck you for letting me think I was the last few days." She shoved past her and stormed into the bathroom.

Alison began pleading through the door. "Kendra, I swear I wanted to tell you, but I was afraid you'd act...well, exactly like this. It's over between Vanessa and me. I'd ended it well before you and I met. She's not what I want. You are."

"I do not deal well with dishonesty, especially from someone who says they can see a future with me."

"I totally understand, and I do apologize for the poor way I handled this. It was only out of fear of losing what we've started that I tried to blow it off as nothing. She means nothing to me, but I should've given you the truth. It wasn't my place to make the choice for you."

The silence from the other side of door unnerved her. "Kendra?"

Still nothing.

"Kendra, darling. I'm sorry." She laid her head against the door in surrender. She'd really cocked things up this time. She swallowed hard against the lump of sadness lodged in her throat and whispered Kendra's name once more. Silence. Finally, she said, "I'll give you time alone with your thoughts, but…but I hope you'll understand and still choose me."

Alison dressed quickly and left Kendra's house.

On the drive back to the Dillfords', she vacillated between the fear of never hearing from Kendra again and what life would be like in an American women's prison after she was convicted of throttling Vanessa to death in her own home.

If Kendra was gracious enough to accept her apology, she would put in her two-week notice with Mr. Dillford despite the looming expiration of her work visa.

CHAPTER ELEVEN

Instead of spending a gorgeous summer Saturday afternoon with the woman she was hopelessly in love with, Alison spent it with Danni. She was sad and anxious waiting for Kendra to mull over whether they had a future together anymore, and she certainly wasn't in a mood to tangle with Vanessa. After a bike ride on a trail in southwestern Connecticut, they picked up deli sandwiches and took them to a brewery.

Alison sat cross-legged in the grass minding the plastic cup of some tart IPA Danni had convinced her to get as it rested against her crotch. They were eating in silence, not just because they were starving from their workout, but because she was certain Danni was bursting at the seams to fire off a rebuke.

"You were right, Danni," she finally said. "You warned me, and I didn't listen."

Danni glanced over at her as she sipped her beer. "I didn't say anything."

"You didn't have to. Your whole countenance is screaming, 'I told you so.' I just wanted to show you that I'm big enough to acknowledge my mistake."

"Okay." Danni shrugged as though it wasn't a big deal. "So after the Vanessa cat was let out of the bag, I'm assuming you also came clean about your secret identity as the Poison Pen."

Alison was aghast. "No. Why would I? It's got nothing to do with her."

"Why wouldn't you? You have quite a following. If she works in publishing, she'd probably find that interesting."

"They produce nonfiction works, technical books, and all that sort. She's never even mentioned reading lesbian romance. Frankly, I think she's too highbrow for it."

"If lesbian fiction was lowbrow, your blog wouldn't have all those followers," Danni said. "Wit is a sign of intelligence."

"I've already told her about the freelance pieces I've published on women's rights and the culture of politics. She seemed impressed with that, so I quit while I was ahead."

Danni gave her a skeptical glare as she bit into her sandwich.

"What?" Alison said defensively. "There's nothing duplicitous in my motives. I just don't want anything to detract from my credibility as a journalist. Once I land a regular spot at a news outlet, then I'll show her the blog, and we'll have a good laugh over it."

"Sounds like a foolproof plan to me," Danni said.

Alison thought she detected some gratuitous sarcasm but let it pass. "So what's happening in your world lately?"

She shrugged. "Nothing. Working. I'm in the process of developing a color formula for a revolutionary new foundation that will hide dark circles and blemishes."

"You're doing God's work," Alison said flatly, more interested in checking her phone for the hundredth time for a text from Kendra. Nothing. The wait was excruciating. Worse was the idea that she was waiting for something that might never come at all.

"And I've been chatting with a woman," Danni added, as though it was an afterthought.

Alison perked up at the promise of a distraction. "Is that so? Do tell."

"We became friends on Facebook, and she messaged me."

Alison waited for the rest of the details, but Danni resumed eating and gazing around the industrial park. "Isn't there more to the story? Like a name, for instance?"

"Violet."

"Violet? As in Kendra's friend?"

Danni nodded casually.

"How did neither of us know our friends were getting to know each other? How could you not have told me?"

"We're private people."

Alison furrowed her brow at Danni's weird response. "Well, do you think you can ask Violet if Kendra's said anything about me, like whether she's through with me or not?"

The suggestion seemed to appall Danni. "I'm sure I cannot. I will not be a party to your illicit schemes."

"It's called being a wingwoman, Danni. That's how it works between friends. Have you met Violet in person yet?"

Danni shook her head.

"Well, then if you help me out in my dilemma, I can certainly help you by facilitating a double date amongst us all." Alison felt satisfied with her clever suggestion.

"I'll pass."

"What? What do you mean, you'll pass? You've finally got someone interested in you after who knows how long, and you're just going to pass?"

Danni nodded again as she sipped her beer.

"This is preposterous. I cannot believe you won't even entertain the possibility of doing me this favor."

"As you know, I'm not very reliable in awkward situations."

"Yes, I learned that about you straightaway, but this doesn't have to be awkward. You just casually bring it up to Violet whilst you're chatting, you know, sort of like, 'so, have you heard about Kendra and Alison?' Then gather what she knows."

Danni seemed to give the suggestion serious consideration. "I suppose I could do that."

"There you are. I'll forever be in your debt. Now when will you be chatting again?"

"Later today probably."

"Excellent. Now let's review what you'll say."

"You just told me what I'll say. 'So, have you heard about Kendra and Alison?' "

"Right. And then she'll say yes, and then you'll launch into how remorseful I am and how marvelous a person I am, and then—"

Danni held up her hand. "Whoa. There is no 'and then.' I'll bring it up to her, see how she responds, and pass it on to you. That's that."

"Well, can you message her now so we can get this over with? I'm so gobsmacked by it all that I can barely think straight. Better still, give me your phone. I'll fire off the message for you."

When Alison reached for it, Danni's lips tensed up into a tiny butthole, a sure indication Alison had triggered her anxiety. "I'm officially not having fun anymore," she said with a scowl.

Alison sat back in the grass in defeat, ready to liquefy from the heat and her intense desire to evaporate in it. Danni was not the type to be pushed. She was just going to have to bide her time.

❖

Kendra sat alone at the Mediterranean bistro's bar and glanced around at the couples talking and laughing over dinner and drinks on a Saturday night. This sucked. It had been so long since she'd met a woman who'd captivated her and made her want to be part of a romantic twosome again. She loved the new things Alison was teaching her, like how to make sushi and modern British culture, among others. Her job as an au pair had afforded her the opportunity to live in several different European countries over the last decade. Recently they'd talked about a trip to Europe so Alison could take her to the best wine bar in Barcelona and the best non-touristy place for an alfresco dinner in Paris.

Now she was swirling a Spanish red around in her glass waiting for her best friend to rescue her from acute loneliness. Together they could analyze all the nuances of what lies were red flags versus which ones were harmless omissions. She'd missed the flags in her previous long-term relationships, and she wasn't about to go color blind again in exchange for a guided tour of Europe with a stunning, sexy Brit.

"Hey." MJ finally breezed in and climbed up on the stool next to her.

"Thank you for meeting me," Kendra said. "I'm sure you must've canceled a date to come."

"I did not." MJ signaled for the bartender to bring her a glass of what Kendra was having and immediately started picking through the olive assortment in the dish in front of them. "I tried to get Violet to join us, but she gave me the same excuse she gave you."

Kendra scoffed and then sipped her wine. "Pressing engagement? What pressing engagement does she have?"

"Why is she being cryptic?" MJ asked. "If she's fucking someone, just tell us."

"It's probably more along the lines of playing in one of those cyber video-game tournaments."

MJ tapped her finger to her temple at Kendra's astute deduction. "Speaking of cryptic, why are you with me and not Alison tonight?"

Kendra sighed at the thought of rehashing the situation. She'd calmed down since texting MJ earlier in the day, but she still wanted her opinion, knowing how unabashedly honest she was when asked—and even sometimes when she wasn't.

"So, I'm not with her tonight because I caught her in a lie, one I consider pretty big."

"What's she, married?" MJ buttered a slice of bread, seemingly unfazed by whatever the answer would be.

"No, but she had an affair with her boss. And she still works for her and lives there."

MJ grimaced. "Oh. That rich broad. You said 'had.' Does that mean it's over?"

"Alison swore it is. She said she ended it before we even met."

"Okay, well, do you believe her?"

"Yes, I do actually, but it bothers me that she's still living there. And the woman texts her constantly when we're together, so it gets me thinking." She hated how confessional she sounded. "Am I just being insecure?"

"Wait. This chick's always texting her when she's with you?"

Kendra nodded slowly, not liking where MJ's mind seemed to be veering.

"And what does Alison say to you when she texts?"

"Up till this morning when I confronted her, she'd say they were work-related and that Vanessa is just pushy and spoiled."

"That's the lie you were referring to?"

"That and the fact that she'd never even told me about the affair in the first place. Is that bad? It's bad, isn't it?"

MJ sipped her wine and seemed to ponder the answer like an Ivy League philosophy professor. "It's not the worst thing she could've lied about. If it really is over, and she's into you, I can understand her wanting to avoid letting you in on the situation. I mean, how can she leave if that's her job?"

Kendra quietly contemplated the irrefutable point.

"Did you break up with her, or is this just an 'I'm mad at you and need to cool down' thing?"

"I didn't actually name it, but this morning I was so heated I threw her out. I just wanted all of it over." She sighed deeply at the thought of a permanent breakup. "But now I don't know what I want."

MJ twisted her mouth in sympathy. "You know what you want."

Kendra nodded. "I do."

"Look. I know you're super into her. If you trust she's telling you the truth that the affair's over, let it ride."

"Really? Is that what you'd do?"

"Yeah." MJ finished chewing and assumed a reassuring demeanor. "It's a tricky situation, Ken. I see your point about being uncomfortable with her still living there, but she can't just walk out on her job because a woman she just started dating doesn't like it. She'll never get hired anywhere else."

"She can start looking for a new job. Would I be out of line to suggest it?"

"Uh, yeah. You're barely two months in. If you're that rattled over the boss, have her stay with you."

"Are you nuts?"

"I don't mean like officially move her in. Just have her sleep over every night."

"Whoa, whoa. Let's pump the brakes here." The angst brought on by that suggestion helped Kendra fine-tune her perspective. "Maybe I overreacted this morning. We had an especially romantic day yesterday, so I was like 'woooo.'" She waved her hands around her head. "She told me she loved me."

MJ halted the wineglass before it touched her lips. "She did? Did you say it back?"

"Yes. And it was a natural response, just rolled right off the tongue. But I'd definitely say moving in is not on the table right now."

MJ's smile was more reassuring than any words. "I'm happy for you, my friend. Don't let this glitch wipe the shine off this beautiful thing you're in."

"Thanks," Kendra said. "What would I do without you?"

MJ playfully nudged her in the shoulder. "I guess there's a valuable lesson in all this."

“Yeah? What’s that?”

“If we ever fuck, I’ll have to terminate you immediately afterward.”

Kendra chortled into her wineglass. “Then obviously I’ll need to control my urges around you.”

“Good luck with that,” MJ said.

❖

The next morning Kendra lay in her crowded bed staring at the ceiling as some show about people who sell obscenely lavish mansions droned on the TV. With Sergio asleep at her feet and Lois and Harriet crawling over her, she replayed her conversation with MJ at the wine bar the night before. She’d been friends with MJ forever and trusted nobody’s advice more. If MJ thought Alison had a legit reason for omitting that information at this early stage in their courtship, then Kendra had to acknowledge the possibility that her harsh reaction was mostly about unchecked emotion.

After all, Alison had mentioned several times she was planning to leave the job soon. That had to count for something. She was actively trying to change careers, so naturally, she’d have to stay on at the Dillfords’ until she’d found a way to pay a rent on her own and secure an extension on her work visa.

Besides, she missed her. The sudden absence of Alison’s vibrant aura, her sensual touch, and adoring blue eyes staring back her left her feeling lost. Yesterday, she’d woken up draped in her arms. This morning instead of a gorgeous, sexy woman in her bed, she had a menagerie of a cat and reptiles, all of whom seemed rather ambivalent toward her. Not that she didn’t love them, but it would be infinitely better if Alison had been there, too.

Later that afternoon, Alison arrived at Kendra’s condo with a bouquet of roses. She was more nervous now than when she’d come over for the first time. That was before she’d fallen hopelessly in love with her, although the jury was still out on whether love at first sight was really a thing. She’d never believed in it before. She couldn’t recall if she’d felt that way with any previous girlfriend, but none of her relationships had made it beyond a year or two.

With Kendra, though, everything felt different.

When the door opened, Kendra's smile nestled in her supple Mediterranean skin floored her. No prior girlfriend had ever left her speechless by simply opening a door.

"Thank you," Kendra said when Alison shoved the bouquet at her. "Come in."

"I'm so glad you called."

They stared at each other in the foyer.

"You can kiss me if you want," Kendra said.

"I do want." Alison moved forward until she felt Kendra's warm lips against hers. Finally her breath returned when she sensed the shared longing in their kiss. She was forgiven whether Kendra wanted to say it or not.

"Would you like a glass of wine while we talk?"

"Of course." She followed Kendra through the condo out to her deck, where a chilled bottle of wine and a small charcuterie plate awaited them. "You shouldn't have gone to any trouble."

"I figured it would prevent me from dragging you into bed before we had a chance to talk." Kendra's look, her whole manner as she poured their wine, was sexier than usual. A mix of desire, vulnerability, and caution danced in her eyes.

"Not that I would've objected, but I do agree it would make a serious conversation more difficult." She sipped the chilled sauvignon blanc and savored the pinch of grapefruit essence in her throat. The fear that she'd managed to stave off since Kendra called and asked her to come over for a chat was rising to the surface. Was this how a classy woman broke up with people? Eased you into it with some sexy innuendo and a wine buzz? She swallowed hard as dread began crawling up from her throat. "I know I hurt you by neglecting to tell you about Vanessa from the start, but—"

"I wasn't upset that you hadn't told me up front," Kendra said. "I was hurt by your lack of honesty when I first asked you about her."

Alison bowed her head, feeling like a total shit. The mea culpa she'd planned to offer vanished at Kendra's cool, rational resolve, and now it was simply a matter of not breaking down and begging in front of her and the platter of meats and cheeses. "This is where you say you never want to see me again, isn't it?"

"You think I would've gone through the trouble of making this fine spread if I was gonna kick you to the curb? I don't have time for that." Kendra's playful smile changed the stifling air between them.

"I was afraid, you know." She took Kendra's hand. "I knew there was nothing between Vanessa and me anymore, but I was scared that, given we still lived in the same house, you'd want to stop seeing me. I made the wrong decision in a split second of panic, and I'm sorry."

Kendra sipped her wine. "I can see how that could happen. But I need you to understand that I also don't have the tolerance for lies in a relationship that I used to. Been there and definitely learned the hard way."

"I respect that. I wouldn't want to deal with it either, especially because you're so special to me."

Kendra brushed her fingers over Alison's forearm. "I'm glad we talked."

"Me, too." Alison leaned in and kissed her cool, tangy, sauvignon-blanc lips. "This was the longest twenty-four-hour period I've ever experienced. I believe I'm hooked on you, Kendra Blake. As long as we're being honest, I might as well confess it."

"And it's more than just sex?" Kendra asked.

"My God, yes," Alison said. "My heart flutters at the thought of you, and not just when I'm thinking about making love with you. We keep saying how fast things are moving, but I can't seem to slow my feelings down."

"I can't either. Something keeps telling me to follow this wherever it leads, and that's what I want to do."

Alison gazed at Kendra's lips as they landed on her wineglass while the wind pushed her hair around. "You look so beautiful tonight. I'd follow you anywhere."

"How about inside?" Kendra asked.

They stood at the same time and faced each other. The desire in Kendra's eyes was arousing beyond words, and the breeze kept taunting her with wafts of Kendra's scent. She picked up the charcuterie tray and carried it into the kitchen.

Kendra came up behind her, pressing her breasts into Alison's back as she stroked the sides of her hair from behind. Alison whirled around, and Kendra pushed her against the counter and kissed her. She held her face, and Alison went limp, submitting to Kendra's forcefulness, as though they hadn't had each other in months. Each flick of Kendra's tongue against hers weakened her legs, swept her up in an uncontainable passion.

Once shirts and bras started dropping on the tile floor, Alison swung Kendra around, tugged her shorts down, and hoisted her onto the counter. She couldn't wait to dive in and taste her, to satisfy her desire, and that was exactly what she did.

She loved nothing more than hearing Kendra moan and then cry out in the pleasure she'd given her.

Chapter Twelve

As Kendra drove to work Monday morning, her spirit felt as light and wispy as the daisy curtains her mother had in the kitchen in summertime. She used to be the happiest kid. Before her mother got sick, she'd worked in a library part-time, affording her plenty of time and energy to dote on Kendra and her brother as they were growing up. With so much attention and encouragement from her mother, she hadn't realized how absent her father was, often working overtime shifts at the factory. Her parents loved taking them on summer trips, and their mother was always signing them up for lessons for this or that. Someone had to put in the long hours to pay for it.

What made that train of thought enter her head? Could it be that this was the first time as an adult she'd felt that level of pure, uncomplicated happiness only kids understand? She'd been in love before, several times. But she struggled to remember if any of the women she'd loved had ever filled her with that fluttery, head-spinning joy of new love. They had to have. At least one of them…at least at one time.

A spark of apprehension singed her as she realized her connection to Alison was much deeper than she'd realized. Hopefully, Alison was on the same page.

When she pulled into her parking space, she shook away the heaviness from the turn her thoughts had taken. It was a beautiful morning for a positive outlook. She brought the tray of coffees and breakfast into MJ's office.

"Well, well, well," MJ said. "Someone's got a glow this morning. I take it the reconciliation went well."

"It did." Kendra grinned, then tore into the bag and split an order of mini-omelets between them. "After someone reminded me how I occasionally hold people to unreasonably high standards."

"Oh. You'll have to introduce me to this genius someday."

"Simmer down, Chief." Kendra chewed a forkful of her egg. "If your head gets any bigger, your little body won't be able to support it."

"Go ahead. Make fun of my stature," MJ said primly. "But I realize your snark comes directly from knowing I'm right. Once again."

Kendra couldn't help laughing at her. "You're a jerk."

"So I have a reservation for four at the Halcyon Café Friday at six. Violet and I are stoked to actually spend some time hanging out with Alison and getting to know her better."

"Yeah. Now that we're a thing, I guess it's time I show her who I surround myself with."

"Have you told her about your book yet?"

Kendra shook her head.

"Are you fucking kidding me?" MJ almost spit out her coffee. "You're having sex with the woman, but you're not close enough to bypass your superstition rule? I don't understand how you can keep such a huge secret."

"I'll tell her this weekend when it's officially released. I'm going to hand her a signed copy along with a long-stemmed rose."

"Aww, how romantic. I'll bet that's exactly what Shakespeare would've done."

Kendra frowned. "It's cheesy, isn't it?"

"It's adorable." MJ reclined in her chair. "I take it, then, you haven't told your father either."

"I'm sure he knows. You think Ryan kept this mouth shut?"

"He didn't call to congratulate you?"

"I made it pretty clear in our last argument a couple of years ago that his opinion on anything I do is neither required nor welcome. Besides, he'd never call me out of the blue. He's stubborn as fuck."

"No kidding. Someone related to you is stubborn as fuck?"

"I never said I didn't inherit some of his qualities…as unflattering as they may be."

"Recognizing you have a problem is the first step."

"I have the problem?" Kendra shook her head. "That train left the station a long time ago, MJ. I don't need him. My brother, his family, and my close friends are my family, my tribe." The bitterness of the past hit the back of her tongue. "The wrong parent went first."

When MJ's jaw dropped, Kendra heard the words that had rolled out of her mouth. "What? You know my mom and I were best friends."

MJ's lingering horrified stare started to unnerve her.

"Okay. That was a shitty thing to say. Of course I don't want him to die, but frankly, how much will my life change when his time does come?"

"That depends on what you do to change things while he's still alive."

Kendra scoffed. "What? Are you and Ryan secretly texting?"

MJ leaned forward, resting her forearms on her desk. "My father's been gone four years next month, and even though we always had a good relationship, I live with the regret that we could've been closer. Sometimes when little girls grow up into women, especially headstrong women, fathers think they have to take a few steps back. I wish I'd had the foresight back then to tell my dad I didn't want him to."

"Our situations are entirely different, MJ."

"I know that. And I respect it. I'm just saying that things never have to stay the way they are, especially if someone really wants them to change."

"Swell," Kendra said, licking the egg grease from the corner of her mouth. "When he gives me the slightest inkling that he cares, I'll let you know."

MJ reached for her mouse and focused on her large flat-screen monitor. "Look. I didn't mean to shit all over your Monday morning. Let's talk some business."

"Oh, we're actually gonna do that today?"

"Yes. When are you gonna send me the outline for your next book?"

"When it's done, obviously, which will be soon."

"In order to do that you'll have to get your face out of Alison's panties first."

"Eww, you're so gross." Kendra stood, deciding the staff meeting was over. "I thought you were setting up readings and signings around town for *The Winding Road*."

"I am, but that doesn't mean you can't start on number two. They say that's the hardest book to write."

"Well, now you're just making me want to dive right in." Kendra headed to the door.

"You know you're my favorite human," MJ said sweetly.

"Some days I'd be scared to see what would happen if I weren't." Kendra pretended to leave in a huff, but deep down she knew MJ was the ride-or-die she could always count on.

As she walked across the reception area to her office, she smiled, thinking about the wave of awesome she'd been riding the last couple of months. Although MJ got under her skin whenever she preached to her about fathers, she refused to let her baggage flatten her positively effervescent mood.

❖

After Alison dropped the kids off at arts and music camp, she planned to take advantage of the few hours she'd get alone to do some writing. She'd researched the transformation of women's interest in American politics, both casually and professionally, after the first hundred days of having the first female vice president in history and couldn't wait to dive in.

She went inside, grabbed her laptop and some sunblock, and headed for the expansive outdoor patio surrounding the in-ground pool. The Dillfords' property was so quiet and tranquil, she was sure to complete the first draft of her article.

After she closed the sliders, the quiet tweeting of sparrows was marred by a spit-out spray of pool water and a shrill, "Last one in's a rotten egg!"

"Jesus!" Alison swung around to see Vanessa peering up at her from the side of the pool. Her big eyes and bigger smile were drippy and dazzling.

"What took you so long to drop off the kids?"

"I had to run a few errands." She set her things down on an umbrella-covered table. "I thought you had one of your luncheon thingies today."

"I canceled. It's too gorgeous a day to waste inside with a bunch of stuffy women trying to out-rich each other. Come join me."

"It's a little chilly for the pool today."

"Not a heated pool. Come on," she purred. "Don't make me play with myself. That's no fun. Oops. I meant *by* myself." The unmistakable seduction in Vanessa's voice set her on high alert.

"Well, I do need to get this article written. I have a deadline." She hoped the lie would make a difference to Vanessa, but it didn't.

"I'll make you a deal. You come for a little swim, and I'll go pick up the kids this afternoon so you can finish your little story."

"It's an essay, not a story."

"Okay, well…" She ran her fingers through the water's surface. "You really should take a dip with me. Once we sign off on your renewed work visa, I know you plan to take off to New York. Then you'll never have time to relax in a pool in the middle of the day."

Relax? Swimming with a barracuda? Hardly. Vanessa clearly needed to fine-tune her subtlety when it came to issuing threats about Alison's work visa in order to get her way.

Alison sighed heavily. "All right. Let me get into my suit."

Vanessa clapped her fingertips together, grinning.

"But only for a bit. I have to get this piece written while it's fresh in my head."

Vanessa nodded condescendingly and waved her off toward the house.

Alison ran upstairs to her room while texting Kendra to tell her she was thinking of her. If ever there was a moment in history when a surprise visit couldn't have been more awkward, this was it. She'd just moved mountains to convince Kendra there was nothing between her and Vanessa anymore. She couldn't bear to imagine the optics if Kendra walked into the backyard and saw them frolicking in the pool.

After ensuring that Kendra was sufficiently busy editing and such at work, she ran back outside and descended the steps into the pool at the end opposite Vanessa.

Vanessa must've been able to smell the fear because she'd swum over straightaway.

"You should stay over there," Alison said. "I feel a cold coming on." She faked a cough for effect.

"A cold? Seriously?" Vanessa arched an eyebrow as she floated on her back. "Could you be more obvious about wanting me to keep away from you?"

Alison grabbed one of the kids' inflatable tubes and used it as a barrier. "I don't need to make up an excuse to keep you away. You know I'm in a relationship with Kendra."

Vanessa grimaced as she kicked in the water, splashing Alison in the face. "Ugh. How could I forget? You mention it every waking moment." She flipped over onto her stomach and approached the tube. "I was in a relationship with Brandon, and that didn't stop you."

"Yes, well, that was one of my less virtuous choices, but it didn't stop you either, and you're the one married to him."

"In name only. But it's not like I'm some gold-digging hussy. He's the one who checked out on me first."

"Well, that's for your divorce attorneys to sort out, but I love Kendra. I wouldn't betray her like that."

"Sounds like things are pretty serious…for such a short amount of time. Does she know you're moving to New York?"

Alison suddenly felt like a fly that had unwittingly flown into a spider's web. "That's not definite. It was a dream of mine when I came here, but I was single then. And, of course, I would only move if I had a job there."

"Two months together and already you're abandoning your dreams. Sad." Vanessa sucked her teeth, clearly enjoying needling her.

"I am not." She paused to reset her reaction. "I'll gladly take a full-time writing job in Connecticut as well. Location doesn't matter as long as I'm working as a journalist."

"You'll probably do better if you move to the City and pound the pavement there. I'm sure Brandon manages the money of a media mogul or two. He could help you. Maybe."

Alison's blood was starting to boil in the heated pool water. She was tired of defending her relationship to Vanessa. She was obviously just being petty, trying to get under her skin. "I'm sure Kendra's boss knows people as well. She'd be happy to put in a good word if I asked her to."

Vanessa shrugged ambivalently. "Provided you're not just an exotic summer fling to Kendra."

"What do you mean?"

"She's a lot older than you, been around the block a few times. What if she's just into you now because you're the dish du jour? Sexy, much younger, blond European immigrant. That's a nice notch in her belt."

"That isn't even remotely Kendra. She doesn't care about notches in belts. She's perfectly sincere, and we happen to get on brilliantly."

"Yeah, huh. Time will tell," Vanessa said, swimming closer to her. "But nothing's guaranteed…except this." She tugged at the tie on her bikini top. It tumbled down, slowly exposing her round, succulent breasts.

Once Alison pulled her eyes away from them, she began backing away. "Vanessa, this is not a good idea. Someone could walk back here at any moment."

"Like who? Martha Stewart? I canceled my lunch with her, too."

"I mean Octavio, the landscaper. Doesn't he usually come today?"

"Stop fighting this, Alison. You know you still find me attractive. You miss having my body and teaching me how to have yours. Admit it. It still turns you on to think about our rendezvouses, doesn't it?"

In the deepest recesses of Alison's most basic desires, yes, all of those things were true to an extent. But truer was the fact she'd stopped thinking of all that once she'd fallen for Kendra. Now whenever her mind was idle, it would instantly drift toward thoughts and fantasies of Kendra. While Vanessa was ravishingly sexy, Kendra was, too, and she was also intelligent, inquisitive, sensitive, and kind, along with other endearing qualities she was discovering all the time.

"As I've said before," Alison said politely, "I ended our affair before I met Kendra. It's nothing against you. I just didn't want to be a party to your adultery-for-spite campaign against your husband, who also happens to be my boss."

"Is that a no?" said the voice above the glistening boobs coming toward her like Royal Navy ballistic-missile submarines.

"Yes," Alison said, backing up in the tube until a cold, tiled wall stopped her.

"Oh, it's a yes?"

"No, it's a no. I was answering your question."

"I thought my question was do you still find me attractive?"

Before Alison could make another attempt to clear up the confusion, Vanessa lurched over the inner tube, grabbed Alison's head, and planted an extra-wet kiss on her.

For fuck's sake, Alison thought. If she was about to refuse this massively hot woman literally throwing herself at her, she might as well propose to Kendra immediately. It had to be true love. In the meantime, she slid out of Vanessa's slippery grip and out the bottom of the tube, resurfacing near the steps.

"Bloody hell, Vanessa," she said, once she was safely on the patio. "What's gotten into you?"

With her bikini top back in place, Vanessa giggled as she backstroked away. "You can't blame a girl for trying."

Alison toweled herself off as she responded. "Actually, if we can blame movie producers for trying, then millionaires' wives don't get a pass either."

"Not even cute ones?"

"Ugh. You're horrible," she replied, meaning it. "I'll go write at the public library." She trudged across the patio to the sliders.

"Alison," Vanessa called out. "I'm sorry. I'm just teasing you. I promise I'll respect your boundaries."

"I know what an enormous sacrifice that would be for you. I'll pick up the kids at four p.m."

After showering and getting ready, she was still so irked at Vanessa for ruining her quiet time to write, she had to get out of the house and away from her. She'd pay a surprise visit to Kendra at work. Even though they'd established seeing each other a few times a week, she needed to see her face now, if only for a quick lunch break. That was, by far, the best antidote to a pisser of a mood.

She picked up some veggie wraps and a pretty crown-of-thorns house plant that would brighten up her office. Then she walked into the reception area and stuck her head around Kendra's open door. "Delivery for Ms. Blake."

Kendra looked over from her computer screen, her face brightening the office tenfold over the vibrant plant as she took off her reading glasses. "Hey, you. What a nice surprise."

"I was a bit nervous you wouldn't find it so nice. I remember you saying you hate surprises."

"Get over here," Kendra said. After Alison placed the plant and bag of food on her desk, Kendra pulled her onto her lap and kissed her tenderly. "I was so ready for a break. Your timing is perfect."

"You're perfect." Alison gazed into Kendra's eyes and brushed her hair over her ear.

"This is the kind of surprise that could make me start loving them."

"I miss you," she said, playing with Kendra's hoop earrings. "I simply couldn't wait till Wednesday to see you."

"I'm glad, because I've missed you, too." Kendra's smile turned her to absolute puree inside. "What's in the bag?"

"Lunch. I brought wraps. There's plenty for MJ as well if she'd like to join us."

"She already likes you, but food offerings will win her over completely. That's sweet of you."

As much as she didn't want to, Alison got off Kendra's lap and opened the bag. "Would you like to ring her office and see if she's hungry?"

Kendra got up and turned Alison toward the office door. "'If' is never a question when it comes to MJ and food."

Alison tagged along as Kendra barged into MJ's office. "Look who brought us sustenance today," Kendra said as she began setting up on the conference table.

"Hey, Alison. Nice to see you again." MJ stood up and came around her desk to give her a light hug. "This is great. Thank you."

"No problem," she replied. "I've always wanted to see the stimulating inner workings of a fast-paced publishing house."

"Sorry to disappoint you," Kendra said playfully.

"Don't listen to her," MJ said. "We're going to be branching out very soon. In fact, Kendra's going to be—"

Kendra's sudden hacking cough cut off MJ mid-sentence.

"Are you okay?" Alison handed her a bottle of water. "Here. Wash it down."

MJ rolled her eyes and bit into her sandwich, an odd reaction to your mate choking, Alison thought. But who was she to judge the nature of their friendship?

"What MJ meant was," Kendra said, "I'm going to be editing a new self-help and well-being series written by an up-and-coming wellness guru."

"Fascinating," Alison said. "Well, perhaps someday when I'm

asked to write the biography of some famous artist or entertainer, I can publish with Labrys as well."

"For sure," MJ said. "We'd love to sign you for that."

"But first I have to become well-known for my journalistic integrity," Alison said.

"How refreshing it would be if that trait became important in the media again," Kendra said. "Nowadays, anyone can call themselves a writer. It's easy to make a buck off sensationalism when truth and accuracy become mere afterthoughts."

Alison's stomach bottomed out. Good God. Had Kendra come across the Poison Pen blog? Worse than that, had she figured out it was Alison, and now they were both attempting to ensnare her in her own web of lies?

"Is your sandwich okay?" MJ asked.

"Oh, yes. Quite," Alison said, chiding herself for her paranoia. No way would they be able to piece it together without someone telling them outright.

Unless…

That bloody Danni!

She leapt up from the conference table. "Would you excuse me for a moment? I have an important phone call to make."

She ran outside to call Danni and began pacing in front of the building. When she answered, Alison wasted no time blurting out, "Did you tell Violet I'm the Poison Pen blogger?"

"What?" Danni said, then made the gurgling sound of a straw sucking up what likely was left of another iced coffee.

Alison took a deep breath, exhaled, then spoke slowly. "Did you say anything to Violet about me being the Poison Pen?"

"No," she said, sounding annoyed. "I promised I wouldn't mention it to anyone. You practically made me swear it in blood. What's the big deal anyway?"

"I've told you before, my blogs are brazen and irreverent and unbecoming of a writer who wants to be taken as a professional journalist. That's why I don't use my real name."

"Okay. I get it. I swear I haven't told anyone."

"All right then," she said, tamping down her spinout. "I suppose it's entirely possible that I'm just being paranoid. Let me go now before they think I'm weird."

"Yeah, because you being on the phone is the thing that would make them think it."

Alison ignored the sarcasm and ran back inside.

"Is everything okay?" Kendra asked her as she plunked down next to her.

"Oh, yes. I'd just remembered that I had to call Danni to remind her of something important. Those brilliant-scientist types would forget to put on pants if they weren't reminded."

MJ looked at her quizzically. "Isn't early afternoon a little late in the day to remind someone they have to put pants on?"

Alison nodded and bit into her sandwich, hoping this absurd discussion would soon fizzle out.

"So anyway," Kendra said, "do you have the afternoon off?"

"Only part of it. I have to pick up the children from music camp at four."

"That's a nice little break."

"Indeed. I only hope I won't have to pay for it by listening to the little one play 'Hot Cross Buns' on the recorder all the way home like last week."

❖

After they finished lunch, Kendra walked Alison out to her car to savor every last second with her. She was so thoughtful to drive out of her way to bring both her and MJ lunch. She could've spent the time off lounging by the Dillfords' pool, but instead she chose to spend it with her.

"What are you grinning at?" Alison asked as she grinned back.

"You." Kendra slipped her hands around Alison's waist and gave her hips a playful shake.

"Have I said something unwittingly witty?"

"No. You just make me smile," Kendra said. "And I could just stare into your dreamy blue eyes for days."

Alison threw her arms around Kendra, squeezed her like a vise, then released her only enough to kiss her passionately. "I'm so happy you feel that way, Kendra," she said when she finally came up for air. "I just can't seem to get enough of you." She assailed her lips and cheeks with more kisses before finally letting her go.

Kendra shivered at the intensity of emotion Alison showered on her.

"I better let you get back to work before MJ dismisses you."

"She wouldn't dare," Kendra replied, glancing around the strip-mall parking lot. "Besides, I think we're terrorizing the waspy old ladies coming out of Talbot's."

Alison chuckled. "Good enough for them. They don't know what they're missing, do they?"

Kendra smiled as Alison hopped into her late-model convertible. She loved that she was getting to know Alison's dialectical manner of speech well enough to recognize that she often ended her sentences with a rhetorical question. She had the cutest little quirks.

Once Alison peeled out of the lot and her car disappeared down Route 1, she forced her feet to carry her back inside and back to work.

When she walked in, MJ lay sprawled out on the reception area sofa looking at her phone. "Boy, are you two cute."

"Don't try to make me blush," Kendra replied, as she texted Alison that she missed her already. After hitting send, she looked up at MJ. "You don't think we look a little mismatched? You know, with her being so much younger."

MJ shrugged. "It's not like you're thirty and she's fifteen. You guys are both mature and attractive women. You make a gorgeous couple."

"Thanks, buddy." Kendra was elated to hear that. She slid down on the arm of the sofa's matching chair, preoccupied as she waited for Alison's reply. "Things are going so well, but I have to stop anticipating that some phantom relationship goblin's going to jump out at me from around the corner."

"Judging by your chemistry with her, I don't think that's gonna happen. Please let yourself enjoy this. You deserve it. You've been single for so long."

Kendra demurred, allowing her vulnerable side to peek out. "You really like her? I mean, she gives off a good vibe and all that?"

"One hundred percent," MJ said as she rose from the sofa. "I'm glad we're all going to dinner this Friday. It'll be a chance for Violet and me to really get to know your lady and, more importantly, for her to see how divine we are. I can't wait."

Kendra smiled and went back into her office. She smiled even wider when she saw Alison's *I miss you more* reply.

CHAPTER THIRTEEN

All week Alison had kept her cool about the night out with Kendra and her friends, but now that the evening had arrived, she was a quivering heap of nerves. Even though they'd already started saying "I love you," it was a major step to be included in group outings with the girlfriend's best friends. And she loved the Halcyon Café in downtown New Haven, a historical gay landmark that dated back to the early struggles for LGBTQ equality in America. With its creaky wood floors, low ceilings, and shoulder-to-shoulder occupancy on weekends, it reminded her of the local pubs she and her mates haunted back in Milton Keynes.

"I've been here to drink a few times but never thought to come for a meal," Alison said as they walked down the street to the bar. "I didn't even know they served food."

"Sure. Upstairs," Kendra said. "It's a limited menu, but the good stuff—shepherd's pie, Irish stew, everything that'll put you in a food coma after."

"I love all that, but if I'm spending the night at a beautiful woman's flat, I'd prefer they bring the stew, hold the coma."

"You're cute," Kendra said as they descended the stairs to the entrance. She went ahead of Alison to the gorgeous trans woman stationed at the reservation podium. "Hello, Josephine. We have a dinner reservation under MJ's name."

Josephine nodded, then glanced rather obviously toward Alison. "You and your *date* look gorgeous this evening."

Kendra gave her what seemed like a conspiratorial nod of

confirmation. "Thank you. Of course, Alison can make anyone look good."

Alison chimed in. "I think you've got it mixed up. I came here with Kendra so I'd look fetching."

"Ooh, *fetching*! I love your accent." Josephine smiled, then gave them some side eye. "You two are gross. It must be love. Enjoy your dinner, ladies."

Alison delighted in the idea that others could see what she felt for Kendra—and apparently, what Kendra felt for her as well. She followed her up the stairs to the small dining area. As soon as Kendra reached the top landing, a roar of "surprise" resounded from the room.

Surprise? Was it Kendra's birthday, and she hadn't even known? That would be rather awkward.

Alison stepped up on the landing, and instead of seeing MJ and Violet seated at their table for four, the room fairly bulged with a group of at least twenty people, mostly women. Kendra had already been swallowed up in the mass of well-wishers. What in the hell was happening?

Emerging from the din of laughter and chatter, she picked up the word "congratulations" as it was shouted and reiterated throughout the room. She looked toward the wall facing the street, and beneath the window was stationed a table adorned with a gold tablecloth, a colorful bouquet of flowers, and two stacks of soft-cover books.

As she walked toward the table to investigate, she tried to puzzle this whole thing out. Yes, MJ was a publisher, so a stack of new books was no great mystery. But why were they shouting "congratulations" to Kendra and not MJ?

She picked up a pristine copy of the novel and felt light-headed when she read the title. *The Winding Road*. Good God. This was the subject of her most recent review, the story she'd loved but had done a particularly wicked job on. The puzzle pieces suddenly cascaded down on her, and she didn't like the scene they created.

"Ladies and ladies," MJ shouted from the corner of the table.

A pair of gay men called out, "Hey, we're here, too."

"Hail to the queens?" MJ said without missing a beat. "If you can release Meredith Hodges, I need her to come up here so she can begin what you all came for." She paused as the crowd cheered. "Meredith, get on up here."

Kendra surfaced from a pocket of women and clutched Alison's arm on her way to the table. "I can't believe MJ did this. I'm still in shock." She joined MJ at the table.

"So am I," Alison muttered, trying to regain her bearings. This can't be happening, she thought. Kendra Blake was Meredith Hodges? How could she not have told Alison about this? How could she have kept something this tremendous a secret?

The word "secret" triggered a bomb in her brain. She plucked a glass of champagne off a tray as a waitress passed her on her way to the table. *Kendra's a novelist, and I'm a book reviewer known for trashing novels. What a disaster*. Thank God Alison had had the foresight to use a fake moniker of her own.

Kendra could never find out about this. She'd never understand, especially as she had already caught Alison being shifty with her about Vanessa. Not to mention the fact that she'd utterly flayed her novel.

MJ took a glass of champagne and backed away so Kendra could have the crowd's full attention.

Kendra took of large gulp of hers, then glanced around the room. "Wow. This is so…" She sounded breathless. "I'm in awe that you all came out for me, and I can't believe MJ was able to pull this off without me finding out. I mean, we're together every freakin' day."

"It wasn't easy. Believe me. You're into everything at work."

"She's not kidding. I really am," Kendra replied. "Anyway, I'm so honored and grateful to all of you for coming out tonight. This is way better than the book-launch party I had in mind—cheese and crackers on a table at the office."

"We couldn't let you debase yourself like that," Violet said.

"You were in on it, too?"

Violet and MJ laughed along with the rest. Kendra was so natural up there, so charismatic as she worked the room, that Alison almost forgot about her part in her girlfriend's book debut. She remembered again, and a pit formed in her stomach. She slunk toward the bar at the back of the room and ordered something much stronger than champagne.

She had to take that review down from her site. If Kendra found it, she'd be crushed. All this euphoria would evaporate into utter disappointment. She ordered a Jameson on the rocks and tried to get on her phone app to handle the situation, but she met an immediate delay as the service was spotty down in the room.

"Hey, baby." Kendra's hand appeared on her shoulder. Alison stuffed her phone in her pocket and spun around. "I wanted to introduce you to everyone before I started signing."

"Sorry, love. I wanted a drink. I was about to text you to get you one, too." Alison felt bad about that lie, too, but the situation was nearing crisis level in its urgency.

"Aww, thanks. I'm just going to finish my champagne, then have something stronger after I'm through signing."

"Righto," Alison said with a constipated smile. She grabbed her drink from the bar, and as soon as Kendra turned around, she downed half of it.

They made their way to the table where the guests had gathered to purchase their signed copies. Alison kept her head down, desperately avoiding eye contact with any of Kendra's friends. Kendra was positively jubilant in her ignorance of Alison's treason.

"So before I start signing, I just wanted to introduce everyone to my beautiful new girlfriend and journalist, Alison Chatterley."

At the sound of the group's applause, Alison downed the rest of her drink before Kendra turned her around to face the audience.

"Hello," she said meekly.

"I'd never have taken you for shy," Kendra muttered while giving Alison a comforting rub on the back.

"I'm not," she whispered back. "This is your night, darling." Alison waved to everyone with a gracious smile as a wave of nausea swept over her. She felt her face bead with sweat as she stepped back out of sight when Kendra commenced her signing.

Alison again skulked to the back of the room, trying to remain calm. This was a nightmare. She got on her phone again in an attempt to destroy any evidence of the review, but when she noticed her review had received over three thousand views and had also been disseminated throughout the web, she knew it was too late. She couldn't just delete it. It wouldn't look good to her advertisers.

She ordered another Jameson on the rocks and assessed her options. Maybe she could write a retraction? Say she'd read the novel again and found that it was actually splendid. That she was drunk when she'd read it the first time; therefore, her initial impressions were grossly inaccurate.

The bartender handed her the drink and arched an eyebrow when she downed half of it in one gulp. Again.

"What?" she said. "I'm British. I could do this all night and still be standing."

"Great," he said. "Just make sure you drive home on the American side of the road."

She snarled at him and glided off toward another corner of the room. Leaning against the wall, she determined that a retraction was out of the question. It would undermine everything her followers and advertisers loved about *The Poison Pen.* She only hoped that neither Kendra nor MJ would come across the review and that it would soon slip into obscurity. Now that the book's wide-release day had arrived, Kendra was sure to get lots of glowing reviews.

In the meantime, she'd just have to act natural. She gulped down the rest of the drink and milled through the throngs until she'd made her way into Kendra's line of vision. When she caught a glimpse, Kendra gave her the sweetest, most heart-melting smile.

❖

By the end of the evening, Kendra was as sober as a nun, too high from the adrenaline of her first-ever book signing to need anything else. Alison, however, seemed to have imbibed enough for both of them. She laughed to herself at Alison quietly humming as she seemed to measure her steps out carefully along the sidewalk.

"Are you sure you're all right?" Kendra said, trying to maintain her own balance from Alison bumping into her.

"Fabulous." Alison slurred the word. "Why do you ask?"

"Well, you're leaning on me pretty good there—not that I mind." She squeezed Alison even closer.

Alison stopped and clasped both of Kendra's hands in hers. "I am a bit tipsy, but it was a fun night. I'm so glad I got to share this special event with you." She looked into Kendra's eyes, squinting against the streetlight, then gave her a tender kiss.

"Me, too," Kendra said. "Even though it was just supposed to be dinner with friends. We'll have to try the dinner foursome again soon. I really want you and MJ and Violet to get to know each other."

"I'd love that," Alison said. "But I'm not complaining about how tonight turned out." She walked around to the passenger door, grazing her hand across the car for support. "Why hadn't you told me you're Meredith Hodges, romance-writer extraordinaire?"

Kendra shrugged as she started the car. "I hate to admit it because it sounds kind of kooky, but I'm superstitious about talking about things before they happen. I just wanted the book to be out before I opened my mouth."

"Really? I wouldn't figure you as the superstitious type. You're so rational."

"We all have our Achilles' heels. Mine goes back years to when my mom was sick." Kendra left it at that. She wasn't sure how much detail she felt comfortable going into about that memory, especially since she'd already told Alison about her shitty relationship with her father. How much emotional baggage should one dump on a new girlfriend all at once?

"Oh, right. You'd mentioned your mum passed from cancer?"

Kendra nodded as she drove through downtown New Haven's congested streets.

"Well, if you ever want to talk about it, I'd be interested to learn how you became superstitious from the experience."

"It's not really that interesting or climactic. But when my mom was diagnosed with ovarian cancer, they gave her a hysterectomy and chemo and all that. After a grueling year, she seemed to have beaten it. They said she was cancer-free. I was fifteen at the time, so I assumed that meant it was gone forever. I went around telling all my friends that she'd beaten it and would be fine and would throw us the biggest, best party when we graduated high school." Kendra stopped herself when she felt her eyes pooling and that familiar knot crawl into her throat.

Alison placed a comforting hand on her thigh. "I'm sorry."

Kendra took a deep breath and pulled herself together. "Anyway. She hadn't beaten it. It came back in her pancreas, and she was gone by the end of junior year."

"Terrible," Alison said as she gently rubbed Kendra's leg. "I shouldn't have brought it up."

"No. It's okay. I like talking about her." That was true—after so many years she sometimes felt people had forgotten her mom. "Anyway, that taught me a lesson about bragging about things before they came to fruition. That's why I hadn't told you. Meredith Hodges was her maiden name, by the way."

"That's beautiful. What an honor."

"Thank you." Kendra patted Alison's thigh in return for her comforting words.

"I'm sure she'd be so thrilled to have her name on such a wonderful story."

"How do you know it's wonderful? You haven't read it, have you?"

"What? Well, no. How would I? I just got my copy tonight. I mean it sounds like it from the blurb on the back."

"Oh." Kendra giggled. "Sorry. I didn't mean to grill you while you're lit up like Times Square."

"Bloody Jameson. I have to remember I'm not eighteen anymore." Alison rested her forehead in her hand.

"I don't know. That's not such a bad thing. Sometimes when I'm with you, I feel like a teenager…a little bit."

"I hope it's not because I'd have to sneak you up to my bedroom if we wanted to shag at my place."

"No," Kendra said through hearty laughter. "I didn't even think of that."

"That's a relief. I was concerned that might become an issue."

"You mean with Vanessa? Look, the unenlightened side of me is a little uncomfortable with you still living with your ex, but the rational part knows that your situation is unique. In a couple of months, you'll renew your work visa and won't be tied to Vanessa anymore."

"That's the plan," Alison said. "It's also why I've had to kiss Vanessa's arse so much lately. I need Mr. Dillford and his political connections to renew the visa. Otherwise, it's quite difficult to prove that my skill as a nanny is an exceptional ability."

"Well, I don't have any political connections, but I think you're exceptional." Kendra's euphoric mood from her book-release party was enhanced by Alison's further explanation. At that point, she couldn't tell Vanessa to piss off even if she'd wanted to, which it sounded like she did.

"Thank you." Alison leaned her head on Kendra's shoulder.

"Hopefully, I'll get the extension, establish my journalism career, and start the citizenship process so I can be done with her once and for all."

"That all sounds exciting," Kendra said. "You know what else does?"

"Does it have anything to do you with you taking me back to your bedroom?"

"In fact, it does."

"Finally I have a woman I'd love to be tied up by."

The suggestion titillated Kendra, but she played it cool. "Ha-ha. I see what you did there. But I said you were tied *to* Vanessa, not tied up *by* her."

"*To*, *by*, tomato, tomahto. Do you have a bathrobe tie or not?"

Kendra accelerated as they neared the exit for her condo complex. When she'd said Alison made her feel like a teenager sometimes, it was partly because she was introducing her to so many new and delicious sexual experiences.

❖

With the sobering conversation on the ride home and the promise of a little light bondage with a woman she was insanely attracted to, Alison's sloppy Jameson drunk had faded. Yes, the sobriety brought intense physical arousal, but it also brought back the haunting reality of what she'd discovered earlier in the evening.

Meredith Hodges.

What an absurd, unfortunate coincidence. She should've known all that wicked joy she'd experienced every time she cleverly skewered another novel would come back to get her eventually. It was simply the law of averages.

Kendra unlocked her front door, and when they spilled into the foyer, she pushed Alison against the wall and kissed her hungrily—almost hard enough to get her to forget what she'd done to her debut novel. The one she was so pumped about, and rightfully so. It was a brilliant book, but Alison, in her need to squirrel away rent money, had turned to torching authors in a genre she loved reading.

"Come on." Kendra took Alison's hand and towed her toward the stairs.

Her ass looked so luscious, Alison tackled her on the stairs and grabbed a handful of it as she kissed her wildly. Kendra was so amazing that everything about her drove Alison out of her mind. What would happen if she ever found out Alison was the Poison Pen?

Kendra giggled. "I'm supposed to be in control here. Don't you want me to tie you up?"

"Yes," Alison whispered. "Oh, God, yes." She kneeled on the step and pulled Kendra's shirt over her head.

Kendra then ripped Alison's bra off and sank her teeth into the top of Alison's breast. She undid the front clasp so Kendra could get more of a mouthful. God, this was exquisite, she thought as she held on to Kendra's head as she tongued her nipple.

She knew exactly what Kendra would do if she ever found out who wrote that review. This and everything else wonderful she'd been experiencing since they met would be over. She suddenly opened her eyes and stared at Kendra's face. "I love you so much, Kendra."

Kendra looked like she'd melt onto the wooden steps. "Aww, I love you, too, baby."

Alison loved nothing more than when Kendra called her "baby." She couldn't lose her. She had to come up with a way to fix what she'd done.

Kendra stood and dragged her, half-naked, up to the bedroom.

Alison jumped on the bed and started to undo her own pants. "I just want you to know I don't need any foreplay."

"What are you doing?" Kendra asked over her shoulder as she rooted through her closet. "I'm supposed to do that. Stop it." She came at her with the tie from a silky bathrobe.

Kendra climbed on top of her and raised both hands over her head. She wound the silky tie around her wrists and fastened them through the headboard slats. Alison was so turned on by Kendra's dominant side that the tight binding squeezed the panicked thoughts right out of her head as she submitted to the glorious pleasure of their encounter.

❖

The next morning at the office, Kendra sat down at her desk, checked her business email for anything pressing, then took her first sip of coffee. She needed one of MJ's pods of dark roast since Alison had stayed over last night and kept her up way past her bedtime. She treated herself to a quick recap of the whirlwind night they'd had that began with the surprise book-launch party and ended with a few hours of hot sex. Really hot. Bondage? Who ever thought Kendra had a dominatrix hidden inside? She never had. Another one of the surprising things Alison had brought out in her.

She shook the provocative image from her head and downed more of the steaming coffee as she waited for MJ to come in for their staff meeting.

While she waited, she decided to google herself, something she'd wanted to do ever since she found out the release date for the novel. She'd actually be googling Meredith Hodges, but it was the same thing. She'd poured so much of her heart and hopes and fears into this story that she couldn't wait to see how others would perceive it. Her friends had been so gracious in their feedback as beta readers, but she just wanted one objective, unbiased opinion on her writing chops.

She typed "The Winding Road Meredith Hodges" in the search bar and, after a dramatic pause, hit the enter key. She scrolled through the first few hits that included the Amazon website, their Labrys Publishing site, and a couple of other online vendors. Then she noticed her novel title and her pseudonym on a reviewer's blogsite.

"My first review," she whispered as excitement rippled through her.

Her heart raced as she clicked on the link to a blog called *The Poison Pen* and began reading.

> The Winding Road*: Meredith Hodges is a new author... and it's quickly apparent. However, before I begin the word carnage, I will say that this newbie knows her way around a lesbian love scene. For sure. Now plot and characterization? Let's just say she needs a refresher course at the community college where this unfortunate soul must've learned how to write fiction. The story's mains are Lila Braddock, a high-priced defense attorney, and Philomena DiRuvo-Kerns, an Italian heiress she defends when she's "wrongfully" accused of murdering her philandering, fracking, executive husband, Frederick Doyle Kerns. SPOILER ALERT: Lila and Philomena fall in love, despite the screaming lack of professional ethics on Lila's part. What a shock! The novel*

opens with a court scene in which DiRuvo-Kerns is found not guilty to the gasps, horror, and shock of a packed courtroom. (Yawn). The story then takes off with Lila and Philomena supposedly set to live happily ever after until an anonymous letter arrives at Lila's house suggesting that she'd helped a notorious black widow get away with murder. Oooh, what's not to love about a greedy, bitchy lawyer who gets off criminals in court and in bed?

That's when the road gets real winding, so winding that I needed a Dramamine to get through Chapter Five! Yes, lots of twists and turns in this one, if you like the feeling of being on a carnival ride operated by an alcoholic with vertigo.

Needless to say, the sketchier and more dangerous Philomena becomes, the more in love with her Lila falls. Oy. Delusional, party of one? Then Lila takes a secret trip to Bari, Italy, where the letter originated, to try to prove to herself the lying, scheming, conniving, murderous diva she's in love with isn't all or any of those things. And that she wouldn't soon be her next victim. But by the end of the second third, I would've gladly done Philomena the favor of murdering Lila for her.

I'll leave the rest of the plot to your imagination, especially if you like to read while you're high as a kite. As for me, if The Winding Road *had a cliff at the end of it, I'd drive off it rather than read this convoluted story again.*

Kendra finished reading the review and sat frozen in a state of shock, her only tether to reality the bran muffin she'd eaten while driving to work that was climbing up her throat. After a period of indeterminate time, she started blinking at her computer. She couldn't believe she'd read what she'd just read. The words were right there, blurred on the screen, but their meaning had already been branded into her brain. As she drifted back to reality, her bottom lip started to quiver, and her eyes filled with tears.

"Goddamnit, Kendra," she whispered. "There's no crying in publishing." She dragged the back of her hands across her eyes to dry them, but they kept leaking. She couldn't help it. The review was scathing, and it broke her heart. She'd worked so hard and for so long on this story. She'd fought off so many demons of insecurity, and even borrowed from her own well of emotions from her first real relationship with the Italian American girl who'd stolen her heart in their early twenties. Then this reviewer had slashed her feelings apart and suggested she was boring and trite in how she repurposed her personal narrative.

As she licked the last of the salty, drippy tears from her top lip, a bolt of rage ripped through her. Who the hell did that reviewer think she was? Or he. Probably some failed author who decided to write reviews of other people's work only after their hundredth rejection letter.

She jumped on the blog page to see if she could gain some insight into who this appalling human was. Of course no photo. Coward. Oh, how cute. The logo was a quill and inkwell. How Shakespearian. Strumpet! She then checked to see how many followed the page. Oh, shit. Over five thousand. Fucking fabulous!

She checked her phone and saw a text from MJ asking her to come into her office. Still fuming, she got up and stormed in. She slammed her door shut, needlessly, as they were the only two there, but it felt good to release some aggression. Landing in the chair like a meteor rocketing to earth, she breathed heavily through flared nostrils.

MJ studied her as she sat there drumming her fingers on the armrests. "Something wrong?"

"Yes, something's wrong." Kendra leapt up and began pacing behind the chair in front of the desk. "Has our site gotten any alerts on *The Winding Road*?"

"No. Why?"

"Oh, no reason," she said, faking calmness. She then leaned forward against the back of the chair and shouted, "It's only been trashed by a wildly popular lesfic reviewer." She toned it down again after realizing she sounded like a maniac. "It just came out today, and it's already been doomed by this Poison Pen person."

"Oh, no," MJ said softly.

"Listen to this," Kendra said, turning to her phone. "'Meredith Hodges is a Joanie-Come-Lately to the lesfic world. If she was coming this late with this mediocre a work, she should've just stayed home.'"

"Oh, jeez," MJ muttered.

Kendra looked up, feeling as though flames were shooting from her ears. "Wait. It gets better. 'If *The Winding Road* had a cliff at the end of it, I'd drive off it rather than read this convoluted story again.' Can you believe this?"

MJ stifled a laugh at the naughty cleverness of the line. "That's terrible," she said somberly. "I was afraid this might happen."

"Wait. You know about this atrocious person?"

"I'm familiar."

"MJ, you said my novel was great. Why would you put me out there like that if it was crap?" Kendra plopped into her chair, on the verge of tears again.

MJ came over and crouched by the side of the chair. "Kendra, listen to me. Your novel is fantastic. I loved it. I never would've put my company's name or my reputation out there if it wasn't, best friends or not."

"You're lying," she replied, unable to control her emotions. "You felt sorry for me being old, so you gave me this one shot so I wouldn't feel like a total loser."

"Hey, hey, calm down." MJ got up and leaned against her desk in front of Kendra. "You are not a loser, and I've never given out a sympathy publishing deal in my life. Ever." She lifted Kendra's chin. "Look. You have to understand bad reviews are part of the package. Not everyone has the same taste in fiction, and not everyone's going to be nice about it. This person is particularly mean because it's her or his shtick. No one really knows if it's a woman or man, but everyone in the biz has heard of *The Poison Pen*."

"But why did she or he or it single out my work? It's my first book. Nobody's going to buy it now."

"Not true. A lot of times the nasty yet, you have to admit, humorous reviews have been known to bump up sales."

Kendra sniffled and looked into MJ's eyes for more reassurance. "Really?"

"One hundred percent. People get a kick out of them, and then they pick up the novel to see what all the fuss is about."

"You're just saying that."

"I'm not. I swear. I've talked to people in the biz who actually want a Poison Pen review. Look on the bright side. Something about your book caught their attention in the first place, whether it's the riveting cover that yours truly designed or your gripping blurb. They wanted to read your book."

"Yeah, and then destroy it. They mocked me and my story. And *The Poison Pen* site has thousands of followers. I'm so humiliated. How can I face Alison if she comes across it?" Kendra dropped her face in her palms and resumed crying. She was so embarrassed, even though MJ had been her best friend for decades. In this moment, MJ was her publisher who took a big chance on her talent and creativity—which, as it turned out, was a quivering lump of nothing.

"Kendra, listen to me. It's okay to feel hurt and angry about this. It sucks to have your first review be a negative one, but don't ever feel humiliated in front of me. And I guarantee you, you'll see great reviews come through, too. Lots of them."

Kendra sat back and took a deep, calming breath. "Thanks. I guess I'm not the first victim of this wretched reviewer, and I won't be the last."

"Facts. Big facts."

She managed a smile to make MJ feel better.

After they'd discussed account statuses and new acquisitions, Kendra did the walk of shame into her office and plunked down into her chair. She ran her hands down her face and tried to cast off the last miserable hour of her life.

Bad things happened to good people all the time. That was life. But she had to postpone her emotional spiral until later, as a manuscript sat on her desk requiring her attention. She took her phone out of her purse and placed it on her desk. Alison had sent her a message.

She melted into a smile when she read the text wishing her a happy two-month anniversary, saying that she hoped Kendra could join her for dinner at her place. She texted back that she couldn't wait to see her and needed to be in her arms today more than ever.

It was funny how things worked out. She'd been single for so long, and suddenly, when she'd needed someone the most, she crossed paths with an amazing woman who made her feel so much better with a gesture as simple as a text.

CHAPTER FOURTEEN

Alison couldn't wait for Kendra to come over. The Dillfords had jetted off to Boca Raton that morning to spend the weekend with Brandon's parents, so they'd have the entire "Wilton Hilton" to themselves. This included use of the built-in pool, Jacuzzi, fire pit, and outdoor wood-fire pizza oven. And maybe even a glimpse of Christopher Walken, who allegedly lived down the road in the affluent Connecticut neighborhood. Aside from some island paradise, she couldn't think of a better way to celebrate their two-month anniversary all weekend long.

To kick off the festivities, she'd prepared two pizzas to bake outside, a taco-style with jalapeños and a margherita one, with sliced tomatoes arranged into a giant heart. A pitcher of mango margaritas and a big bouquet of sunflowers completed the scene.

When the front doorbell rang, Alison bounded into the foyer. But after she opened the door, Kendra trudged in and basically flopped into her arms.

"Darling, what's the matter?" Alison said.

"The universe hates me." Kendra's voice was muffled against Alison's shirt.

Alison nudged her back to address the concern. She'd never seen her look so sad. "What do you mean? What's happened?"

"Don't read my book. I don't want you to read it now."

She started to panic but wasn't exactly sure what she should be panicking about at the moment. "Blimey, Kendra. Would you tell me what's happened?"

"I got my first review, and it was horrendous."

Alison froze. "You what? Come again?"

"My first official review and this person trashed it. They basically said it was garbage and that people shouldn't waste their money on it."

Alison relaxed a little. Kendra didn't know it was her. A small consolation. "Oh, that's awful," she said. She prayed Kendra couldn't discern the guilt barreling through her as she looked her square in the eye and pretended to share in her dejection. She guided her down the hall toward the kitchen, grappling with the weight of knowing she'd hurt the woman she loved in the worst way possible.

All along she'd been having so much fun writing her acerbic book-review blog and making money doing it, she'd never stopped to think how the author she was mincing might feel. Now she was actually witnessing the massacre for the first time, and it was her very own girlfriend.

Maybe a playful quip might lighten the angst. "Who's the witch who done this to you? I'm going to contact her and give her a piece of my mind."

"I don't know who it is. Some jerk who calls herself the Poison Pen. It could be some dude for all I know. Anyway, thank you, baby." Kendra gave her a gentle kiss. "That's so sweet of you, but it's not necessary. MJ said that this comes with the territory, so you just have to let it ride."

"Yes, yes. I agree one hundred percent with MJ," Alison said. "Forget all about it. Who even reads books reviews anyway?" She croaked out a nervous laugh she hoped hadn't sounded suspiciously contrived.

Kendra glanced absently into space. "I'm just afraid that because it's the first review and by someone with so many followers, word will get out, and nobody will want to read my book. Or worse, no one will ever want to read anything else from Meredith Hodges again." She looked at Alison with pooling eyes. "My pseudonym is my mom's name."

"Right. Your mum that's passed away. I remember that." Alison didn't recognize her own voice coming out in such a robotic tone.

Good Lord. She must've been out of her mind to think Kendra would never find the review. Of course she would. Authors are ego-driven and hypersensitive and probably google themselves all day long. Pseudonyms! What were the odds? Her mind raced. How was she supposed to handle this latest twist? She thought again about a retraction, but now the timing of it would be rather conspicuous. No. That wouldn't do. She could take this present opportunity and confess, go the honest route and laugh it off as a silly coincidence followed by vigorous and sincere apologies.

"It took me so long to muster the courage to put my words, hell, my heart on those pages," Kendra said as she plunked down on the arm of a sofa in the adjoining family room. "I could've published something long ago, but I was so petrified of baring my thoughts like that to the world. I went round and around for years thinking, what if readers hate it? What if everyone rejects it? What if it turns out to be the biggest failure of my life? And when I finally overcame all that, this happens. I don't think I'll ever want to publish anything again."

Leaning against the kitchen island, Alison pinched the skin at the bridge of her nose. Honesty was clearly out of the question—for the weekend anyway. The only thing to do was comfort poor Kendra as best she could and encourage her, in the same vein as MJ had, into forgetting about it.

"I'm so sorry, love." She moved toward her and wrapped her arms around her. "You should listen to your publisher. She knows what she's talking about. In the grand scheme of things, reviews, good or bad, don't mean that much."

"Of course they do," Kendra said, wiping under her eyes. "People read them to see if a book or movie is worth their time. This Poison Pen creature said that by the time they got to the end of *The Winding Road* they wished there was a cliff to drive off."

Alison cringed, as she was especially proud of that wickedly witty line. "I know it must seem catastrophic now, but trust me, most people don't care what others say about someone's creative work. It's all subjective. If I see an ad for a film or novel, I decide whether it's interesting or not. I don't rely on someone else's opinion, especially someone I don't even know."

Kendra looked up with a tentative smile. "That's a good point. I don't either."

"Atta girl," Alison said, only slightly relieved. "Now let's get down to the business of the evening. How does a mango margarita sound?"

"Heavenly. Thank you."

Alison went to the refrigerator and took out the chilled pitcher, exhaling deeply. Her heartbeat finally returned to a normal cadence. After their chat, she felt the matter would soon fade off, especially once Kendra started receiving the positive reviews the book was sure to garner. As she filled their glasses, she decided she'd immediately get to work on a flattering review written under her own name, posted on the professional blogsite she was developing.

"Here's to the weekend," Kendra said, still sounding rather down.

Alison clinked her glass against hers. "Here's to a slew of brilliant reviews for an outstanding work of literature. Let's enjoy these on the patio, shall we?" She rubbed Kendra's back, then coaxed her off the sofa arm, leading her out through the sliders.

Kendra dropped into a cushioned patio chair, flung off her flip-flops, and propped her feet up on a nearby chair. Alison began giving her shoulders a deep massage.

"Ahhh," Kendra said. "How do you always know what I need?"

"I don't. I just like to take advantage of any opportunity to get my hands on you."

Kendra giggled as she leaned her head back to look up at her. Alison bent over to kiss her upside-down mouth, then sat down across from her.

"Okay, good," Kendra said. "For a minute there I thought I was dealing with some mystic mind-reader…who, by the way, makes a killer margarita. This isn't a mix, is it?"

Alison shook her head, feeling modest. "Fresh pureed mango, Cuervo silver, Cointreau, and fresh lime juice. I worked my way through university as a bartender."

"Girl, you are a keeper." As Kendra licked her lips after another sip, Alison noticed her sad expression had seemed to melt away into the chilled, fruity cocktail.

"You ought to reserve judgment until you taste my pizza," she said. "I know how you southern New Englanders are about your pizza."

"Bring it on." Kendra's smile was wide and flirty, and her first drink was already almost gone.

After a rocky start, this was shaping up to be a good night.

❖

The next morning, the world seemed brighter, if not in actual reality, then from the cloudless blue sky above Kendra. They'd slept in after a night of lovemaking, and after Alison made her breakfast in bed consisting of Scotch eggs, fruit cup, and piping-hot coffee, she floated in the pool, her fingers playing at the cool water's surface. If she were honest, she couldn't blame Alison for not rushing to move out of the Dillfords' luxurious home. The sprawling yard ensconced in privacy pines and outdoor patio complete with a movie-projection screen made her feel like she was spending the weekend at a lavish B&B in the mountains. As the sun's heat prickled her skin, she tried hard to delay rolling off the raft into the water.

"You look so comfy," Alison said. "I was tempted to do a great big cannonball on top of you but hadn't the heart to disrupt your Zen." She leaned down and handed her a spiked seltzer on the rocks before entering the pool.

"That wouldn't have been nice, considering how much you've spoiled me since I arrived yesterday."

"I like spoiling you," she replied. "I only wish it were my place in which I was doing the spoiling."

Kendra rolled off the raft and waded through the low end to join Alison, submerged to her waist on the pool steps. "This setup isn't so bad in the meantime, especially when your employers go away." She sipped her seltzer and gave her a kiss.

Alison nipped at Kendra's lip before she could pull away. "But I know you'd be more comfortable if I weren't cohabitating with an ex-lover."

"I'll admit at first it was jarring to find out, but now I understand your situation and know this is only temporary."

"Yes. That work visa haunts me. It's coming up for renewal, so as much as I'd like to, I can't leave the Dillfords' employ until I either find another job or get the renewal through them."

Kendra squeezed her knee under the water. "I know you're in a tough spot, so we'll just continue to take each day as it comes."

"Thank you. I appreciate that. Actually, I appreciate you coming into my life, especially now."

"The timing is rather interesting."

"For me, with things getting so complicated here, I'd been missing home, my friends back in Milton Keynes, familiar surroundings. But then I met you, and suddenly, I had something brilliant and beautiful to focus on, so home didn't seem so far away after all."

Kendra's heart felt like it could float away. "That's the sweetest goddamn thing I've ever heard."

Alison chuckled. "No. It's true. I really had been homesick, but I dunno. Being here feels different now. You and I click on so many levels."

Kendra couldn't keep from smiling. Alison was saying everything she'd been thinking over the last few weeks but hadn't the nerve to admit. They were so different in so many ways, but they seemed fully cohesive on the things that mattered. Initially, she'd been disillusioned with her when they'd had their first misunderstanding about Vanessa, but the more she got to know Alison's character, the more she felt sympathy for her. It couldn't have been easy to up and leave her home and move to a different country and culture with people she hardly knew. But Alison had done it to forge ahead with her dreams. That was a bold, impressive move, to say the least.

"I feel that way too, the clicking part, I mean." She tapped her red Solo cup against Alison's, and they kissed.

"I'm glad to hear you say that. I thought maybe I was feeling too much too soon."

Kendra stared into her pale-blue eyes, noting the light freckles the sun brought to her skin's surface. God, Alison was so good at taking emotional risks. Where had she gotten the courage at such a young age?

"What are you staring at?" Alison broke into a nervous smile. "Have I gone and purged too much from my heart again?"

She shook her head. "You always seem to know exactly how much to purge."

"You bring it out in me, Kendra. Honestly, I've never known anyone who makes me feel like you do. If you asked me run away with you to some exotic locale right now, I'd be crazy enough to go."

"Exotic locale." Kendra chuckled. "I've never even been to Europe."

"Really? I would've thought you've experienced quite a lot of the world. You're able to talk about such a variety of topics as though you've had firsthand knowledge."

"I read a lot. Besides, it's not that I haven't wanted to tour

Europe. It's just that the early twenty-first century has been somewhat of a shitshow what with terror attacks and global pandemics…but it's definitely on my bucket list."

"Well, when you're ready, I happen to know an experienced tour guide who'd love to show you all around London and Paris."

"That sounds like a dream. Consider yourself hired." She leaned in, and they shared a sweet kiss.

Alison began rubbing her toes along Kendra's lower leg, narrowing her eyes suggestively. And Kendra liked what she seemed to be suggesting.

"If you tire of the pool, there's a Jacuzzi tub in the master bath," Alison said. "Then we wouldn't need these bathing suits confining us."

Kendra ran her fingers along the inside of Alison's extended leg. "Hmm. I thought you were trying to seduce me here in the pool."

"I certainly would be if the Dillfords didn't have outdoor surveillance cameras recording the grounds twenty-four-seven."

Kendra retracted her hand so fast she dragged a spray of water with it that soaked her own face.

Alison laughed. "I'm sure the camera can't pick up your hand on my leg." She threw her arms around Kendra and dragged her into the pool like a bride carrying her wife through the threshold. "But if it can, it serves Vanessa right for spying."

Kendra rubbed her nose against Alison's. "Then maybe we should go inside…"

"If you're game, I'd love to. I kept you awake rather late last night."

"Yes, and I enjoyed every minute of it—every minute until I passed out. I have no recollection of falling asleep."

"You were quite knackered last night, but I must say, when you decide to rally, you come back with the energy of a Scottish rugby team."

"That sounds like a compliment. Is it?"

"The highest."

Kendra tightened her grip around the back of Alison's neck and kissed her sensually, all bantering aside. Despite the magnificent release last night, desire began stirring in her again. She loved how Alison was holding her, partly like she was about to throw her down on a bed and ravish her, and partly as though rescuing a damsel trapped in a bell tower.

Alison seemed so masterful and in control of everything she did, and Kendra just loved falling under her power.

CHAPTER FIFTEEN

After their romantic weekend together playing house at the Dillfords', Alison hated watching Kendra drive off that Sunday night. Her fingers had trembled as she pulled the drapery aside to watch the car's taillights fade in the distance. Her heart was dark and cavernous as she'd thought about having to wait three days to see her again for their standing Wednesday dinner date at Kendra's, which usually consisted of either cooking together or ordering in, then making love until they'd exhausted each other. More and more, days between their dates seemed to drag on, even though she was occupied with her nanny duties and writing her blogs. The midweek date buoyed her until the weekend, every one of which they now spent together.

This weekend was no different. However, Kendra's plan was rather out of the ordinary. She'd instructed Alison to show up promptly at six thirty p.m. on Friday, but rather than go inside and decide what they would be doing, Kendra was standing at the driver's side of her car waiting with her passenger door open.

"Are we going somewhere?" Alison asked.

"No questions. Just get in."

"Ooh, I like this." Alison tossed her overnight bag and a bottle of Kendra's favorite wine in the bask seat, then buckled up. "The woman who hates surprises is yet again involved in one."

"I hate receiving them, but orchestrating them is lots of fun." Kendra clearly tried to seem serious as she backed out of her parking space. "Here. You'll need this."

Alison picked up the fabric Kendra dropped in her lap. "Good God. Is this a leftover pandemic face mask? Where on earth are you taking me?"

"It's for your eyes. I'll tell you when to put it on. And no peeking."

"This is quite exciting." Alison folded her hands in her lap and tried to anticipate all the possible scenarios in which a blindfold would be needed—outside of the bedroom, that is. It wasn't her birthday, and they'd just celebrated their monthly anniversary last weekend. What did Kendra have in mind?

She was actually quite good at being cagey. She'd held their conversation to the minutiae of their workdays as she drove, and when there seemed a lull, she cranked up the radio. This tactic left no idle moments for Alison to pursue guessing games.

When they got off the downtown New Haven exit, Kendra told her to put on the blindfold. "No peeking."

"You've already said that. I can't see a bloody thing."

Downtown New Haven had some elegant, romantic restaurants, Alison thought. Suddenly, her stomach roiled with exhilaration as she was seized by the wildest idea yet. Was Kendra? She couldn't possibly be…This wasn't a…Was Kendra planning to propose tonight?

"You're not peeking, are you?"

"No, no. But I have to say I'm dying with suspense. Would you please give me a hint?"

"You went the whole car ride without asking. Now that we're a minute away you're dying of suspense?"

"You were talking so much I couldn't get a word in to ask. Have you parked, or are we sitting at the longest traffic light in history?"

"Let me get out and feed the meter, and I'll come around for you."

Alison's hands were shaking and clammy. This was ridiculous. She was getting herself all jazzed up over nothing. Kendra wasn't at all the impetuous type. She was a sober, rational woman who thought out even the minutest decision like it was a quantum theory. She certainly wouldn't be so bold as to propose marriage only two months in. Would she?

What would she reply if that was Kendra's plan?

The passenger door opened. "Ready to go?"

"I do," Alison blurted. "Em, I mean I am." She let Kendra help guide her out of the car and onto the sidewalk. "When can I take this blindfold off? I'm afraid I'm going to fall through a sewer grate."

"You won't. Just keep holding on to me. I won't let you fall."

"You didn't stop me the first time," Alison said.

"Wait. I didn't..." Kendra said, then: "Ohhh." Her voice rose and fell in a Bell curve. "I see what you did there. Very cute."

Alison giggled. "It was, wasn't it? Are we there yet? I'm getting a bit dizzy not seeing where I'm going."

"Almost. Just about another block." They took several more strides before Kendra tugged at her to stop. "We're here." She turned Alison's shoulders slightly, then slipped off her blindfold.

After Kendra picked at the part of Alison's hair the mask had disturbed, she stepped aside. Alison looked up at the lettering on the building: YALE CENTER FOR BRITISH ART. The sight and the sentiment behind the plan made Alison's eyes pool. She turned to Kendra, whose eyes sparkled in clear anticipation of her reaction.

"You said you were homesick, so I—" Kendra shrugged as a blush glinted off her cheeks.

"This is utterly brilliant. And so thoughtful." She lunged at her with an embrace on the sidewalk befitting her level of exuberance.

"Come on," Kendra said. "Let's go in."

As they walked farther into the lobby, Alison thought it odd that they seemed to be the only visitors in the building except for a security guard, who exchanged a knowing glance with Kendra.

"Are we the only ones here?" Alison asked.

Kendra nodded. "They close at seven, but my friend, Tanisha, the security guard, did me a solid."

When they rounded the corner, Alison gasped at a table set for two with a tall, lit candle, a single rose in a thin vase, and a container of take-out food at each place setting.

Alison needed a moment to take it all in. "Whatever this is, I'm sure it's the most romantic thing anyone's ever done for me."

"We had to have fish and chips. It's a British staple." Kendra slipped her arm around Alison's waist and led her to the table.

"It smells delicious, just like my favorite pub back in Milton Keynes."

They sat down, and Kendra slid a small cooler out from under her chair. "Speaking of pubs…" She took out two beer glasses and two bottles of Smithwick's ale.

Alison nearly swooned. "How on earth did you remember that Irish red ale is my favorite? We hardly ever drink beer."

"What can I say?" Kendra said while doing a proper side pour. "Everything about you is unforgettable."

"Kendra, I can't believe you did all this for me just because I mentioned I'd been homesick once. It's incredibly thoughtful."

"It's not a big deal. When I told Tanisha what I wanted to do, she was all in. We only have an hour, but I think that's enough time to eat and browse around."

"It's just so kind of you." She sprinkled some malt vinegar on her fish and dug in. "It's funny, because I talked to my mum on Skype this week, and we had a really nice chat. I think living on different continents for nearly two years has done us both some good," she added with a chuckle.

"Hmm. That must be where I've gone wrong with my father all these years. Maybe if I move to another continent, we'll appreciate each other more."

Alison chuckled again at Kendra's adorable, dry sense of humor. "It couldn't hurt. Although if you're planning to go in the next few months, let me know. I won't bother with the visa renewal."

Kendra rewarded her retort with a sexy smile. "Aww. You wouldn't stay here if I moved away?"

"How could I possibly?" Alison played along with her in a theatrical tone. "You've colored my world here in America. If you left, it would be insufferably dull and gray."

Kendra studied her, her lips puckering back a smile. "If you weren't a blonde, I'd swear I was sitting across from Audrey Hepburn."

"Oh, who doesn't love her?"

"Nobody, I'm sure. Nah. It's safe to say that fleeing the continent would be among my last resorts to fix my relationship with my dad. But I'm glad you had a nice conversation with your mother. I remember you saying it was always difficult feeling heard when you were growing up."

"Very much so. But it was different this time, like she's finally ready to view me as an adult. The judgmental tone was entirely gone, and she actually did more listening than talking. It's funny how we always want our parents to see and hear us, but sometimes we forget that they're human beings. They've struggled or are struggling with their own shit just like we are."

Kendra nodded and smiled.

"I'm glad I reached out to her," Alison said, hoping Kendra would want to talk more about her dad.

But she just smiled again and replied, "That's great." Her expression had lost some of its spirit, and she'd become pensive.

Well done, you twit, Alison thought. You had an epic night ahead, and you had to go and suck all the life out of it blathering on with all that bollocks about your mum. She took a long swig of her ale, slipped her foot out of her sandal, and tickled Kendra's feet with her toes.

Kendra's expression began to soften. "There must be a rule about making sexual advances on someone in front of priceless works of art. It might steam the paint right off the canvas."

"I'm sure there is." Alison giggled as she continued tickling Kendra's feet. "How do you like breaking it?"

Kendra flashed a mischievous grin. "I can't wait to get you home."

When she closed her empty take-out container and began gathering their trash, Alison stood to help her. She loved watching Kendra doing anything—any movement of her statuesque physique grabbed and held her attention. With her short, wavy hair perfectly coiffed and tailored dress-casual clothes, Kendra herself was a captivating work of art.

❖

After dinner, they toured an exhibit of paintings from the Enlightenment Age that featured industrial scenes by Wright and portraits by Hogarth. Kendra held Alison's hand, sneaking glimpses of her as she studied paintings and read the descriptions beside them. She admired so many things about Alison—her worldliness, emotional maturity, and zest for new experiences.

"Did you read the caption on this one?" Alison seemed a bit indignant as she pointed at a Wright painting.

"About the scientific experiment with the bird?"

Alison ran her finger over the words. "It says the people kept watching the experiment even though they knew the bird would die if the demonstration wasn't stopped."

"Three hundred years later, not much has changed. You know. You follow American politics."

"Yes, I do. The dynamic is quite intriguing. And it certainly explains your cynical view of people."

Kendra stopped walking. The observation both stung and fascinated her. "I am a cynic, aren't I?"

Alison had the expression of a cornered animal. "Well, sort of, but not in an obnoxiously negative way. I think your level of cynicism is the perfect foil to my hopeless optimism."

"Ugh," she replied as they continued walking. "I was hoping I fell somewhere in the middle."

"I'm sure you do about most other things." Alison smiled and slipped her hand back into Kendra's.

Kendra appreciated her attempt to reassure her, but she kept revisiting their conversation about Alison's mother. She'd struck a nerve when she said that their parents were just like anyone else struggling through life, doing the best they could with what they knew. But had her father tried hard enough to do what was best for his children after his wife died? Or had his grief so consumed him that all he could think about was finding a replacement for her so he wouldn't have to be alone and reminded daily of his first love's absence?

Grief, she knew, was powerful, consuming, frightening at any age, but at sixteen she hadn't been prepared to manage it on her own. She and her brother should've been their father's number-one priority, but they weren't. And now she was supposed to be the "adult" and forgive a man who'd never even thought of asking her for an apology? No. That wasn't happening.

"Are you okay, love?"

"Yes, fine." Kendra slathered a big glob of perkiness on her reply.

"You've been quiet since I talked about my mum. I feel like I keep saying the wrong thing tonight."

"No. You're fine." Kendra sighed, not wanting to get into it, but Alison deserved an answer. "You did get me thinking about my dad and me, though."

"That's what I was afraid of. I'm sorry. I should've been more sensitive."

Kendra stopped her in front of the exit to the lobby. "No. Please. You didn't say anything to apologize for. My brother's been trying to get me to think about it, too, so maybe it's time I act like a grownup and face my issues."

"You're also grown up enough not to need anyone to shove you into something that doesn't suit you."

"I wouldn't call it 'shoving.' It's more of a gentle nudge. I think the universe does that for us when we're unable to do it ourselves."

"That's so cosmic. I love it."

"I love you," Kendra said and swept her up in a kiss before she could even respond. Alison's warm lips and delicate touch as she ran her fingers up Kendra's arms soothed the angst their conversation stirred in her.

When Kendra released her grip, Alison stared into her eyes for a moment.

"If what you say is true, the universe might be pulling at me, too—to move on from the Dillfords. I agree in principle, but in reality, I'm still sort of stuck."

"I hate that you have to feel that way, baby," Kendra said. "I realize it's way too early to talk about moving in together, but I just want you to know, my door is open if staying there is stressing you out."

"You're so generous." Alison draped her arms around Kendra's neck. "I'll be fine. I'm sending out query letters and submissions like mad. Something should turn up soon."

"I'm sure it will." Kendra smiled her encouragement, then thought for a minute what it would actually mean when Alison got hired somewhere. Chances were it would be a remote position, so it wouldn't affect the flow of their relationship. In fact, if they continued to get along as well as they had been, they'd be ready to move in together by then.

They walked out into the lobby and stopped at the guard post.

"Right on time," Tanisha said as she checked her watch. "Did you ladies have a nice tour?"

"It was the best surprise ever," Alison said. "Thank you."

"Yes, thank you," Kendra said as she hugged her friend. "I owe you big time for this."

"Just don't forget me when you become a *big-time* author."

"That's a deal," Kendra said. She looped her arm through Alison's as they walked out of the gallery, leaving behind all the concerns for the future that had intruded on her earlier.

What she knew for sure was that she had the whole weekend ahead with this amazing woman. And for now, that was enough.

CHAPTER SIXTEEN

The night of the Youth Alliance scholarship awards banquet, Kendra was the happiest she could recall being. She was in love with a woman who was gorgeous both inside and out, and her book, released nearly a month ago, had risen respectably high in the virtual rankings within her genre. Not to mention she'd just enjoyed a heavily attended reading and signing at a local bookstore. Life couldn't have been any better.

She glanced over at Alison sipping her wine. As if feeling the weight of her gaze, Alison glanced back and extended her arm around Kendra's shoulder. Even the simplest of her gestures gave Kendra the chills. Yes, the goddesses had certainly graced her with their favor this year.

MJ leaned toward her from the other side and whispered, "It's nice to see you smile again. It only took a friggin' month to get over that stupid review."

"I'm not over it," Kendra replied from the side of her mouth. "I'm just choosing not to let it devour me."

"You've had three great reviews by noteworthy bloggers since," MJ said quietly. "I don't know why you keep obsessing over the lousy one."

Kendra clenched her teeth to control both her volume and temper. "I'm not obsessing. You're the one who brought it up."

"And I see what a mistake that was."

Alison leaned across Kendra to address MJ. "I gave it a five-star review on my new pop-culture blog. I keep telling her those are the only ones to pay attention to."

"Listen to your girlfriend," MJ said. "I hate to tell you this, but that's not going to be the last shitty review you're gonna get. Might as well accept it."

Kendra sighed. "I know, but that one was the first, and it was so well-written. You could plainly see that a professional reviewer did it. It's no wonder she has thousands of followers."

"Do you think so?" Alison asked with a weird smile. "Oh, em, what I meant was it probably sounds professional because she was a failed novelist herself. Bashing others makes her feel better about her lack of success."

MJ pointed across to Alison. "A thousand percent. You said 'her.' Do you know if it's a woman?"

"Well, no. I just assumed—"

Kendra drew her arm around Alison and squeezed her close. "Brains and beauty. How did I get so lucky?"

"Ugh," MJ said. "Here they go."

"No." Alison protested. "I scored myself a beautiful, brainy, published author. I'm the lucky one."

Kendra kissed her on her cheek. "I left out the most important attributes."

"What's that then? Great titties?" Alison asked.

She chuckled in the midst of the tender moment she was attempting to create. "The most warm, loving, nurturing woman I've ever met."

Alison responded with a kiss a bit too passionate for such a public venue.

"C'mon. Save that for later," MJ said. "It's starting."

A hush fell over the room as the emcee, a dashing butch in a perfectly tailored tux, walked across the portable riser and adjusted the podium mic before clearing her throat.

"I think I know her," Alison whispered.

"Nearly everyone does," Kendra said, recalling the time the woman backed her against a bathroom stall in her earlier bar years.

"Oh. Then it appears I'd exercised poor judgment having a one-nighter with her once," Alison said casually.

Kendra whipped her head toward her. "What?"

"Good evening, everyone," the emcee said. "For those of you who don't know me, I'm Grace Witten, director of the Greater New Haven LGBTQ Youth Alliance."

The crowd roared with whistles and cheers.

"As you know, tonight we will award three very deserving high school graduates scholarships to help them continue their academic pursuits this fall as college freshmen." She paused again to allow a wave of applause. "Each year, thanks to the generosity of business leaders in our community, we select Connecticut LGBTQ high school students who've stood out among their peers for not only their academic success but also their efforts to help improve their local communities through volunteerism. I want to thank all three of our benefactors who've donated a scholarship of two thousand dollars for a student who's excelled in STEM, in arts and literature, and in athletics. So, without further ado, I'd like to call up our first presenter for the arts-and-literature scholarship, the owner of Labrys Publishing, MJ Del Vecchio."

The crowd applauded as MJ made her way to the stage.

Upon her arrival, Grace wrapped her in a lengthy hug. "Now, MJ, before I turn the mic over to you, I have to know, we *all* have to know something."

"What's that?" MJ asked.

"We all want to know what it's really like inside the relationship of your debut lesfic author, Meredith Hodges, and her unlikely significant other, blogger extraordinaire, the one and only Poison Pen."

The spotlight swung to their table and flashed in Kendra's eyes, obscuring her view of everyone in the room. When it returned to the stage, MJ stood with her mouth agape, seeming as broadsided with the announcement as she was.

Kendra turned to Alison, dumbfounded. "What is she talking about?"

"I dunno know," Alison stammered, her face as white as the cloth napkins bunched up by their dessert plates. "She must be drunk."

The world stopped short, and Kendra felt like she'd just slammed into the windshield. "You're the Poison Pen?"

Alison clearly struggled to gather herself. "Kendra, please, let me explain…"

Kendra stared at her. "It was you?"

"Well, yes and no. You see—"

Seething, she stood up so abruptly, she nearly knocked her chair over behind her. "I…I don't know what to say…"

"Then give me a moment to—" Alison leapt up and tried to reach for Kendra's hand, but she pulled it back.

"I can't believe this. You're the one who wrote that epically shitty review?"

"I'd just met you then. I didn't know you'd put out your own book. I'd only found out at your surprise party."

"Why didn't you ever tell me you're a nasty reviewer instead of acting like you're some professional journalist?" Kendra glanced up and realized MJ was trying to signal her from the stage. She turned back to Alison's frightened eyes and felt nothing but disgust. "God, I don't even know you. I feel like such an asshole."

She bolted off through the standing-room crowd beyond the table seating. She thought she heard Alison yelling something like, "Kendra, wait. Please talk to me," but the din of the room drowned her out.

Propelled by an inexorable force, she burst through the door, jogged down the street toward the parking garage, and didn't stop until she was seated in her car. When she finally allowed herself to breathe, she broke down in the dimness of the garage, done in by a combination of humiliation and a broken heart.

This was the final straw. First it was Vanessa and now this. How many red flags did she need waving in her face to realize Alison couldn't be trusted? She was the worst kind of con artist. Young and immature, she just didn't understand how important honesty, trust, and communication were in a relationship.

She turned the ignition but couldn't go anywhere until her eyes stopped blurring with tears. How could she have been so stupid, so naive, so vain to think she could tame a wild thing like Alison Chatterley? The woman made her own sushi, for God's sake.

She rolled down her window as her face overheated with anger and despair. Now she didn't know who she was more upset with, Alison or herself for being fooled into falling for a player.

"Kendra."

Her name echoed inside the parking garage. She looked over toward the stairwell door, and when she saw Alison heading toward her, she threw the car into reverse. She backed up quickly but couldn't go forward as Alison ran in front of her car.

"Would you please let me explain," Alison said.

"Get out of my way."

"Kendra, please. If you'd just hear me out."

"I am not interested in yet another after-the-fact explanation for your bad behavior."

"But you don't understand."

"What don't I understand? That you're a terrible person, a fraud, and a coward?"

"Em, no. That's not what I was going to say."

"Of course it wasn't. That would be honest and brave, two things you're absolutely not. Now step aside before I run your lyin' ass over."

"I'm not moving until you promise to stop acting like a drama queen."

Oh, the fuck she didn't.

"Drama queen?" The question screeched out of her as she started losing her grip. "I'm the last person in the world you can label a drama queen."

"Well, you're certainly earning the title right now."

Kendra held up her cell phone. "Get out of my way before I call the cops on you. Getting arrested for harassment won't look good for someone applying for a new work visa."

Apparently realizing she was beat, Alison moved aside. Kendra slammed her foot on the gas pedal, and the tires shrieked across the concrete as she drove away.

Halfway home, she realized Alison wasn't the only one she'd left stranded at the banquet. She voice-texted MJ's cell and said she'd be on her way back to get her after the event.

Alison leaned against a grimy wall in the parking garage, trying to wrap her head around what had just transpired. This was the second time she'd tried to take the easy way out of a dodgy situation of her own making and the second time it exploded in her face. Unfortunately, the lessons had both come with the same person, and her stomach sank with dread. She'd really fucked up this time. Had she pushed Kendra too far? She'd laughed off Danni when she told her older women usually didn't tolerate any shenanigans. Why hadn't she taken the warning seriously?

She took out her phone. Perhaps Danni would trade a ride home for a chance to say I told you so. But on the way back to the Dillfords' house, Danni was eerily quiet as she squinted at the road ahead of her.

After a solid fifteen minutes of silence, Alison said, "You're not going to give me a lecture?"

Danni shook her head, her eyes trained on the road.

"Why not?"

"I've never seen you this quiet," she replied. "You're miserable. There's no fun in kicking someone when she's down."

"That's very kind of you, Danni." She let out an exaggerated sigh, waiting for an offer of solace. When none came, she added, "I can't believe I've lost her. How could this have—"

"Bup, bup, bup," Danni said, holding up her hand practically against Alison's face. "I said I wouldn't kick you when you're down. I didn't say you could host your own pity party in my car at eleven o'clock at night over something you completely brought on yourself."

"There's the Danni we all know and love. Do we have to sit here in this dreadful silence all the way home?"

"Yes, if the only other choice is you obsessively changing the stations to avoid love songs. You'll be home in twenty minutes. Now you can just sit there and think about what you've done."

Alison groaned, then rested her head against the passenger window until they pulled into the Dillfords' driveway. "Thank you again for coming out to get me. An Uber would've cost me a queen's ransom."

Danni smiled warmly. "Get a good night's sleep. In the morning you can figure out if there's any way on earth you can salvage this."

Alison chuckled. "I don't see how I'll get a good night's sleep—at least not for another decade or so." After hugging Danni good-bye, she walked up the long driveway and around the back of the house, hoping to make it inside without waking anyone. After checking her phone for the millionth time for Kendra's response to her series of lengthy apology texts, she gently pushed open the back door.

Fantastic. Only the stove light was on as she traipsed through the mudroom and crept into the kitchen.

"What are you doing home?" Vanessa was perched at the island with what looked like a half-full brandy glass.

Alison removed the hand she'd used to stifle a yip of fright. "I had a bit of a tiff with Kendra and decided it best to come home."

Vanessa took an elaborate sip from her glass like an old-time actress in a black-and-white movie. "I'm sorry. Are you okay?"

Alison shook her head.

"Have a seat." Vanessa got up and grabbed another brandy glass from the cabinet. "Have a little. It'll settle your brain so you're not tossing and turning all night." She poured two fingers of raspberry brandy. "This is from Brandon's father. A gift from a senator and ridiculously expensive."

"Thank you." Alison took a sip and puckered her lips at the sweetness. "I think I'd need a few bottles of this if I'm to forget about what happened tonight."

"Did you and Kendra break up?"

Alison hesitated. Was it wise to answer that truthfully? Vanessa was being suspiciously gracious, but was her sympathy genuine? She shrugged. "I hope not."

"What happened?"

"She found out about me, that I wrote her Poison Pen review."

"Oh, no." She clutched Alison's hand in sympathy, and her reaction seemed sincere. "Why did you pick tonight to tell her? Weren't you at some awards party?"

"I didn't pick tonight or any night to tell her. I tried my hardest to keep it from her. At least until she was a best-selling author and we'd been married for thirty years."

"Then how did she find out? A scorned lover hatched a nefarious plot against you, didn't she?"

"No. Nothing like that. It was actually all very innocent. An acquaintance of mine, who didn't know or had forgotten I keep my reviewer identity secret, was the emcee of the damned awards banquet. She knew I'm with Kendra but apparently also knew that Kendra is an author. She outed me right there in the middle of the ceremony, but only for a laugh. The whole thing went to shit in record time."

Vanessa's eyes widened. "That's quite a cluster-fuck you have there. And Kendra won't let you explain?"

"She nearly ran me over with her car."

"I like her style," Vanessa said as she flipped her hair behind her ear. "I'd definitely give her time to cool down."

"I don't have much choice in the matter. She hasn't responded to any of my texts."

Vanessa took a gulp of her drink. "You're going to need to up your game from texts if you want to fix this."

After they finished their brandies, Alison was calmer.

"One more?" Vanessa asked.

Alison shook her head. "I need to at least try to get some rest. I have to look at three apartments tomorrow afternoon."

Vanessa leaned on the counter and wrapped her hands around her empty brandy glass. "You know, you don't have to move out. You could stay here until you land that full-time reporting job you want. You never know where it might take you. I promise I won't lose my shit on you over Kendra."

Alison managed a listless laugh. "I know. You've been well-behaved lately. But it's time, Vanessa."

As they walked upstairs together, Alison assumed Vanessa would take a left and go to her own room since Brandon was home. Instead she followed Alison to her door.

Alison tensed as she anticipated having to fend her off. "Vanessa, we can't. Your husband is across the hall."

"Like that ever stopped us before," she said in a sexy drawl. "I know we can't, but Brandon's not the reason."

Alison was confused.

Vanessa placed a warm palm against Alison's cheek. "We can't because you're in love, truly in love."

Alison hung her head, trying not to tear up.

"I let my chance with you slip away. I hope Kendra isn't dumb enough to make the same mistake."

"Thank you." Alison tried to stop her lip from quivering.

Vanessa wiped the tear that rolled down Alison's cheek with the back of her hand and gave her a delicate peck on the lips. "Try to get some sleep."

She watched Vanessa walk down the hall to her bedroom. She had such a sexy sashay and was amazing in bed. Strangely, though, it never felt like just sex with Vanessa. She touched the place on her cheek where Vanessa had caressed her and realized why.

She closed her bedroom door and collapsed on her bed, vacillating between heartache and slow, simmering anger. Why was Kendra being such a hard-ass? It was all an innocent misunderstanding that could've easily been explained had she given Alison a chance. Kendra had reacted like she was some double agent who'd knowingly trashed her book and was laughing about it behind her back. Alison was the one who should be furious. All that talk of being madly, hopelessly in love and looking toward the future. What about that? Apparently, you were only allowed one mistake with Kendra Blake. After that, she'd kick anyone to the curb who displeased her.

The more she stewed about it, the more she wanted to text Vanessa across the hall with an invitation to join her in bed. If Kendra wanted a reason to be cross with her, Alison should give it to her. She picked up her phone and texted Vanessa.

Can you come back for a minute?

She waited for Vanessa's reply, half expecting not to receive one, given the hour.

Then Vanessa's answer popped up.

You want to use me for a revenge fuck against Kendra?

If you wouldn't mind...

Alison waited again but nothing appeared. She'd assumed she'd taken it too far for Vanessa, so she turned off the light and rolled into a ball on her side.

She hadn't heard the door open and jumped when Vanessa crept into bed with her. She couldn't see her features but knew her unmistakable scent and the feel of her silky auburn hair as it grazed Alison's shoulders. Without a word, Vanessa started kissing her neck. When she rolled onto her back, Vanessa climbed on top of her and kissed her hungrily as she groped her chest.

"I've wanted this so bad," Vanessa whispered. "You don't know how my body's ached for you."

It should've been so easy. She should've let herself get washed away in the abandon of dangerous, sensual sex with such an enthusiastic partner. She should've done it so she could forget Kendra and her impossible standards. That's exactly what she would've done in the past. But she wasn't that woman anymore, not since meeting Kendra. Casual hook-ups didn't seem to offer the same thrills they had before she'd fallen so deeply in love.

Vanessa was kissing her so hard she could barely breathe. This could've been the wildest night of sex she'd ever experienced—if only she could stop picturing Kendra's face.

"Vanessa, I can't," she whispered.

Vanessa stopped. "What do you mean, you can't? You told me to come in here."

"I know, but my heart just isn't in it."

"Your heart isn't the organ I'm interested in at the moment."

Alison wriggled out from under her. "It's Kendra. I can't get her out of my mind. She's ruining it for me."

"She's not doing me any favors either." Vanessa got up and headed toward the door.

"I'm sorry," Alison said. "I shouldn't have dragged you into my drama."

Vanessa sighed. "I shouldn't have let you. I hope you can figure your shit out soon."

Once Vanessa closed the door, Alison buried her face in her pillow as the dam holding in her tears finally broke free.

Chapter Seventeen

That Monday morning Kendra walked into work to see a bouquet of red roses sitting on the coffee table in the reception area. MJ was standing in her office doorway sipping from her coffee mug.

"Morning," she said.

"Morning," Kendra replied.

"These are for you."

"Are they?" Kendra knew full well that they were. She snatched the card from its plastic holder and read that they were indeed from Alison. She stared at MJ as she slowly tore the card into tiny bits, sprinkled them on top of the roses, and headed into her office.

"Come on, Kendra," MJ said as she followed her in. "That's it? You're totally done with her because of a review she gave your book when she didn't even know it was your book?"

Kendra landed in her chair and turned on her computer. "I only wish it were even remotely as simple as you're making it sound. It's a question of character."

"Character?" MJ sounded dumbfounded.

"You don't get it. She's a sneak and a liar and I caught her. Twice." She held up two fingers for emphasis. "How many other things is she hiding from me? You know what? Don't answer that. I don't care."

"Oh, you care. You just don't want to admit it. I also think a bit of ego is at play here."

Kendra stopped riffling through papers on her desk and stared at MJ. "Why are you sticking up for her? Have you forgotten you only recoup the money you laid out for my book if it sells?"

"Oh, is that how it works?" MJ glared at her.

"Yeah, it is," Kendra replied snippily. Her mood was growing foul and running away from her. "And I don't believe for one second what you said about how when she trashes a book, it results in more sales. That's ridiculous."

"Mmm. So I take it you haven't peeked at your sales lately."

"No…" The statement piqued her curiosity, but Kendra was determined not to let it show.

"Okay," MJ said coolly. "Well, have a look when you get a chance," she added as she slithered out of the room like a snake.

Kendra sat fuming. Against her own best interests, she didn't want MJ to be right. After an extensive period of staring into space, she logged into the program that tracks orders from their website and was pleasantly surprised to see she had over two hundred orders shipping this week. Impressive for a new author with little notoriety.

Maybe she had to admit that the review hadn't completely sabotaged the book, as she'd initially feared. But she preferred to credit the marketing plan she, MJ, and Violet had developed for the sales rather than Alison's comedy roast of a review.

She strolled out of her office and tapped on MJ's open door.

"Can I help you?" MJ said with an exaggerated perkiness.

"It's not just the review, you know." Kendra crossed her arms over her chest and leaned against the door frame. "It's the omissions of truth. That's what hurts the most. I caught her twice during the first three months. She used questionable judgment in both instances. How do I move forward trusting that whenever she tells me something, it's the full story?"

"I wish I could answer that."

"I wish you could, too."

"Have you talked to her?"

Kendra shook her head. "She's texted me a bunch of times. And the flowers."

"Maybe you should respond. If your feelings for her were as authentic as they seemed, don't you owe her that? Don't you owe yourself that?"

"I need more time to think. I don't know. I mean, maybe the age difference is something we can't overcome."

"How so?"

"I'm just not in a space where I want to train someone on how to be a good, adult girlfriend. If she doesn't know how to do that by now, then she's not the one for me."

MJ studied her like she wanted to refute her claim. Kendra was waiting, hoping she would.

Instead, she said, "I can't argue with you on that. I can only say what I'd do, but I don't know if that would help you."

"You'd go run and jump in bed with her, that's what you'd do."

MJ shook her head with sincerity. "I wouldn't jump into bed with her, but I wouldn't write her off just yet either. I'd give myself more time to cool down."

Kendra sighed, too worn out to keep debating the merits of their relationship. MJ had a point. While she did love Alison, more than she could remember loving anyone, the red flags were waving at full mast. She owed it to herself to trust her process and not repeat the mistakes of her past. It was too easy to allow her rose-colored glasses to turn those flags transparent. She needed to climb out of her own head for a while. Alison would just have to understand.

And if she truly loved her, she would.

❖

That night Kendra was glad to meet her brother for their dinner-and-billiards meet-up. She'd needed the distraction and normalcy of routine more than ever. Her talk with MJ definitely gave her much-needed perspective, but she simply refused to normalize the lies Alison had told her. They set her on edge and left her wondering what else was waiting to leap out at her if she took her back. Two big, fat lies. Should she give her another chance? Should she approach it with the "three strikes and you're out" rule or go in faith that it was only two and would only ever be two?

As if reading her mind, Ryan asked, "You're really done with Alison," as he leaned over to line up his shot.

Kendra felt like a Pez dispenser as her head fell back in despair. "I wish people would stop asking me that."

"I only ask because I've never seen you happier than when you were with her, and now you seem miserable. Damn it," he added after missing a shot.

She stared at him as she chalked up her cue. "It's that noticeable?"

"Well, yeah," he said. "You weren't all 'I'm gonna stay home and cuddle with my lizards' when you were dating her. You've always been kind of moody, but if you suddenly go from this sunny disposition to below your baseline, people are gonna notice."

"First of all, they're iguanas. And secondly, I only dated her for a few months. It's not that big a deal." She was saddened the minute the phrase came out, mostly because it was completely untrue. It was *that* big a deal. In a short span, Alison had left a major impact on her, one she wasn't going shake off like crumbs on her comforter. She leaned over to take her shot.

"Who are you trying to convince?" He timed the question impeccably.

After the cue ball went sailing off the table, she whirled around on him and slammed the handle-end of her stick on the floor. "I don't like liars. You, of all people, should understand that. You grew up with the same one I did."

"Wow. I always wondered how lesbians dealt with daddy issues."

"Don't be a jerk, Ryan. I don't think my intolerance for dishonest people falls into the category of emotional baggage. It's called learning from your experiences."

He shrugged, apparently not looking for a debate. "I get all that, Ken. I just think you're being extra hard on her. So, she was keeping a couple of sketchy things about herself from you. That's what you do when you start out with someone you're really into."

"That may be what *you* do, but I don't."

"She came clean when you called her on them, didn't she? That should count for something."

"She had to. She was caught red-handed in both situations."

"She could've disappeared when you called her out, but she didn't. She owned up to it all." He shrugged and set up his next shot. "You gotta do what feels right."

"I am," she said primly. Her decision felt right in her head. It was her heart that still needed convincing.

"While we're on the subject," Ryan said. "Dad is coming to the championship game Saturday."

"Thanks for the warning."

He rolled his eyes at her. "You know, this could be a chance for you to start letting go of some of your crap. Maybe learn to go easier on people."

Suddenly, all the fun drained out of the evening. Was he serious? Her normally sensitive, compassionate little brother was really giving her the "get over it," toxic-masculinity dismissal?

"Well, I didn't realize I'm such a pain in the ass to deal with."

"Don't put words in my mouth, Ken. Can't we just talk about him without you getting bent out of shape?"

"I only got annoyed, dear brother, because I don't recall asking your opinion on any of my issues, yet I got it anyway. This is supposed to be a fun, chill night a couple of times a month. Let's keep it that way."

"Fine." He turned to sip his beer and muttered, "I'll just add myself to the list of people who need to walk on eggshells around you."

"You know what? Why don't you do that?" She returned her pool cue to the rack and gathered her wristlet and phone.

"What are you doing? Where are you going?"

"I'll be in the car. I wouldn't want my childhood traumas to keep bubbling over and ruining your game." She stormed off.

"Jesus, Kendra. Get back here," he shouted, but she wasn't stopping until she reached his car.

As she leaned against the passenger door waiting, she continued stewing about Ryan's comments. He had a hell of a lot of nerve judging her like that. Yes, they were raised by the same father, but their experiences were not the same. He was essentially dismissing her feelings, something she'd finally learned not to tolerate, from anyone.

She folded her arms over her chest and watched him through the window as he returned the equipment at the front desk. He was her brother, and they'd always been close, but he shouldn't have said what he had.

Ryan was about to walk through the door but stopped to hold it open for an old man and let him walk out first. He was always a good kid. And he grew up to be a good guy. Maybe he wasn't dissing her feelings as much as he was encouraging her to process them so she could move on. Maybe he was just being exactly the brother she needed when she needed it.

Ugh. Now she was really annoyed.

He walked to the car, and the doors unlocked with a click. "I'm glad you didn't call a Lyft back to the house."

She got in the car but still wasn't ready to make nice.

"Look. I'm sorry," he said. "All that stuff is your business. I shouldn't have said anything. Truce?" He extended his hand.

Kendra sucked at her teeth before shaking it.

"Ken, I said I was sorry. I won't bring it up anymore. Just…" He stared straight ahead before starting the car. "Can you please not let it interfere with your relationship with my kids? They're getting older now, and they're picking up on stuff."

She closed her eyes and exhaled. How could she possibly argue with that? She loved her niece and nephew dearly and wanted for them what she and Ryan never had—the most normal upbringing humanly possible.

And frankly, she was tired of arguing with everyone. "I hear you, little brother." She held out her hand to him. "Truce."

Chapter Eighteen

Kendra sipped her ice water as she scanned the lunch-and drink-specials menu. She was so thankful when MJ suggested they sneak out of the office for lunch and meet Violet. It was a gorgeous summer day, and when MJ announced she was in the mood for seafood at a restaurant overlooking the marina, Kendra recognized it as another of her tireless tactics to help cheer her up. Getting over Alison wasn't as easy as she'd thought it would be, despite the dishonesty.

Violet rushed out onto the deck to join them and hugged Kendra from behind, apparently another show of solidarity.

"Now that we're all here," MJ said, "I'm happy to announce that *The Winding Road* has cracked the Top Twenty on Amazon's romantic-intrigue list. Number nineteen, to be precise."

"Woo!" Violet broke into applause.

"As a result," MJ added, "I can pay for this lunch on Labrys's corporate card, so get the lobster rolls if you want."

Violet clapped and wooed again.

Kendra offered a flaccid smile and a halfhearted fist pump. "I'm ordering the top-shelf vodka in my martini."

"I insist you do." MJ summoned their server. "But I thought you'd have a bigger reaction to the book making that list. Do you realize what a major deal it is to break any top twenty on your debut novel?"

"I think Violet is reacting enough for the both of us."

Violet beamed, danced in her seat, and resumed silently clapping her fingertips together. "I'm clapping for the free lunch," she said.

"I totally knew that," MJ replied.

Kendra turned to the menu, her heart not into the banter. She'd eaten there before, so she knew their food was outstanding. But nothing seemed appetizing at the moment. Except the martini.

"I'm just kidding, you know," Violet said. "I'm so proud of you, Kendra. I said from the start how much I loved the book."

"I know," she said and chucked her in the arm. She then turned to MJ. "I guess Alison's horrible review didn't sabotage me after all."

"Now you finally believe me. If anything, she gave you free promotion. You're averaging four stars on all your reviews. Aren't you checking for them?"

Kendra shook her head, completely soured on the whole review experience. "I've been busy working on my next novel."

"When are you going to tell me what it's about?" Violet said. "I'm your beta reader."

"I'm betting someone's getting murdered in this one," MJ said.

Kendra couldn't help chuckling. She narrowed her eyes at MJ. "It's a mystery. A highly successful but irritating publisher gets beaten to death with a bag of her own books, but with so many suspects, the sexy detective goes insane from trying to narrow down the list."

MJ stared at her. "That's disturbingly specific."

Kendra regarded her with a menacingly glare. "I've been plotting it in my mind for a long time."

Violet snorted. "That's a guaranteed best-seller."

"I'll bet the Poison Pen will tear it to shreds before it's even released." Kendra couldn't have masked her distaste if she tried.

"I don't think she's gonna have much time for that anymore," Violet said.

Surprised, Kendra turned to her. "Why?"

"*Modern Women* picked her up for a ten-week column. If it does well, it'll become permanent."

The server arrived with their drinks as an array of emotions bombarded Kendra into silence. First, she was so happy for Alison and proud that she was on the verge of making her dream come true. Not that Kendra ever doubted she would, but it was such a lofty goal, she'd assumed she'd have to spend a lot longer paying dues and building toward it. Not so. She was too talented and smart for a savvy media outlet not to notice and snatch her up.

Then it was sadness's turn. Her initial impulse was to call her immediately and congratulate her, but that would be too abrupt after the last few weeks of ignoring her. Maybe she'd text her later on and offer her best wishes.

"Did she quit her nanny job?" MJ asked.

Violet nodded. "Danni said she has a week left with the Dillfords, and then she's out."

That remark retrieved Kendra from her near-catatonic state of contemplation. "Did she get her own apartment?"

"No. Danni said she's staying with a friend in the Village until she decides where she wants to settle."

Kendra's heart dropped with a thud. "She's moving out of Connecticut?"

"For now," Violet said. "She said she's wanted to live in New York since before she came to America, so she'll probably end up staying."

"*She said?*" Now an emotion she wasn't familiar with hit her hard and ugly. "Did Danni tell you that, or did you talk to Alison?"

"Well, she met Danni and me out for happy hour recently and—"

Betrayal. Yep. That was the unfamiliar emotion descending upon her. Her insides roiled at the idea that Violet was there and hadn't even mentioned it to her. "Why didn't you tell me?"

"I don't know." Violet's gaze darted between her and MJ. "It was just happy hour. You've been acting like the breakup was final all this time, so I didn't saying anything 'cause I didn't want to get you upset."

"I'm not upset," Kendra said brusquely. She then toned it down after catching the less-than-subtle look Violet and MJ exchanged. "We weren't right for each other. We're both better off now." The hollowness of her statement made her even sadder.

MJ sipped her mojito, then sat back in her chair so her face was in the sun. "I may be speaking out of turn, but I don't think Alison was ever convinced she was better off without you."

"She's young. She doesn't realize how much easier it'll be establishing her career in New York without any other distractions."

"Well, aren't you just a happy little martyr." MJ's tone was devoid of all playfulness.

Kendra's hackles rose. "I'm not happy about not being with her anymore. You of all people should know that. But I'm not so selfish that I'd stand in the way of her pursuing her dreams."

"You could go with her," Violet said. "You can totally do your job remotely, couldn't she?" She looked at MJ for affirmation.

In return, they both stared at her like she'd sputtered out sacrilege at a holy altar.

"I have no interest in moving to New York City, thank you very much, especially to chase some girl who still has a lot to sort out in her own life."

"I hope you'll at least have the decency to text her congratulations," MJ said.

"Yes, of course I will," Kendra said. "I really am happy for her. She's gonna be great at a weekly column. And lesfic authors will be immensely grateful for the reprieve if she doesn't have time to eviscerate novels anymore."

"So how are things going with Danni?" MJ asked. "And will I ever get to meet her?"

Violet demurred. "You'll meet her. She's really shy, and we've decided not to rush things."

"Shy is a nice, diplomatic term," Kendra said. "I found her to be delightfully odd…the one time I did meet her. Are you okay with how she never wants to leave the house?"

"She leaves the house plenty," Violet said with a hint of protest in her voice. "I love how she's a homebody. She has a garden, she loves to cook, and she dotes on her two dogs."

"I've never met two people who are more unlikely to be best friends," Kendra said fondly. "Alison is so worldly and loves to explore one adventure after another."

"Opposites attract, right?" MJ said.

Kendra knew MJ meant that as much for her as she did for Danni and Alison's friendship, but she didn't take the bait. Even if she was willing to roll the dice that Alison's situational lying wasn't an indicator of a more sinister character flaw, this new bit of information about her moving to the Village for her career felt like a sign that their breakup was meant to be.

"I'm happy for you, Vi," Kendra said.

"Thanks," she replied. "I know she's not my usual type, but since I turned forty, I like the idea of spreading my wings in life and love. I'm not sure it will lead to a happily-ever-after, but I like talking with her and spending time together."

Kendra smiled at her friend, genuinely happy for what she'd

found and envious of her courage to venture off into the great romantic unknown.

❖

That night Kendra had brought Sergio home from work for emotional support. She was planning to text Alison, not call her. Hearing her voice might be too much. She'd be too likely to fall for something like a farewell Connecticut cocktail or some other maudlin bid for closure Alison might suggest. Kendra still found her too attractive to resist her if they'd made it to a face-to-face meeting. Besides, she wasn't exactly forthcoming with Violet and MJ at lunch when she'd suggested she'd made peace with the end of their relationship.

MJ had to know she was full of shit but was a true enough friend not to call her on it.

She grabbed a yogurt out of her fridge for dinner and plopped down in front of the TV. She turned on the local news and went "psst, psst, psst" for the cat to jump into her lap. After Sergio completed his kneading routine against her stomach, she picked up her phone and began crafting the congratulatory text.

She'd typed a rambling paragraph saying she wasn't the least bit surprised about Alison's success and potential to do big things and all kinds of other sentiments that just made it seem like she was trying too hard. After delete-keying the entire thing, she settled on, *Congrats on the* Modern Women *gig! So happy for you!* She dropped the phone into her lap and waited for Alison's prompt reply, which did not happen.

Emotionally drained from thinking way too much about everything since lunch, she'd nodded off until sometime during *Jeopardy*, when Alison's text startled her awake.

Thank you so much!!! How are you doing? Well, I hope.

Hmm. Should she send off a generic "fine, and you?" Or be more original and risk getting into a full-on conversation? She could be totally authentic and tell Alison she was missing her and became unspeakably sad when she'd heard she was moving, but that would just make things messy. Why do that to either of them? They were in different places in their lives. It was as simple and as convoluted as that. Kendra was the one who wanted a simple life, while Alison's age and passions and curiosity had her off on a course of adventure that seemed a perfect fit for her personality. Kendra wasn't fool enough to try domesticating a wild spirit.

Doing well, she wrote. *Busy working and writing.*

Another best-seller, I'm sure. ☺

Thank you. Fingers crossed. Well, good luck on your new adventure! You'll be great!

Kendra stared at their text as the three dots floated. And floated. Wow. She must've been typing a paragraph. Was it a final plea for a second chance? A weepy, regretful good-bye laden with emotion? How would Kendra respond if it was?

Then the dots vanished.

"*What?* No," Kendra shouted, causing Sergio to jump off her lap. "You get the final word. You can't just leave—"

Suddenly, *Thank you!* followed by a smiley face, popped up.

"Oh." Disappointment churned inside her. She stared at the screen, trying to decide if she wanted to have the last word, maybe a *You're welcome* that would vex Alison for hours as she attempted to decipher its hidden message. Well, yes, she wanted to, but again, not the right time. She was still vulnerable, and Alison was, too. Maybe. Hard to say since she was so ready to dig into the next phase of her life—rightfully so.

She should probably accept the fact that while she had truly fallen in love with Alison, she was just a pit stop along the way in Alison's journey.

Before she'd finished contemplating should she or shouldn't she, the three dots appeared again. Alison was adding something else but was clearly putting thought into her wording. Kendra's heartbeat accelerated in anticipation.

Finally it appeared.

If you're free this weekend, would you like to have a cocktail before I go? It might be nice to have a proper good-bye, but if you're busy, I'd understand.

Kendra sank farther into the sofa cushions. Alison had moved on…from her and whatever promise the future held for them.

Thanks. I'll let you know by the end of the week.

She placed her phone on the end table and scooped up Sergio, who'd returned to sit on the coffee table. She held him to her chest, and when his sleepy purr started, she closed her eyes and listened.

❖

Alison felt like shit after receiving Kendra's last text reply. She thought she could at least count on a yes right off, some sort of indication that she'd want to say good-bye. If Kendra let her leave for the City without a hug or a handshake, well, then, their three months together couldn't have meant that much to her. She rolled off her bed, walked into her poofy Union Jack slippers, and headed to the kitchen for some tea.

Standing at the counter, she bobbed an Earl Grey teabag in her mug, and for the life of her, she simply couldn't decide between milk and honey. So she kept bobbing.

Vanessa walked in from the family room carrying an empty wineglass. In the past, that meant only one thing, but Alison's heart, or any other body part, wasn't in it.

"They conked out in front of the TV again," Vanessa said. She stepped past Alison and placed her glass in the dishwasher.

How unusual, Alison thought. She must've gotten started on the bottle earlier than normal. "Want me to help you get them to bed now?"

Vanessa shook her head. "After your tea." She leaned over on her elbows at the island and flipped through a country-living magazine.

"Are you all right?" Alison said. "You're usually only halfway through a bottle at this hour."

"I made it halfway through. The rest is in the fridge if the tea ain't doing it for you."

"The tea is fine," she said, then took a sip. "Are you?"

Vanessa shrugged as she pulled out a stool and sat. "I know this was your last week, but you don't have to rush out of here. You can stay rent-free until you get settled at the new job."

"Thank you, but I won't be settled in until I can establish a readership that'll allow me to keep the column. That could mean at least several more months."

"I wouldn't mind," Vanessa said without looking up from the magazine.

Alison pulled out a stool across from her and sat. "Vanessa, why don't you divorce him? You're far too young and vibrant to be languishing alone in this big house."

She finally looked up, and with that sanctimonious glare, Alison recognized the old Vanessa again. "Divorce him for what? You're moving to New York."

"I don't mean for me. You and Brandon aren't happy. Why don't you free yourself up for what will make you happy?"

"I already explained to you about the pre-nup. If I divorce him while the kids are still minors, he gets custody of them, and I get visitation. I won't stand for that."

Alison shook her head. "That's ridiculous. What's he gonna do with them full-time? He only likes popping in and playing father of the year a couple times a week. Another nanny would be raising them."

"That's exactly my point. It's a power game rich men play. It's all about preserving their wealth and control…at any cost." She closed the magazine and tossed it aside. "I wouldn't even mind it so much if he'd put more of an effort into hiding his affairs."

Alison was about to chastise her again for signing a pre-nup in the first place but thought better of it. No sense in antagonizing a cornered creature. They're scared enough by the predicament they got themselves into. She offered a sincere "I'm sorry" instead.

"Thanks." Vanessa gazed at her intently. "Is that how I made you feel, like a pawn, lording your work visa over your head?"

"If I'm honest, at first I found it quite hot shagging the mistress of the manor, so to speak. But then when you started with the veiled threats, I thought to myself, for fuck's sake, someone like you was the last person I'd suspect would pull a Harvey Weinstein on me. You were so classy and seemed to have it all together."

Vanessa scoffed at the assessment. "*Seemed* being the operative word. I think now you see me for who I am—or was. A dreamer who believed marrying a rich man would afford me everything I wanted in life. Don't get me wrong. I love my kids to death, and I truly loved Brandon when we married, but it's all pretty much turned out to be an empty vault."

An impromptu confessional was the last thing Alison had expected of the evening, but she went along with it anyway. "What was I to you then?"

"Evidently, the escape I'd been looking for. It was such a turn-on to be the one with power for a change, but I let it go to my head. It was shallow and stupid and just plain wrong, and I really am sorry for the way I treated you. Can you forgive me?"

"How could I not after such a heartfelt apology?"

"I meant it—and not just out of fear of the massive lawsuit you're probably going to file against me anyway…but because I really did love you, Alison." She looked away and muttered, "I still do," under her breath. She then exhaled deeply, seeming to gather herself. "Under different circumstances, I would've liked to have seen where we could've gone."

"For a time, I was willing to see it through under these." Alison hadn't anticipated getting swept up in the confessions, but when in Rome… "But it got to a point where the pleasure our affair brought to my body was no longer worth the pain it brought to my heart."

"Is that your way of saying you loved me, too?"

"I *love* you, too. Just not in the way I fell in love with Kendra." She chuckled ironically. "Karma's slapped me about pretty good, then, hasn't she?"

Vanessa's face oozed sympathy. "I'm sorry it didn't work out the way you hoped and for my role in it, whatever it was. If you think it would help, I'd be willing to talk to her."

Alison shook her head. "It wasn't your fault. I'm the one who mucked it up because the truth was too inconvenient. I'd never been too keen on doing the work involved in commitment. Now it's finally caught up with me."

"I guess we both should dig for the lesson in the rubble of our current situations. You've gained some important insight about yourself."

"Gaining insight and losing Kendra is not my idea of a fair exchange."

"Some people go their whole lives never getting it. You're only thirty-two. The next time you fall in love, you'll be ready for it."

"But I don't want to fall in love with anyone else. I want Kendra."

Vanessa's eyes conveyed what she was too sympathetic to utter in words. But if she had said it aloud, it would've roughly translated to something like, "I know, sweetheart, but you fucked that up royally."

"Promise me something," Alison said.

"What?"

"That someday on one of your jaunts to the City with your girlfriends, you'll have me join you for a drink."

Vanessa smiled warmly. "I'd like that."

Alison returned a smile over the rim of her mug. At least she would be leaving Connecticut with one unburnt bridge.

CHAPTER NINETEEN

The Little League championship game had begun ordinarily enough except for the attendance of Kendra's stepmother, Joyce. She had such mixed feelings about her stepmother. Other than the obvious resentment she'd harbored as a kid when this woman had replaced her dead mother, she'd always wanted to dislike her. But as she'd matured, she found there wasn't a lot to dislike about her. She was a petite woman who wore a sour expression, but she was actually nice and never said a bad word about anyone, even on the occasions when Kendra lashed out at her. Despite her expression, she was attractive, stylish for a woman pushing seventy, and always wore pretty costume jewelry. She'd made a few attempts to win Kendra over when she'd married her father, but her mousy personality was no match for an angsty, wounded teenage girl.

Kendra secretly despised how, whenever she saw her father and Joyce now, she seemed to emotionally regress into that same difficult teen.

After the game, Kendra ran up to her niece and gave her a huge congratulatory hug, saying all the words to show her auntly pride while keeping an eye on her father and Joyce, who were making their way over. As they approached, she pivoted around to leave, only to find her brother's wall of a physique standing behind her.

"Oh, Ryan. Great game, huh?"

"Yes. Awesome. We're all going over to Duke's Drive-in for hot dogs and ice cream now." It wasn't a question or a polite invitation. It was an imperative Kendra couldn't refuse.

"Fuck," she whispered, loud enough for Ryan to hear. He ignored her reaction as he stared at her expectantly. "Great. I'll meet you guys over there."

"Why don't you take the guest of honor with you in your car?"

Kendra chuckled. "Do you seriously think I'm gonna brazen an escape once I'm out of your sight?"

"No, of course not. She's all sweaty, and I just had my truck detailed." His sly smile eased the tension—a little.

"Hey, Alyssa," Kendra called out. "Want to ride shotgun with me?"

The girl nodded and ran over to her.

"How about you, Hayden? Want to come with us?"

"No, thanks," her nephew replied. "I'm going with Grandpa to show them how to get to Duke's."

Kendra looked at Ryan, who was leaning against his shiny pickup truck with an irritating smirk. "Evil genius," she hissed at him, then grabbed her niece's hand. "Come on, 'Lyss."

The drive-in was jammed with team members and their families. Although the picnic table where the adults were sitting had room, Kendra opted to sit with the kids. She placed her tray down and squeezed out packets of mustard and ketchup onto her hot dog, ignoring Ryan, who was trying to send her signals to join them.

Nope. Not happening. She was enjoying the afternoon and wasn't about to place herself in a situation that would steal her joy. She was all about self-care, and Ryan would just have to deal with it.

Once everyone had moved on to ice cream, Kendra stood off to the side in a patch of shade a large oak tree provided. Carefully smoothing out her two scoops of pistachio with her tongue, by the time she noticed her father's approach, it was too late to escape.

"Congratulations on the book," he said. "How can I get a signed copy?"

"You've come to the right place, but I highly doubt it'll be your cup of tea."

"It's a romance, isn't it? Joyce loves those."

"It has elements of romance in it, but this isn't quite what she's used to reading. There's no shirtless, muscled dude riding bareback with his long hair flowing in the wind."

"I know. You write the gay stuff."

Kendra couldn't prevent her face from contorting with condescension. "Yes. The gay stuff. Exactly."

"Joyce isn't gonna care. Nobody cares about that anymore."

"Except the people still dealing with the prejudice. I'll make the book out to Joyce." She attempted to leave for the trunk of her car, but her father gently held her arm.

"Kendra, wait. I didn't come here to argue with you or cause any tension. Please don't walk away again."

She poked her thumb over her shoulder, not quite registering her father's earnest engagement. "The books are in my car."

"Oh. Okay. Maybe we can talk more before you leave."

She turned on him with suspicion. "What's the matter? Are you sick or something?"

"No. Why? Do I look it?"

She shook her head, trying to process what was happening. Who was this guy masquerading as her father? The guy who never showed emotion, who never gave an inch?

"No. You look fine," she said. "I'm just wondering why you picked now to show interest in my life again."

"I've always been interested in your life. You're the one who stepped away from us. After enough declined invitations, you kind of get tired of asking."

What a bunch of bullshit. And she was just about to call him out on it, too, when her niece Alyssa ran up to them.

"Aunty Kendra, can you come back to the house for cornhole? Please?"

She stroked Alyssa's ponytail and glanced at her father.

"Don't worry," he said. "I'm not going. Give Joyce the book, and let me know what I owe you."

She watched him walk off, annoyed at his audacity. He was acting like the wounded party? Really? She wished she had a violin so she could play him off with some maudlin exit music. "Sure, I'll come for cornhole," she replied, still watching as he sat down next to Joyce.

When everyone was done with their ice cream and bathroom breaks, they all headed to the parking lot. Ryan caught up with Kendra and followed her to her car.

"Thank you for doing this," he said.

"You don't have to thank me. I know what today means to Alyssa."

"Yeah, but I also know how Dad gets on your nerves, so I just wanted to thank you for taking one for the team."

"He wanted to buy a signed copy of my book for Joyce. Did you put him up to that?"

"No way. Christy must've. I heard her telling Joyce about it."

"Oh. Wow." Was that her father's way of trying to communicate that he was proud of her accomplishment?

"I told you he's mellowed in his old age," he said. "See you at the house."

She watched as Ryan headed to his own car and put his arm around his daughter before they all got in. He was a happy guy, and clearly his family brought him much of that happiness. Then she thought about Alison. Kendra was the happiest she could remember being when she was with her—until the shine faded and Alison's deceptive ways rose to the surface. But was she really all that deceptive? If she spun it the right way, it was understandable that Alison wouldn't want a new girlfriend to get upset that she had still been living with her ex. And as for her secret identity as the Poison Pen, was it fair for her to be upset about that when she'd kept her Meredith Hodges pseudonym a secret from Alison? Probably not.

She sighed as she started her car. Was it a good idea to be with someone she had to spin things for to justify questionable behavior? Probably not. She'd done that in a previous long-term relationship whenever her ex had made a new "friend." It only ever led to disappointment.

Kendra was on her couch binging episodes of *Super Girl* when she heard knocking at her door. She detested unannounced company, so it took her a moment to decide whether to bother getting up and seeing who it was. Then the knocking grew harder, and MJ's voice rumbled outside the door.

"Stop pretending you're not home, Kendra. I need to talk to you now."

Kendra leapt up, straightened out her sweatpants, and answered the door. "I wasn't pretending. I just didn't hear you at first," she lied.

"I have news so stupendous I just had to deliver it in person."

MJ swept past her and into the living room. "Is that your dinner?" She pointed to the pile of trash on the coffee table.

"Ice cream is a good source of calcium, and the white-cheddar popcorn provides roughage," Kendra said primly, then turned snotty. "Don't judge me."

MJ pushed the junk aside, dropped onto the couch, and crossed her ankles on the coffee table. "Are you ready for this?"

Kendra sat down next to her. "Lay it on me."

"Okay, remember me telling you about Anita McDaniel, the artist and filmmaker I met at the Harlem Art Expo last year?"

Kendra nodded as she poured cheesy popcorn crumbs from the bag into her mouth. "Didn't you sleep with her that weekend?"

"Well, yes, but that's neither here nor there." Her eyes as radiant as the stars, MJ repositioned herself like she was about to launch off the couch. "She read your book and loved it. She wants to talk about optioning it for a film."

"Are you serious?"

"Very."

Kendra allowed her mouth to hang open for a second as she analyzed the contrast of the moment. There she sat, depressed, carbed-out on junk food, and looking like an overall mess, while MJ informed her that her novel could possibly, one day be made into a movie. She grabbed an open bag of peanut M&M's from the coffee table. "I don't know what to say. That's amazing. But it definitely sounds too good to be true." She shoved a handful of candy into her mouth.

"Well, not that I want to kill anyone's buzz, but yeah, just because she wants the option of adapting it to film doesn't mean it's guaranteed to happen."

"What does it mean that she wants to option the novel?"

"She has a boutique production company, so basically it means that she wants to make it a film but needs a partnership with another production company and/or a financial backer to go ahead with it."

Kendra let what little hope that bubbled up in her fizzle out. "In other words, she liked it enough to think it could be a movie but will probably never be able to make it happen."

"I don't like the phrase 'probably never.' That suggests an eighty-twenty split that it won't happen. I think your chances are much better—fifty-fifty."

"Fifty-fifty? Would you be satisfied with those chances if you were having open-heart surgery?" Kendra leaned back and let her head sink into the cushion. "I almost wish you'd never told me. False hope is worse than never knowing you had any hope at all."

"Come on, Ken. It really is something worth being optimistic about. Anita wouldn't have approached me with the idea if she didn't have a reasonable amount of hope. Now that I think of it, your chances are better than fifty-fifty."

Kendra stared at her with a wan smile.

MJ sprang up from the couch. "Christ. I've run out of ideas on how to cheer you up."

"You don't have to cheer me up. I'm fine. I'm just in a little rut when I'm not preoccupied with book stuff."

"Have you heard from her?"

Kendra shook her head.

"Why don't you text her? I'm sure she'd love to hear from you, being all by herself in the City."

"Please." Kendra sucked at her teeth. "She's gotta be living her best young, single, and gorgeous life in New York City."

"She's gotta be missing you, too. Don't you think?"

"MJ, a wound won't heal if you keep picking at the scab."

"Truth," she replied and held out her hand for a fist bump.

"Besides, I'm sure I hardly ever cross her mind anymore."

"I don't believe that for a minute." MJ headed to the door. "Listen. Snap out of this funk. You have your reading tomorrow at the Pride Center. You don't want to make your audience all depressed and what not."

Kendra got up and followed her to the door. "You're leaving already?"

"I'm meeting Violet and the ladies from her softball team for cocktails. Wanna come? You might meet a hot jock. That's why I'm going."

Kendra made a face as she shook her head. "I don't want to see Danni."

"I don't think she's going. Violet said something about her working late."

Kendra shook her head again.

"How about I text you when I get there and let you know how it is?"

"That sounds like a plan," Kendra said.

MJ gave her a quick kiss on the cheek and headed down the steps to leave. "Don't forget to check your phone. About a half an hour."

"Roger that." Kendra knew she wasn't going anywhere for the night, but she so appreciated MJ's efforts to make her feel better.

❖

Alison had thought once she'd settled into her friend Carmen's apartment and her new routine of researching and writing, the clouds would've lifted from her heart. This was so unlike her. She'd had numerous relationships that were fine while they lasted, but each time they came to their natural conclusions, she was happy to set her ex-lovers free with a sentimental text or a hug.

With Kendra it was completely different. She found no freedom in being apart from her, only a longing that pulled at her heart and taunted her with regret. She should've fought harder for her. She should've been unrelenting in showing her how much she meant to her before running off to New York. But when she'd gotten the call from *Modern Women*, something Vanessa said that had burrowed into her brain came to the surface: was she willing to table a dream she'd had for years for a woman she'd just met?

Forced to make a life-changing decision at an unsettled time in her life, Alison chose the dream—mainly because Kendra wouldn't talk to her. Once she'd settled into Carmen's and her new job, anger had taken over. How dare Kendra cut her off like that? Nothing she'd done was so severe in its consequences that they couldn't overcome it if they'd loved each other enough. Alison had, but it was a horse-tranquilizer-size pill to swallow to realize that Kendra hadn't.

One night Carmen dragged her out to a popular lesbian bar in the Village. Alison wasn't the least bit interested in diving into the City's lesbian social scene without first having observed a proper mourning period. But Carmen convinced her that it was all about her witnessing the history of the struggle for LGBTQ rights in America.

"Alison, you're in Henrietta Hudson's in the Village," Carmen said as she slid a shot toward her at the bar. "With the possible exception of West Hollywood, you'll never find a more eclectic lesbian scene in America."

Alison chucked back the hot cinnamon shot, and after making a sort of grunt as her throat recovered, she felt even sadder. "Connecticut's was pretty interesting, too," she said, recalling the dance where she'd met Kendra.

"Connecticut is a mere microcosm of queer life here," Carmen said. "A third of the women who come here on any given night come in from Connecticut."

Alison shrugged. She simply didn't care no matter how much Carmen hyped it up. Being back out on the singles circuit wasn't fun or titillating anymore like it was before Kendra. Now it just sucked. It reminded her of the night she'd met Kendra and her whole world had shifted. She just wanted to be with her.

"Listen," Carmen said as she pushed another shot toward Alison. "I get that you're not into this on a personal level, but if you're writing a column about politics and pop culture from a lesbian's point of view, you have to start here."

Carmen was spot-on. A segment producer for a local morning show, Carmen indeed had her finger on the pulse of pop culture. Alison needed to muster up some of that stoicism Brits were famous for and sink her teeth into some lesbian culture.

For their third shot, they decided on a car bomb, in honor of Alison's heritage. This was going to be a cheap evening since the bartender seemed enthralled with her.

"I could listen to you talk all night," she said as she dropped the shots of Jameson into the pints of Guinness. "This one's on the house."

"Another one? My goodness. You're a generous chap, aren't you?"

"Chap?" The butch bartender's face lit up. "I love it."

"Cheers," Alison said and looked at Carmen for the signal to chug.

After they recovered from that one, Carmen pulled her aside. "Listen. We should probably slow down, or we'll end up passed out in the street."

"Over in the UK, that's how we know it's been a great night." Alison giggled and hiccupped. She was tipsy now and really enjoying the high in her head and the numbness of her emotions.

Carmen clapped Alison on the back. "I have an early meeting tomorrow, so I'm gonna take one more lap and then wrap things up."

"Oh, no. You're breaking up the party already? I've just started to enjoy myself."

"I'm Lee," the bartender said, extending her hand. "I'll get you home if she has to leave."

Alison's instinctive flirtatiousness kicked in. "Whose home?"

"Any one you say," Lee replied.

"Aren't you cheeky? I'm Alison." She gripped Lee's hand and shook.

Carmen pulled her aside. "I really do have to get myself to bed, but feel free to stay if you want."

"Okey-dokey. I think I'll stick around for one more."

"Atta girl," Lee said. "This must be your first time here. No doubt I would've remembered that beautiful golden hair and regal accent."

"You're quite observant. And yes, this is my first time. Oooh, it's been a while since I've said that to anyone." Alison got silly at herself, then picked up her phone to check for messages.

"I certainly hope it won't be your last."

"I've moved here to start a new job, so I'm sure it won't be." As her next pint of Guinness started further wearing down her faculties, she opened the last text exchange she'd had with Kendra weeks ago. After focusing her bleary eyes, she reread their last convo and was struck with the notion that she should reach out and send her a text. Kendra would love to hear from her. Who doesn't love receiving a text from an ex at eleven thirty p.m. that's filled with misspellings and drippy sentiments that never would've been expressed had alcohol not been involved?

"Well, I've lived here for over twenty years," Lee said. "If you'd like to go for dinner this week, I'd love to show you around to some of the favorite places of the locals."

"Pardon me for one second. I have to send a text to my ex-girlfriend."

"Before you do, can I give you a little free advice?"

"Why not? Your free drinks have worked out splendidly."

"Don't."

"Don't what?"

"Don't text your ex while you're intoxicated. I've been in this business since cell phones came out, and I've never ever heard from one patron that texting their ex while drunk at my bar was the smartest decision she ever made."

"Of course it's not a smart decision. Had I been good at making those, she wouldn't be my ex then, would she?"

Lee gestured like her mind was just blown. "I've never met a drunk who is as self-aware and insightful as you are. It's refreshing."

"I've recently had an epiphany of sorts, and now I'm trying to maintain an all-honesty policy. Although I've never lied to intentionally hurt someone, I've found that people don't consider lying to avoid a conflict any less offensive."

"Is that what lost you this woman you want to text?"

"Unfortunately, yes."

"What did she say when you explained your epiphany to her?"

"I hadn't. It's just sort of come to me recently. She'd caught me twice in rather sketchy situations and wasn't particularly receptive to a third chance."

"She sounds like a quality woman," Lee said.

"Indeed." Alison sipped her beer and rested her chin on her hands folded on the bar.

"What did you lie about?"

"The first time I tried to hide the fact that I'd had an affair with the wife in the family I'd worked for as an au pair. The second time, I neglected to tell her that I had written a beastly review of her debut novel on my rather highly traveled review site."

Lee stared at her in stunned silence.

"What?" Alison asked innocently.

"I don't know where to start." Lee shook her head, apparently trying to clear it. "Okay, yes, I do. Why would you write such a vile review of your own girlfriend's novel?"

"I didn't know it was her novel when I'd written it. She uses a pseudonym, Meredith Hodges."

"You were dating Meredith Hodges?" Lee beamed. "Are you kidding? I loved her book. It was awesome. Why would you trash it?"

"It's what I do…or rather I did. I didn't get paid to write glowing reviews. Readers loved the comically wicked ones and came to expect them from me."

"Wait—don't tell me you're the Poison Pen?"

Alison raised her hand. "Guilty as charged."

"Holy crap. This is amazing." Lee said. "I read your blogs all the time. You might not know it by looking at me, but I'm a real big reader. Now that I'm thinking of it, you haven't posted for a while."

"When it all went down with Kendra, I posted that I was going on holiday for the summer, but the truth is, I just can't bring myself to read another romance with a happily-ever-after ending when my own relationship went to shite."

"That's a real shame. Sorry, kid. I enjoyed your writing style."

"I'm working for *Modern Women* now. I won't have carte blanche to gut anyone's work anymore, but I'm sure my signature snark will be evident when I write about politicians who attack LGBTQ rights. Perhaps you'll check out the site."

"I think I've read articles they've posted, but I'll be sure to subscribe to it. I'd love to keep up with you. I'm a big fan. Oh, excuse me." She moved down the bar to wait on a group of young ladies who had been signaling her as she gushed.

Alison smiled as she finished off her beer. In another lifetime, she would've parlayed the bartender's flirtation into a one-nighter or even a one-weekender, but none of that appealed to her anymore.

She hopped off the barstool but held on to it until her balance recalibrated. After checking that her phone was securely stuffed into her pants pocket, she meandered through the crowd of women, making eye contact with numerous cuties along the way. She stopped in the middle of the dance floor when a woman started dancing with her. *Dance with her, you idiot*. She screamed that in her brain, but she only offered a polite nod and continued toward the door.

Kendra was still entrenched in her heart, and no matter how many attractive women she encountered, she was going to need more time to get over her.

CHAPTER TWENTY

By the time winter set in, Kendra had returned to her comfortable routine as the quiet introvert she was pre-Alison. Immersed in writing her next novel, she was attending writers' conferences and relishing the joy of her first quarterly royalty check plus an honorable mention for *The Winding Road* from a prominent women's writing organization. And as per usual, her best friends had resumed conspiring to get her out to various lesbian social events around town.

While MJ was juggling two women on a dating site, Violet's and Danni's brief romance had run its course, and they came to realize they made much better friends than lovers. Kendra thought that was nice. In her experience, she'd never wanted to remain friends after her relationships ended, usually because a partner had done something that challenged her faith in them or they'd simply grown apart.

As she sat on a bench at the town beach on an unusually warm, sunny December afternoon, it dawned on her that, prior to Alison, she hadn't always been that discerning when picking her partners. They'd always picked her, and she'd just gone with the flow—a decent approach when trying to decide on pizza toppings with a group of friends, but for a relationship, not so much.

Then she met Alison. Although Alison was another woman who'd picked her, Kendra went along with it this time because Alison truly interested her from the moment they'd met. By this stage in her life she had finally learned that her time and attention weren't things she should give away to any well-meaning drifter who came along seeking them. Alison had not only interested her, but she had also inspired her to want more for herself by virtue of her own grand ambitions. Alison went for what she'd wanted rather than letting her life float along like dandelion spores in spring.

If she allowed herself to think honestly about it, her life, as good as it was, felt empty without Alison in it. They'd ended on decent terms, so it was conceivable that they could still be in each other's lives to some degree. Could she manage a friendship with her the way Violet and Danni did? Danni was almost a regular at their gatherings now, and everyone got along great. Maybe she should give it a shot—if Alison was on board, of course. But how would she go about initiating it? She couldn't just call her in New York out of the blue and suggest it. That would be incredibly weird. Perhaps in this situation she needed to call upon the expertise of her friends.

And within hours of her text, MJ and Violet had met her at their favorite local brewery overlooking the river. As they passed around a take-out container of salad and picked through the boxes of small pizzas, they watched the football game playing on the big screen.

"I think the Giants finally have it together this season," MJ said.

"It's about time," Violet said. "I was beginning to lose faith in my New York teams and ready to switch over to Boston."

MJ skewered her with a look over her beer glass. "You better be joking."

Finding an opportunity amid their banter, Kendra tossed her pizza crust into the box and wiped her mouth. "So speaking of New York, I was thinking—"

Violet and MJ both groaned.

"You didn't even hear my idea."

"Please, not another one of your 'I'm so over Alison that I just have to bring it up again and tell you how over her I am' soliloquies." MJ shook her head in distress. "I can't handle it."

Taken aback, Kendra fought to control her facial expression. "My goodness. I had no idea," she said calmly and turned to Violet. "Violet, have I been going on as relentlessly as our dear friend here is suggesting?"

Violet glanced at MJ before responding with a meek, "It does kind of come up a lot."

"Oh." Kendra looked down at her beer flight and pouted, waiting for them to prompt her.

MJ exhaled loudly. "I'm sorry. I've had a stressful week. What's your idea?"

"Well," Kendra said, aligning her beer samples in front of her. "I was thinking about seeing if Alison wants to be friends."

MJ and Violet exchanged cynical looks.

"I saw that," Kendra said. "What's the matter? You don't think it'll work?"

"Well, I—" MJ said.

"How is this not a good idea?" Kendra asked. "Violet and Danni were involved once, and now they're the best of friends."

"I wouldn't say we're the best of friends," Violet said. "And our situation was different from the start. Danni and I never had the level of passion you two had."

"What does that have to do with anything?" Kendra asked. "It's been six months. I don't expect to hang out with her all the time like we do. It just seems like a waste not to have a cool person in my life simply because we weren't compatible romantically."

MJ snorted, apparently louder than she'd intended, drawing Kendra's attention back to her.

"If you have something to add, MJ, please, by all means…"

She shook her head. "Listen. If you think it could work, then I'm behind you one hundred percent."

"Thank you." Kendra raised her little glass of beer and took a dainty sip.

Violet looked up from her phone. "You can put your theory to the test this weekend. Alison is coming in to stay with Danni Saturday."

The flutter in Kendra's stomach caught her by surprise. Maybe it was the beer sampling on top of all the food. "Is she? How's that for a coincidence."

"You know what Freud said about that," MJ said, then turned to Violet. "Are you going to hang out with them Saturday?"

A sly smile spread across Violet's face. "I haven't talked about it with Danni, but I can always find out where they'll be, and we can crash."

"Yesss," MJ said, hissing like a snake. "This is exactly what you need, Kendra."

"Um, I was thinking more along the lines of I'd send a friendly text asking how it's going first."

"Lame," MJ replied. "You'll never have a better opportunity than this—in person, face to face, no misinterpreting tone. Plus, unlike in text, you'll experience all the nuances of the nonverbal cues. It's the ideal scenario."

Kendra didn't like the way they were hijacking her idea. This was a delicate situation that could go very wrong if not handled carefully. "Uh, I don't think Violet wants to be dragged into the middle of this. Besides, it's kind of a shady thing to do to Danni, don't you think?"

"I don't mind," Violet said. "And I don't think Danni would either, especially if it makes her friend happy."

"It's not like we're gonna commandeer their entire night," MJ added. "Violet will let us know where they're going, and we'll all just pop in for a quick drinkie, then be out. Kendra, you'll know by the end of the round if Alison is interested in a friendship."

Kendra flipped her gaze between both of them as she struggled to poke holes in their ideas. But she couldn't. They both made solid points, and if Kendra truly wanted this, her friends were actually helping her, not meddling.

Violet placed a hand on top of Kendra's. "But if you really want to handle this on your own, MJ and I will stay out of it."

MJ nodded begrudgingly.

"I love you guys," Kendra said. "Let's wait till the end of the week and see what happens."

"Sure," MJ said. "You may feel differently in the sober light of morning."

"I'm not drunk," Kendra said. "I don't know why you're making this out to be such a big deal." The indignation in Kendra's voice made her sound more confident than she felt—at least to herself.

"I'm not," MJ replied. "I'm just looking out for you."

Kendra's hackles spiked as she felt like MJ was more needling her than playing protective big sister. "I don't need looking out for. You, on the other hand…"

"Kendra, please don't." Violet lifted her beer to her mouth and stared at the TV screen.

"No, no. Please do, Kendra," MJ said. "I'm so curious as to what you're referring to."

"You know…all your little game-playing on the dating sites. You know you're still attractive enough to land any woman you want. Why do you feel like you have to prove it? You're not twenty-one anymore."

"Oh, Christ," Violet murmured. "I have to go to the bathroom." She leapt from the stool and jetted off to the ladies' room.

MJ slammed down the lid of the pizza box before grabbing another slice. Kendra rolled her eyes. *Fucking Scorpios*.

"First, I don't have to prove anything to anyone," MJ said, waving a finger in front of her face like Rhianna. "And secondly, I'm not playing games. I'm up-front with every woman who contacts me. I happen to enjoy getting out and playing the field again, meeting people and doing different things. If I meet someone I click with, great. If not, I'm gonna get the most out of my nineteen-ninety-nine a month."

Kendra folded her top lip under and stared reproachfully back at her. She felt like a jerk.

MJ's stern face broke into a smile. "You're an asshole. You may be fooling Violet with this 'I wanna be friends' bullshit, but you're not fooling me."

"Really? You think Violet is buying it?"

"Violet is a humble, genuine soul. Even if she knew you're completely full of shit, she'd go along with every bit of your nonsense because she's that cool."

"That's so true," Kendra said as she downed the rest of her stout sample. "Let's play Saturday night by ear. If I'm meant to see Alison again and have a friendship with her, the universe will make it so."

MJ studied her. "Come on. You're not even a little drunk?"

Kendra pinched her thumb and forefinger almost together. "Maybe just a little."

They broke into laughter, and Violet returned to the table.

"You're gonna regret breaking the seal," MJ said.

Kendra giggled again as she downed the rest of her IPA sample.

"I was around the corner watching you guys," Violet said. "When I saw you both start laughing, I knew it was safe to return."

"Get over here," Kendra said and grabbed her in a sisterly hug around the waist.

❖

As Alison rode the train from Grand Central Station to New Haven, she used the time to work. She arranged interview notes and ideas on her laptop for a column she was working on about young women finding their voice in the corporate world. The idea had come from a recent virtual staff meeting in which a male editor at the predominately female-run media outlet she worked for had a lot to say on that particular day. Many of his points were valid and appreciated. However, the problem that Alison identified was the way in which he dominated the discussion, often mansplaining concepts that Alison thought a keen but young female editor had clearly communicated.

When the woman seemed to back down from presenting her own idea, Alison got to thinking about other young women who worked in male-dominated professions and businesses. Was this a generational thing or a societal construct, this business of young women allowing men to grab the reins in a business setting even if they were driving the carriage just fine? Her boss had found the concept engaging enough to suggest she stretch it into a series of columns rather just a one-and-done analysis.

Before she knew it, the train pulled into the station in New Haven. She jumped into Danni's car waiting in front and hugged her until the driver behind them laid on his horn. Delighted to see Danni again after a few months, she'd soon forgotten work and focused entirely on catching up.

"I'm so happy our schedules finally synched," Alison said.

"Me, too," Danni said as she drove through the city. "I was starting to think you'd never come back."

Alison frowned at the wistfulness in Danni's voice, something she'd never express in actual words. "Of course not. I've met some fantastic people here, Danni, present company emphasized. I'm not through with Connecticut at all."

"Shall we begin with a round at our old stomping grounds?"

"Naturally," Alison said with a chuckle. "Especially since that's exactly where you're headed."

"Creature of habit." Danni smirked as she scanned for street parking near the Irish pub Alison loved.

Once inside, they settled at a high-top table in the bar section and placed their drink and app order. Alison performed a cursory scan of the

Saturday-afternoon crowd of mostly young men there for the college basketball games airing on multiple TV screens. She tried to appear casual in front of Danni, but she was hoping, by the workings of fate, that Kendra might be there with her brother, as they shared a love of college ball.

"You look great," Danni said, redirecting Alison's attention to the table. "You were made for city life."

Alison smiled out of habit rather than agreement. One thing she didn't want to do on a rare trip back to Connecticut was to appear like life was anything less than spectacular in New York, but here they were. Luckily, their waitress was quick to return with their drinks.

"That's what I'd thought, too, but thanks for the compliment." Alison sipped her Bacardi and Coke.

"I don't understand," Danni replied. "Whenever I text and ask how things are going, you always reply 'fantastic.' Is something wrong?"

"It's not as though anything's wrong per se. I just, well, it's just not all I thought it would be. Perhaps it's my fault for having built up such high expectations."

"Is it the job? Your roommate situation?"

"No, no. All that's fine. Carmen's been quite hospitable, and I rather enjoy the job. I get to write for a living. What's not to enjoy? That part's been everything I've dreamt of since before I left the UK."

"Then what?" Danni said. "Are you dating anyone?"

Alison shook her head and took a large swig of her drink. This conversation was making her anxious, and it wasn't that she didn't want Danni to know she wasn't happy. The prodding was forcing her to pinpoint and discuss what exactly was lacking in her new urbane life, something she'd avoided doing for the last six months.

Danni tapped her knuckles on the wooden table top. "I'm too sober for a one-sided conversation."

"I'm sorry. I just don't want to bore you with the same old story."

"Oh. My. Goodness." Danni halted lifting the drink to her lips. "It's Kendra, isn't it?"

"What? No." Even Alison knew it was too late to walk it back.

"Have you been involved with anyone since you've been there?"

"No."

"Have you slept with anyone?"

"No."

Danni furrowed her eyebrows as she clearly tried to digest the meaning. "You, Alison Chatterley, have gone without the companionship of a female for six months now?"

"I mean I've been on a few dates…first dates." Alison gazed off into the bar crowd, regretting she'd opened that floodgate. But how was she to pull it back now that her misery had rushed through? "So, how are things going with you? Have you seen Violet? Do you think you'll get back together?"

Danni licked the beer foam off her lip as she seemed to process the rapid-fire questions. "Uh…fine, yes, and no."

"That's it? Can't you expound on any of those subjects?"

Danni shrugged. "Which one?"

"Violet. Have you seen her since you split up?"

"Oh, yeah. We're friends."

"Friends? As in hang out together?"

Danni nodded. Once she'd homed in on the waitress bringing over their apps, Alison had temporarily lost her.

"Please tell me it's the food you're lusting over so I know I still have a flat to stay at tonight."

As soon as the waitress set down their apps, Danni grabbed a wing, plunged it into the blue-cheese dressing, and stripped it to the bone in a matter of seconds. "So good," she said as she reached for another. "Now what were you saying?"

As she daintily dipped a zucchini fry in ranch dressing, Alison watched in awe as Danni savaged another wing. "I asked that if by friends you meant you actually pal around with Violet."

Danni nodded and licked buffalo sauce from the corner of her mouth. "She'll text and let me know where she and her friends are having happy hour or dinner once in a while."

"And you go?"

"Sometimes," she replied as she reached for another wing.

Alison thought for a moment and, against her better judgment, said, "So then you've seen Kendra recently."

"About a month ago. She's doing well."

"Fabulous." Alison sipped her drink, trying to slow her roll. She was about to assail Danni with a slew of questions about Kendra, the answers to which she likely wouldn't want to hear. She was annoyed with herself for bringing up the topic. She was only in Connecticut for an overnight visit. Why had she dredged up memories of someone she'd spent the last half a year trying to forget?

"Aren't you going to ask me if she's seeing anyone?"

"I don't care if she is," Alison said defensively. "Whatever makes her happy is fine with me."

"Okay," Danni said as she looked around for the waitress. "You want another drink?"

"Yes. Yes, I do." Alison scanned the crowd again, searching for a woman, any woman, she found attractive enough to contemplate going home with. In the past, it wouldn't have been too difficult a task. When she'd first arrived in America, it was almost too easy to woo women into their own beds with a few eloquent phrases in her British accent. She was a little ashamed of how many American women she'd actually slept with in that first year, but once she'd gotten involved with Vanessa, their complicated affair occupied most of her time.

Then when she'd met Kendra? Other women just seemed to cease to exist. Kendra had apprehended her heart with her mind and body, and, as Alison had figured out, hadn't yet returned it to her.

After Danni signaled their server for another round, she looked Alison directly in the eye. "She's not seeing anyone."

Alison felt as though her heart might burst all over the table. She released the breath that had caught in her throat and managed a cool, "Oh."

"I only said it because it's what you were thinking."

"Well, I wasn't," Alison lied. "But thanks for letting me know."

"Maybe next time you come for a visit—"

"Danni," a familiar voice called out.

They both looked toward it and saw Violet heading toward their table. What they hadn't immediately noticed was MJ and Kendra trailing her single-file into the bar area of the restaurant.

Alison slugged down the last of her drink as all five of them broke into a round of festive greetings and hugs and kisses. When it came Kendra's turn to greet and hug Alison, the din and clatter of the busy establishment fell to the background as Alison drank in Kendra's enticing perfume and the familiar feel of her body.

"Of all the gin joints..." Kendra said as she seemed to take in all of Alison in one lingering glance.

"I can't believe this," Alison said. "I come to Connecticut for one night, and look who I run into."

"Looks like you picked the right night to sneak into town," MJ said. "So nice to see you."

"You as well. Would you all care to join us?" Alison was asking the group but couldn't help staring at Kendra. God, she was so beautiful. She'd convinced herself she was making progress getting over her while living her dream in New York City, but seeing her standing before her in all her radiant glory sent a tidal wave of emotion crashing over her.

"Would you mind?" Violet asked Danni.

Danni shook her head with a smile, and soon all five of them were sitting in a round corner booth talking over each other and indulging in all manner of cocktails and appetizers.

Alison couldn't remember the last time she'd had such fun in a group of women. Several years back in Milton Keynes it had to be. An hour in, she was pretty buzzed but wasn't concerned, as Danni was her driver for the evening. "I hate to ask you to get up," she announced, "but after all these drinks you're plying me with, I'm afraid I must."

The table cheered her on as she slid out of the booth and made her way to the ladies' room. She sat down on the toilet and felt the room spinning. It appeared her app-to-drink ratio was favoring the drink side. Part of her wondered if this evening hadn't been a setup orchestrated with the help of her best American friend, Danni. She also wondered if she should be furious or grateful to said friend. At that point in the evening, she couldn't make a well-informed choice as she was piss drunk on Bacardi, shots, and Lord knew what else.

When she came out of the toilet, she started when she met Kendra outside the stall. "Oh, hello."

Kendra chuckled, then said with a shy grin, "They sent me in to check on you."

"That's nice of them…you." Alison paced her words in an effort not to slur. "I just needed a moment to work this bloody belt." She giggled and lurched into Kendra's arms.

"Whoa. Are you okay?"

Alison tried to suppress another giggle. "Yes. So sorry. I was just trying to make it to the sink. I think I should cut myself off now. What do you think?"

Still holding her, Kendra smiled. "I say as long as you have a safe ride home, you do you."

Alison knew she was supposed to go to the sink but didn't, allowing Kendra to hold her steady. She stared into Kendra's eyes as the room around her undulated in her periphery. Her gaze fell onto Kendra's lips, her soft, juicy lips. She leaned ever so slightly forward and kissed them gently, as if all she'd wanted was to feel the connection to Kendra for as long as she could until she'd pushed her away.

But Kendra didn't.

She kissed Alison back, with purpose and vigor, and Alison began to wonder just how drunk she was. Had she passed out in the stall and all this was a fantasy, or was Kendra actually kissing her? She grabbed a handful of Kendra's hair and really kissed her. This time passion, not the inhibition of alcohol, fueled her. Adrenaline pumped through her as her body and senses absorbed everything about Kendra's physical being. She wanted to tear into her clothes right there in the bathroom until the door opened and MJ appeared, looking uncharacteristically embarrassed.

"Jesus. Go into a stall," she muttered.

Kendra recoiled from Alison and blurted, "It's not what you think."

"I don't care what it is," MJ said. "I'm just here to pee."

After she disappeared into the stall, Alison and Kendra looked at each other, shaken back to reality by the interruption.

"I, em, I just need to wash my hands…" Alison turned away from Kendra and toward the sink.

"Glad you're okay," Kendra said awkwardly. "See you back at the table."

Alison nodded as she washed her hands under the motion-activated faucet. After drying them on paper towels, she dabbed the cool, damp paper on her cheeks and neck.

"My bladder has the worst timing," MJ said as she emerged from the stall and joined her at the sink. "You all right?"

"Yes. Just a little too much, too fast."

"We'll get some food in you, and you'll be fresh as a daisy."

Alison smiled at her as she inhaled the remnants of Kendra's perfume on her shirt. "Right. Food."

❖

When Kendra saw Alison walking toward the table, she felt the need to sit up and seem fully pulled together—even though she was anything but. The kiss had her shaken for myriad reasons, not the least of which was that Alison was drunk, almost sloppy drunk, and she didn't know how to feel about her impetuousness. Maybe when she was that inebriated she'd make out with anyone in a bathroom. Or, worse, it was just one of those stupid things you do when you're drunk, then deeply regret the next day.

Alison slid into the booth, poured herself a glass of ice water, and guzzled until it was gone. Her pallid complexion elicited enough sympathy that Kendra decided never to mention the kiss to her.

"Have we ordered dinner yet?" Alison asked with a perky smile.

"No, but that's a smart idea," Danni said. "You're not going to like hurl in my guest room tonight, are you?"

"I should hope not," Alison replied as she perused the menu. "Do they have any bangers and mash?"

"Come again?" Violet said over the top of her menu.

"It's a popular dish over in Britain," Alison said. "It's like a bratwurst-type sausage over mashed potatoes."

"Oh." Violet seemed to shudder at the mere description.

Kendra couldn't blame her. It sounded revolting. If Alison could eat that and keep it down as drunk as she'd been a few minutes earlier, she truly was a woman of steel. "I think I'm having the house salad with grilled salmon."

"Hey, if you two want to join us at my house after dinner, we're doing a hot-tub soak on my deck."

Kendra couldn't believe MJ just did that. Was she stoned, too? "I'm sure they have their own plans, MJ. It's bad enough we crashed their dinner."

"Don't be silly," Alison said. "It's been a delight hanging out with you all again. Danni doesn't mind, do you, Danni?"

Danni shrugged as she buttered the last roll in the basket.

"Brilliant," Alison said. "We'd love to come with. Just text me your address."

"Excellent," MJ replied. "This is turning out to be such a fun night."

"Oh. Hang on," Alison said. "We don't have our swimsuits with us."

MJ grinned. “You don’t need ’em. Swimsuits are optional.”

At that announcement, the buffalo wing slipped through Kendra’s fingers and wound up in her lap. “Shit,” she uttered in despair.

MJ glanced over at her. “You okay there, Ace?”

“Never better, Ace,” Kendra muttered with a menacing glare.

CHAPTER TWENTY-ONE

Kendra was certain that by the time they'd all finished their entrees, desserts, and last cocktails, Danni and Alison would have thought better of detouring their evening so drastically. But as Kendra stood off to the side of the hot tub, watching her breath float away in the cold night air, she witnessed just how wrong she'd been. Obscured only by a thin layer of steam rising from the hot, bubbling water, MJ, Violet, and Danni—of all people—sat as naked as a litter of hairless cats drinking hot toddies out of Mason jar mugs as they chatted away. Well, Violet and MJ were chatting. Danni was listening and sipping.

"What are you waiting for?" MJ called out to Kendra. "Get in. You'll freeze to death standing out there."

"In a minute," she lied. She had no intention of adding herself to that giant vat of boiling orgy broth. She was only lingering because she was waiting for Alison to come out of the bathroom, so she could say good-bye.

"Come on, Kendra," Violet said. "I need another body to help block the wind."

"Be right there. I'm just gonna make sure Alison is okay."

She opened the sliders and slipped into MJ's family room to warm up. A low fire burned in her gas fireplace, and it struck her how romantic a setting it was. For the life of her, she couldn't figure out why they were out there, a potential human stew to a starving bear prowling the woods behind her house, when this room offered such warm winter ambiance.

"Why aren't you out there having a soak as well?" Alison asked as she walked into the room.

"I thought it would be rude to leave you to have to get into the tub all naked and alone."

Alison's gaze penetrated her from across the room. "That's a proper lady, then. Thank you." She strolled over toward the sofa in front of the fireplace and turned to face Kendra. "Actually, I'm not much for group nudity."

Kendra maintained her position near the door but couldn't help staring at Alison, poised against the back of the sofa and backlit by the glow of the fire. She must've been out of her mind breaking up with her. "I hear ya," she said. "I much prefer my nudity in the company of one."

They gazed at each other for a moment that was both awkward and ripe with possibilities. Alison seemed different these days—sharper, more mature, more focused on her career. Kendra supposed that living in a city like New York could do that to a person. Then again, maybe it was Kendra who was different. These days, her skin felt a little thicker, her heart a little tougher. But oddly, she hadn't felt any resentment or bitterness toward Alison. By now they'd been apart longer than they were originally together. Whatever it was, she was happy for Alison and inspired by her courage and determination to achieve her goals.

A muffled scream from outside shattered the silence.

"You suppose they're all right?" Alison said with a smirk.

"Sounds like it to me," Kendra replied.

"It sounds like someone's been attacked by a wild animal."

"The screaming would've gone on for much longer," Kendra said as she slowly moved closer. "That was more of a screech…like someone's foot accidentally ended up somewhere it didn't belong."

"Would it be wrong to stand behind the curtains and watch?"

"I didn't know you were into voyeurism," Kendra said, approaching Alison's side.

"I'm not. I'm just curious as to what Danni's doing. She must've pulled out a book by now. This evening alone she's done more peopling than she had in the entire year and a half I've known her. I can't imagine what's going through her mind being naked in a tub with Violet and MJ."

Kendra grinned at the thought. "Should we go upstairs and throw things out the window at them?"

Alison giggled. "Like what?"

"I don't know. Let's go see what MJ has in her fridge."

They rushed into the kitchen, and Kendra found a bag of grapes in a vegetable bin. "These ought to get the job done."

"We're actually doing this?"

Kendra nodded with a dastardly grin, grabbed Alison's hand, and they hurried upstairs to MJ's master bedroom above the deck. She carefully slid open the window above the Jacuzzi and turned to Alison, who was now toting their ammunition. "Ready?" she whispered.

Alison covered her mouth and snorted into her hand. She might have found the plan absurd at first, but her eyes were brightening with mischief.

"Shhh." Kendra tugged at her sleeve. "This mission requires stealth. Here. You go first." She picked a few green grapes from a stem and dropped them into Alison's hand.

Alison glanced out the window, apparently positioning herself for battle, and hurled the handful down at them. She leapt away from the window, practically into Kendra's arms.

"What the hell was that?" Violet said.

"What happened?" MJ replied.

"Something hit me on the head."

"It's probably just an acorn," MJ said.

Kendra suppressed her laughter as she leaned closer to the window. "They haven't even noticed this window is open," she whispered to Alison. "They must be so high."

"Here. Let me have another go at it," Alison said. She plucked another handful from the bag and whipped them down at them.

"Oh, what the fuck?" MJ shouted.

"They're throwing grapes at us," Danni said, her soft voice barely audible from a floor down.

"Hey, assholes," MJ said. "Shut my window and stop wasting my food."

"I don't know what you're talking about." Kendra's words were almost garbled in her laughter.

"Would you just get the fuck down here? We're not staying in here all night," MJ said.

"Be right down." Kendra closed the window, and when she turned around, Alison was very close to her.

"Well, maybe not *right* down." Alison threw her arms around Kendra's neck and began kissing her with as much fervor as when she was loaded back in the restaurant bathroom. But this time, she was sober, and there was no mistaking her intent as the misguided actions of a drunk person.

Kendra laid Alison down on MJ's bed and ran to lock the bedroom door. Alison was already stripping off her clothes in the dim glow spreading out from the deck lights. For a moment, Kendra felt incredibly weird having sex with someone on her friend's bed, especially with said friend just outside. But from the shrieks of laughter and steady rumble of voices, she knew they had as least another half hour, maybe longer, depending on how many pot gummies Violet had brought.

Alison flipped aside the covers and helped Kendra join her in nakedness, roughly pulling her down on top of her. She dug her fingers into the flesh on Kendra's back, and the ravenous, urgent way she clutched at her aroused Kendra even more than when she'd leapt in her arms after tossing out the first handful of grapes.

"Make love to me, Kendra," Alison said breathlessly into her ear. "I want to feel your tongue so badly."

"I'm getting there," she replied. Slowly she made her way down Alison's torso, taunting her with swirls of her tongue on her breasts and stomach. As Alison writhed beneath her she couldn't wait to taste her again, feel her body quiver with pleasure.

"Hurry," Alison whispered. "Before they get out and come looking for us."

Kendra submitted to Alison's command and plunged her tongue between Alison's legs, stroking, flicking, and swirling with measured control.

Apparently, Alison couldn't express her reaction to the building pleasure quietly, so she grabbed a pillow to moan into, removing it only to say, "Faster, faster."

Kendra slowed for a moment, then resumed with full-on speed and pressure, causing Alison to nearly leap off the bed from her orgasm. She climbed up and tried to remove the pillow, but Alison was still gasping loudly.

"I forgot how incredible it is with you," Kendra said in her ear.

"I hadn't," Alison replied, dropping the pillow to her side. "That's why I couldn't let this chance pass. Who knows when we'll get another one…if ever."

Kendra was quiet as she kissed Alison's cheek. Whatever Alison had meant by that last part, now wasn't the time to break it down. She was throbbing and needed Alison to satisfy her. She started grinding on her, but Alison nudged her off and slid her hand all the way down, landing exactly where Kendra ached for it. It hadn't taken Alison's fingers long, as they moved inside and out, to bring her to an intense climax.

Instead of holding her afterward, Alison lay back on the pillow beside her. Kendra wanted to reach over and grab her and pull her back on top, but she didn't. If Alison hadn't done it of her own will, it meant she hadn't wanted to, probably to keep things uncomplicated, as after tonight, they'd both go back to their own worlds in different states. She thought about asking Alison if everything was okay, but again, she didn't want to stir things up. She was the one who broke up with her and then, in true douche-bag fashion, seduced her back into bed again. Yes, she needed to let it be.

Especially because she noticed all the noise had stopped outside. Where was the laughter, the low rumble of voices?

"We have to get dressed," Kendra said as she leapt up and foraged for her clothes in the semi-darkness.

"What's going on? Is the house on fire?"

"Worse. I think they're planning to ambush us up here."

"Bloody hell," Alison said as she pulled on her pants and shoes and everything else she came in with. "How was the bed? You have to put it back in order."

"Oh. Shit." Kendra dragged the covers back up and tried to make it seem as pristine as it was before they tore it up. "Turn the light on."

Alison placed her ear to the door. "I think they're coming upstairs."

Kendra flew to the door, unlocked it, and opened it just in time to see MJ and Violet standing there in nothing but towels. "That's how you come dressed to a raiding party?"

"What are you doing up here?" MJ asked.

"Nothing," Kendra said, trying hard to sound casual. "I was just showing Alison around your beautiful home while you guys were in the tub."

"Em, your house is gorgeous," Alison said. "Have you done much in the way of renovations?"

Violet must've noticed how uncomfortable Kendra felt and turned up the corner of her mouth reassuringly. "Come on, MJ. Let's go get changed before we get pneumonia."

"Where's Danni?" Alison asked.

Violet and MJ looked behind them in the hallway.

"She must be getting dressed downstairs," MJ said.

Alison shoved past them and hurried down the stairs, leaving Kendra to face MJ and Violet on her own.

"What were you two doing up here?" MJ asked with a lurid grin.

"Well…" In a fit of panic, Kendra burst through them like a tight end, shouting, "Not now. Danni could be drowning," as she flew down the stairs.

On her way to check out the hot tub, Kendra nearly collided with Alison. "Did you find her?"

"Her car's gone," she replied. "The little twit took off and left me here."

Kendra loved Danni, but she was peculiar to the nth degree, which spoke volumes about Alison's level of patience as a friend. "Don't be upset. I'll take you to her house."

"Thank you, but now you'll have to drive out of your way. I could just throttle her when she does things like that."

"Don't throttle her," Kendra said calmly. "It might ruin your chances at citizenship."

"The way I feel this minute, it would almost be worth it."

As they came down the stairs, Violet asked where Danni was.

"She's on my shit-list, that's where," Alison replied.

"She just took off?" MJ asked. "Did she even dry herself?"

Alison shrugged.

"Do you need a ride to Danni's?" Violet asked, stunning Kendra.

MJ must've read Kendra's expression. "Kendra's probably gonna drop her off."

"Oh. I just figured I'd offer since I'm closer to Danni's than you," Violet said. "It's on my way."

Standing there with three sets of eyes trained on her, all anticipating her answer for a different reason, Kendra downshifted into ambivalence. "Yeah, no problem. Makes more sense anyway."

"Yes. Yes, it does," Alison said with what Kendra read as wistfulness in her voice. "Well, then, off we go." In a quick motion, she leaned toward Kendra and gave her a limp hug good-bye. "Thank you all for a memorable evening. Hope we can do it again soon."

Kendra's heart collapsed as she watched Alison walk out with her friend. She wanted to be furious with Violet for being so clueless and volunteering a ride. But she couldn't. Her friend was only making what she thought was a nice gesture. After all, immediately after making love, both she and Alison seemed to act like it had never happened, so how was Violet supposed to know Kendra wanted to take her home?

"You want to have a seat and talk about this?" MJ asked.

"Not really," Kendra said, but she followed her to the sofa anyway, where they both plunked down in front of the fire. "I screwed everything up. Completely."

"I don't get it. We were all having such a fun night."

Kendra stared at the dancing flames, not in the mood to elaborate.

"So what did she say about your idea of being friends?"

"I didn't get the chance to discuss it with her."

"You never even brought it up? That was the whole purpose of us crashing Danni's evening with her tonight."

"A good deal of our time alone was spent *not* talking. Besides, the way everything turned out, I'm glad I didn't. I honestly don't think it's possible."

MJ turned to her. "Do you want to try again? Does she?"

They stared at each other for a moment, then turned their eyes to the fireplace.

MJ broke the silence softly. "There's only one way to answer that question."

Kendra closed her eyes and exhaled deeply. All night she'd felt like she'd been holding her breath in anticipation. But in anticipation of what? Throwing gas on the fire of her sexual chemistry with Alison? Yes. They did that. Now, after asking the question that had been rattling around in her mixed-up thoughts, the answer seemed further away than ever.

"I need to sleep on this one," she said as she stood up.

"It's late. Why don't you stay over?"

"Nah. I wouldn't be very good company," she replied through a yawn.

"I didn't ask you to stay so you could entertain me." MJ caught Kendra's yawn as she rose from the sofa. "I have to keep an eye on my star author, make sure she doesn't blow out her brain cells thinking too hard. Your draft deadline is this week."

Kendra clicked her heels together and saluted. "Yes, sir, editor, sir. It'll be ready by Monday at oh-eight-hundred hours sharp."

MJ nudged her lovingly with her shoulder as she walked by and headed to the staircase. "I'm going up. You know where everything is."

Kendra smiled to herself, grateful that MJ was and would always be the pillar of support she could lean on when life tossed her predicaments too big to handle alone.

❖

Once Violet drove away from MJ's house, Alison sank into the passenger seat. Laying eyes on Kendra again after so long had buoyed her into a sort of euphoria, and now that she was gone, she felt depleted. God, Kendra was still so breathtaking. In a low-cut camisole under a black blazer and her short hair swept back and off her forehead, her appearance almost dared Alison to try to look away. From the moment she began speaking to her, Alison knew something was going to happen between them if the slightest opportunity presented itself, although ending up at MJ's house and having full-throttle, broken-up sex in her bed was beyond even her vivid imagination.

Violet had a sappy playlist going with the volume low, but echoes of a Brandi Carlisle song tormented her ears. She'd wanted so badly to have Kendra drive her home, but she didn't want Kendra to know that. She'd already played out the scenario in her head—Kendra would take her back to her house, and they'd make love again, even more wildly uninhibited than before. Then she'd fall asleep in Kendra's arms, feel distraught about leaving her in the morning, and have to contend with Danni's wrath for having blown her off for Kendra.

Yes, whether it felt like it or not, Violet had saved her from a most Shakespearean fate.

She looked over at Violet, who'd put on her glasses for the drive home. As lanky as she was, her seat was as close to the steering wheel as could accommodate her long legs. How the hell had she and Danni managed a friendship without jumping into bed whenever they saw each other? Only one way to find out.

"Violet."

"Hmm?" she replied, never taking her eyes from the road.

"Tell me something. How is your friendship going with Danni?"

"It's great. Why do you ask?"

"Well, I'm sort of asking your advice." She paused to organize her thoughts. "I've missed Kendra's friendship, and I wondered if she has as well."

Violet seemed to hesitate, perhaps bound to secrecy by some unspoken friend code. "I seem to recall her mentioning that she wouldn't mind catching up with you now and then."

"Oh. Okay." She found Violet hard to read. Was she being cagey to protect her friend's emotional interests, or was Kendra truly past their relationship but amenable to a friendship like Danni and Violet had?

"I mean it would be cool if we could all hang out together whenever you make it up to Connecticut," Violet said. "Wouldn't it?" she added when Alison hadn't immediately responded.

"Yes, of course. I had a blast tonight."

"Me, too," Violet said. "I've never seen Danni so animated. You really know how to bring out the party animal in people. Kendra was almost as introverted as Danni, but since she was with you, it's a little easier to get her out of the house now."

Alison found her assessment amusing. "I'm glad I've served a useful purpose to you all."

"I didn't mean it like that," Violet said. "We all really like you."

"I know. I was just being facetious. But I am glad you feel that Kendra's come out of her shell more since meeting me. I'd like to think I've left a positive impact on her."

"For sure," Violet said.

As they neared Danni's house, Alison contemplated spilling to Violet that she was still madly in love with Kendra. But luckily, she'd sobered up and caught herself before making the confession. Other than their physical connection, Kendra hadn't seemed overly interested in anything more. She'd assumed that if she had, her friends would've known about it, and Violet would've used this opportunity to tip her off. Instead she only reinforced Alison's suspicions that Kendra had indeed moved on from her romantic interest in her and was cool with keeping a group friendship on the table.

When Violet pulled into Danni's driveway, Alison noted that the lights were on downstairs. This was a good thing. She wanted to run all her thoughts about this night by Danni and get her take, however limited, on it.

"Thank you so much for the lift," Alison said as she leaned over for hug.

"Anytime. It was great seeing you again."

Violet waited in the driveway until Alison walked up the porch and went in through the unlocked door.

As she'd observed, the lights were on, but Danni had apparently left them on for her and had gone to bed. So much for venting. She decided against waking her in favor of having a chat at breakfast tomorrow.

As she headed into Danni's spare bedroom, she lifted the collar of her shirt to her nose and sniffed the traces of scent Kendra's perfume had left.

❖

After Kendra washed her face and brushed her teeth, she climbed into bed with MJ, who was reading. "You don't mind, do you?"

MJ shook her head, never lifting her eyes from her tablet.

Only fifteen minutes earlier, Kendra had hardly been able to keep her eyes open. Now she was wide awake. "You're not supposed to be staring at a screen right before you go to sleep," she said.

MJ shot her some laser-sharp side eye. "If I don't read when I get in bed each night, I'll never calm my brain enough to actually sleep. You know what I'm like if I don't get enough Zs."

"A bear." Kendra shuddered as she snuggled into the comforter and stared up at her. Despite MJ's tough exterior, Kendra knew the real woman better than anyone. She remembered when her marriage to Patty ended, seemingly out of nowhere. They'd been together twenty plus years, and Patty had gotten a huge promotion at work that meant she'd have to move, but MJ didn't want to. It had caused quite a strain on their relationship, but MJ always maintained that they'd work it out. She'd convinced everyone, especially herself, that they could do the long-distance thing until MJ was ready to move her and her business to Chicago to join Patty. But that day never came—mainly because after about eight months, Patty had met someone else.

Kendra had watched the slow, torturous end unfold on the daily, and her heart broke for her friend. But like all strong, capable, driven women, MJ rallied. She'd licked her wounds and came back better than ever, if not a little more cautious and cynical about love. Kendra admired the shit out of her best friend.

"So…what did you think about Alison tonight?"

MJ looked down from her pile of pillows. "What do you mean? I barely saw her."

"What was your impression of her? Did she seem different to you?"

MJ shrugged. "I don't think I truly got to know her in the three months you were together, but she seemed…I don't know, like Alison."

"Oh. She seemed different to me."

"You'd know better than I would," MJ replied with her eyes still on the tablet screen.

"I don't know. I guess I'm just trying to decipher the mixed signals I got from her tonight."

MJ laid her device in her lap and took off her reading glasses. "You fucked her, didn't you? In these sheets we're lying in now."

Kendra's face nearly combusted. That was not where she was going with this. "Um, that is completely irrelevant to our discussion—"

"Is that why you kept stalling me from going to bed? You wanted the wet spot to dry?"

"Eww, no. At least I don't think there was a wet spot. It all happened so fast, we didn't have enough time to make one."

"What are you getting at, Kendra?"

Kendra sighed. "I…I'm not sure. I was just thinking that maybe—"

"You want my opinion about going back with her?" MJ said. "Having a long-distance relationship, you in Connecticut and her in the City?"

Kendra opened her mouth to answer, but MJ wasn't finished.

"I'm the wrong person to ask if you're looking for someone to tell you that your long-distance relationship with someone thirteen years younger than you will work."

"Um, well, I didn't ask for a Julia Sugarbaker angry monologue from *Designing Women*. I was just going to say it felt good being with her again, both in and out of bed."

"I don't suppose you shared this sentiment with Alison."

Kendra shook her head. "The night sort of got away from me."

"You don't say."

"I meant that we originally planned to have a girls' night out so I could broach the subject of being friends. But actually seeing her again screwed it all up."

MJ placed her tablet on her nightstand. "Look. Tonight happened for a reason. Maybe it wasn't the one you intended, but nevertheless. It's up to you to decide what that reason was."

"I think you covered it with your snide remark about long-distance relationships."

MJ began talking with her hands, a sure sign she was getting heated about the topic. "Well, you know my history with that."

"I do…" Kendra wanted to suggest that maybe their decades-long relationship had already been a boat with a slow leak and that the major change they'd experienced forced the water in. But she didn't. At this point, it would be unnecessary cruelty to justify her own argument. Instead she went with, "You'll meet someone again someday, someone who'll show you that true love isn't just a one-act play."

MJ smiled. "Listen to you, practicing your flowery language about love."

"You'll do it, too, once you meet a person who makes you feel it again."

"Shut up." MJ playfully bopped her with her pillow and turned out the light.

"Good night," Kendra sang in the dark.

She rolled over and faced the wall, balling the covers up to her chin. If Alison was the one who made her feel the way she'd just described, was it smart to part ways without letting her know?

Then again, was it smart to put that out there if she wasn't prepared to act on it?

❖

When she and MJ got word that Anita McDaniel had arranged financing and was gathering a production crew of recent NYU film school grads, Kendra knew her life was going to change radically, at least for a while. It was much sooner than expected, and she feared she didn't have enough time to mentally prepare. But in truth, could she ever adequately prepare for something this huge?

Anita paired her with a budding young screenwriter, and together they would work to adapt Kendra's novel into a screenplay.

"Oh, does that mean I'll have to go into New York City to meet with her?" Kendra had tried not to let her excitement seem too obvious.

"No," MJ replied. "That's what's so awesome about the digital world. Besides, Taylor lives in Westport."

"Oh. Great."

MJ came over and sat at the edge of Kendra's desk. "Ken, this is huge on so many levels."

"I know it is."

"Really? Because you don't seem like you do. What's the matter?"

She wasn't about to elaborate on her disappointment at not having to make regular trips into the City and possibly running into Alison while there. "It's kind of overwhelming. I don't know how to write a movie script."

"You're not writing it. Taylor is. But you're going to be her collaborative partner. And look at it this way. While she's learning how to adapt a book to the screen, you'll learn how to write screenplays. It's an amazing opportunity. This project could take us both in a whole new creative direction."

"Don't tell me you want to get into movie production."

"Why not? If this works out, the sky's the limit for us."

Kendra smiled. Alison aside, this was every bit as amazing as MJ made it seem. She'd never entertained the idea of being a screenwriter, but what writer wouldn't want to learn if given the chance?

Maybe this momentous diversion was the universe's answer to her earlier question of whether to tell Alison how she truly felt.

CHAPTER TWENTY-TWO

Eighteen months later, *The Winding Road* had its indie-film premiere in a small, avant-garde theatre in Greenwich Village. The event drew an impressive crowd, as the Independent Film Guild had recently named the director, Anita McDaniel, an up-and-coming African American filmmaker. Also, "Meredith Hodges" had become a name in the LGBTQ literary world, her second novel debuting in the Amazon Top Twenty, so as many attendees were there for her as for the director.

MJ had rented a car service to drive Kendra, Violet, and Danni into the City, joking that she wanted them to roll up all glamorous for the red-carpet opening like stars used to in the days of old Hollywood. MJ escorted Kendra in a curve-hugging black tuxedo with hot-pink shirt and matching tie. Kendra had yielded to MJ's persistence and wore an off-white, off-the-shoulder dress that dipped in front to accentuate her full bosom, while its skin-tight alterations accentuated her firm backside. Her short, dark hair was fluffed out and slicked back like she was a cross between Emma Thompson and Lana Turner. She couldn't bring herself to admit it out loud, but she felt glamorous that night, something she'd never conceived she could ever feel about her appearance.

Violet and Danni hung back but followed along as they always did: enthusiastic and unobtrusive.

Kendra smiled and waved as a small klatch of photographers from various LGBTQ+ outlets called out their names. It was surreal and spectacular and everything she'd ever thought she'd wanted if all her dreams had come true. But still, something was missing. Amidst all the fanfare, and the love and support of her closest friends, an emptiness resounded within her that she couldn't reconcile. She'd made her most profound dream come true, and it hadn't taken her until the end of her life to do it. Only in her late forties, she still held the promise of the best being yet to come. While she'd had her insecurities like any other person, she'd never been a defeatist. She couldn't dwell on the negative when so much positive loomed before her.

Then, as she and MJ approached the entrance of the theater, what was missing gazed at her from the left side of the entrance doors held open by female ushers.

"Ms. Hodges," she said. "Alison Chatterley with *Empowered Women's Journal*. Can you tell our readers how it feels knowing you're about to see your award-winning debut novel on the big screen?"

Kendra stopped short, retracting her arm from under MJ's.

Alison gently tugged her aside by the arm so the flow of patrons could continue into the theater undisturbed.

They stared at each other for an eternal moment—silent, stationary, completely oblivious to the clamoring all around them.

"Ms. Hodges," Alison said slowly. "Can you spare a moment?"

Kendra nodded, still incapable of forming and articulating a fluent sentence.

"How does it feel to have your successful debut novel adapted into a film?"

"Uh, if you haven't gathered by now, I'm rather speechless. This night? Phew. So far, this night is way beyond any and all expectations."

"What had you expected?"

"To be honest, I don't know. I've spent my whole life watching Hollywood awards shows, secretly imagining I was one of the celebrated walking the red carpet. And even though this isn't anywhere near close to Hollywood's magnitude, it feels…I don't know. It just feels amazing."

"Have you seen the finished product in the screening process?" Alison asked. She was so professional, so engaged, that Kendra literally forgot she was in love with this woman.

"I've seen only bits and pieces. I told MJ that I wanted to wait to see it in its entirety on the night of its premiere. And here we are."

Alison's dreamy blue eyes gleamed with happiness. "Yes. And here we are."

Kendra's mouth opened, but no sound issued forth. She pressed her lips together as she replayed a previous thought: The woman she's in love with. Not used to be, but *is*. She was still in love with Alison.

"I know you must leave and get to your seat," Alison said. "But would I be asking too much for an interview with you after the premiere? I'd meet you anywhere that's convenient for you."

Kendra sighed. "Sure. How about in the lobby after the film?"

"Of course. Okay, well, if you're sure it won't be an imposition to you..."

"It's no trouble." Kendra smirked. "As long as you give the film an honest review."

"That's exactly what I'm here to do." Alison's eyes were tempered with regret and sincerity. "If it's anywhere near as amazing as the novel, you'll be quite pleased with the review."

Kendra wanted to act on the opportunity Alison gave her for a stellar dig about her review-writing talents, but something in her heart moved her to let it pass.

"Kendra," MJ called out frantically from the lobby. "Aren't you coming?"

"I won't keep you," Alison said.

Kendra smiled as she walked into the theater lobby and joined MJ by her side.

"Was that Alison?" MJ asked, seeming almost as surprised as Kendra.

Kendra nodded.

"Are you okay?"

She nodded again and added a cautious smile.

They walked inside the theater and sat in the designated area with the film crew, and while everyone was reaching, stretching, and clamoring to share their comments and observations about the evening ahead, Kendra sat quietly staring at the screen, doing the same in her own head.

❖

When the film was over, Alison sprang up from her seat toward the back of the theater to claim a prime spot in the lobby, one Kendra couldn't miss. The movie was spectacular beyond her expectations.

And she loved that the director had changed one of the main characters in the novel to a woman of color for the already multifaceted film.

As she waited for Kendra to exit the theater into the lobby, she used voice text into her phone to jot down some ideas about the stellar review she couldn't wait to write.

She spotted Kendra and MJ as they walked out and dashed over to them, feeling more like a rabid fan than a journalist. Actually, of all the people there for the screening, Alison was beyond a doubt Kendra's biggest fan.

After they all exchanged pleasantries, Kendra said she'd meet MJ at the reception shortly.

"I can't thank you enough for giving me this exclusive interview," Alison said.

Kendra smiled. "That's sweet, but Anita McDaniel is the one you want to land for an interview tonight. She's the brains behind the film. And the soul."

"There wouldn't be a film if it weren't for your brain," Alison said, adding a flirtatious lilt. "I'd rather start with you."

"Fair enough. Did you like it?"

"It was outstanding." Alison was almost cooing, but she couldn't help it. She was in utter awe of Kendra. Not only was she swept away by the film, but she was also swept up by Kendra's talent and vision and arresting beauty. And that dress. She'd never seen Kendra go full-on femme, and she was killing it.

"Phew. I was afraid the Poison Pen was going to butcher it like she did the novel." Kendra smirked like she had earlier.

Alison flushed at the embarrassing reminder of her past, then quickly regrouped. "There's nothing to butcher. The film was brilliant. Besides, the Poison Pen is no more."

"What? What do you mean?"

"I informed my followers that the Poison Pen would post one farewell review and then the curtain will close on the site. I just don't have the time to keep up with it anymore."

"That must be bittersweet. But I bet you're happy for the reason, though."

"Yes, quite. And speaking of the reason, would you like to begin your interview?"

"Of course. Fire away." Kendra straightened her posture and clutched her hands in front of her like she was about to go on the air.

Alison pressed *record* on her phone. "Your character of Lila is portrayed as a black woman in the film, but the novel gives no descriptions of race."

"It was Anita McDaniel's choice, and it was a brilliant one. When I was creating the characters I hadn't thought out race markers, but when Anita mentioned it to me, I was all for it. As a new author, I needed the reminder to think beyond my own world."

Alison nodded. "As readers, we tend to view characters in ways that reflect ourselves. Did you find you did that in your writing process as well?"

"For sure. But sometimes an individual's perceptions don't reflect the wider world we live in. I'm so grateful Anita McDaniel added her vision to the story when she adapted it. She stayed completely true to the story line and creative content, but the film now has an added authenticity that inclusion always adds to an artistic project. I've learned a lot from her."

"At one point, when Lila disappears, Philomena fears she'll never see her again and wallows in regret for the missed opportunities with her. Do you personally relate to that subject? Missed opportunities?"

The question, loaded with subtext, clearly caught Kendra off guard. "Well, uh…sure. I guess we can all relate to regret for things that weren't said or done at some point in our lives."

"Perhaps one of the benefits of writing is that you can work those things out through your characters."

"Sometimes." Kendra glanced around at the now-empty theater lobby, then turned back to Alison. "Although nothing beats getting a second chance in real life."

"What if you got a second chance? Would you take it?" Alison stopped recording and stuffed her phone into her pocket.

"Are we still talking about crafting character and story line?"

Alison shook her head.

"I guess I'd be a fool to miss the same opportunity twice."

"I'd love to discuss that subject, but I don't want to keep you from the evening's festivities."

"Then come with me."

"Oh, I couldn't crash your party."

"You're not crashing. You're the press. We need a reputable journalist there to cover the event so only a factual account makes it on *Page Six*."

Alison laughed. "Well, if you're looking for someone with journalistic integrity, I'm your gal."

Kendra extended her arm to Alison with a level of chivalry that contrasted to her sexy, feminine outfit, and they headed out.

❖

When they arrived at the café down the street for the premiere reception, Alison excused herself to hit the ladies' room. Kendra grabbed a glass of champagne off a server's tray and headed over to MJ, who'd set up her court by the bar.

"Author! Author!" MJ shouted as she approached.

Demurring from the applause, Kendra took a large sip of champagne. "I know what you've been doing while I was gone," she said and walked into MJ's open arms.

"I'm celebrating, baby, and you should be, too." After a tight hug, she released Kendra from her embrace. "I noticed a really hot woman wander in. I've been tracking her movements for you. Let's go check her out."

"I can't," Kendra replied, eyeing the sign for the restroom.

"What do you mean, you can't?"

"I came with an escort."

MJ stared at her in astonishment. "Alison?"

Kendra nodded.

"Did you ask her, or did she just tag along?"

"I asked her. That was probably dumb, huh?"

"Well, yeah, especially since I think that hottie over there is fangirling you."

Kendra followed MJ's eyes across the room to the corner where two extremely attractive women stood staring back at them. One woman, a stunning femme Latina, raised her drink at Kendra. She raised her glass back and gulped down the rest of her champagne.

"She was looking at me, wasn't she?" Kendra muttered out the side of her mouth.

"Without a doubt." MJ shook her head as if lamenting Kendra's earlier decision. "I can intercept Alison when she comes out of the can if you want."

"Uh, no, thanks. That won't be necessary."

"Suit yourself," MJ said. "I'm gonna go see if Anita needs the companionship of a dapper butch."

"Atta girl," Kendra said with a slap on MJ's back for encouragement.

Alison returned from the ladies' room carrying two glasses of champagne and handed her one. "I hope I didn't just drive MJ off."

Kendra jerked in head in MJ's direction. "Definitely not. She clearly has another agenda."

"Those women over there are beautiful." Alison gazed at them, then turned her eyes to Kendra. "Is one of them meant for you?"

"Uh, no. I didn't order either one of them."

Alison giggled. "I didn't mean for it to sound like that. It's just that they keep looking over here. I wouldn't want to stand in your way if you have other plans."

"Tonight is a special occasion. My only plan is to have a great time, and if that includes getting shit-faced drunk, then so be it." She wolfed down her champagne.

"In England that's any occasion, but I hope your plan is successful. Are you and the girls staying in the City tonight?"

Kendra chuckled. "No. You don't get hotel rooms here until you've hit the big time."

"Based on the success of your first two novels, I'm sure that's around the bend."

"Thank you." Kendra offered a sincere smile. "Maybe third time's a charm. We'll see in a couple of months, I guess, after my third release."

"Fantastic. You're on a roll. You must be rather confident in this one since you're willing to talk about it before it's happened."

"Ha. You remembered that little quirk of mine, which I'm happy to say I've been working through."

"I see that," Alison said. Her eyes and smile were beginning to radiate more than just the glow of friendship. "I remember all your little quirks."

"I would imagine the weird ones would be hard to forget."

"Actually, it's you that's hard to forget, Kendra—as much as I've tried." Alison's bravado slipped down, unintentionally or otherwise, revealing vulnerability that Kendra had never been able to resist.

"I know the feeling," Kendra replied. She stared into Alison's eyes, meeting her vulnerability where it was.

"Why don't you stay over at my place tonight so you can celebrate properly without worrying about a long ride home?"

"Thank you, but I wouldn't want to inconvenience you."

"It's no trouble at all. I'd be happy to find spots for your friends as well."

"Something tells me they won't have any problem on their own, whether they head home after this or not."

"My apartment is the size of a closet, but I've learned to manage. However, it's preferable to a cardboard box in the subway terminal."

Kendra downed her second champagne as quickly as the first into her empty stomach, and now her head was feeling just as bubbly. She knew there would be consequences if she didn't decline the offer, but she was too high on the events of the evening to care. And Alison looked so beautiful and deliciously sexy in her black leather pants and denim jacket and plunging V-neck. But this was her night. She was so caught up in the magic of it all, she couldn't be bothered overthinking.

"Let's see how the evening goes," she said. "You're working, after all."

Alison wasn't giving up. "I'm essentially my own boss. And after you were so gracious to give your time for an interview and then invite me to this fab party, it's the least I could do."

Kendra looked around to make sure MJ wasn't lurking. "If you're sure you wouldn't mind…"

"I'd love to have you over." Alison's bright, amiable tone turned into a sexy, solicitous drawl. "Actually, I'd love to have you sleep in my bed tonight and to wake up next to you in the morning, but if all you'd like is to crash on my sofa, I'm cool with that as well."

With perfect timing, Anita, the film's director, sidled up and handed Kendra a glass of rye and ginger ale. She gave Kendra what came off as a flirty grin.

After their lingering visual exchange, Anita walked off, and she turned back to Alison, whose countenance had changed. Oh, shit. Was she that obviously gushing over Anita's attention?

"Well, I think I just got my answer," Alison said and started walking away.

This was not the turn Kendra wanted her night to take. She twisted in a moment of indecision, her mood cranking tighter with every step farther Alison took. "Wait." She sprinted through the crowd after her. "Alison."

Alison whirled around, ready to say something, but her eyes did all the talking.

"My answer is yes," Kendra said. "Do you want to get out of here?"

"I dunno." Alison glanced around the room, seeming unsettled.

"If you still have some interviews, I'll wait. I'm in no rush."

"I don't have anyone else to interview. All I came here for is you, but if you're otherwise attached to someone else, I don't want to keep you from her."

The pieces came together in Kendra's bleary mind. "What? Oh, Anita? No, that's…Nothing's going on there. Actually, MJ is working her charm on that. They have some history anyway."

"Well, you seemed to have had that response queued up rather quickly. Look, Kendra. I came here to work, to write about your meteoric rise in the lesfic world. And if the truth be known, I was also hoping we could speak on a personal level. But I can see now that you've moved on to new worlds, and I don't want to take up any more of your—"

Kendra couldn't bear to listen to her any longer. She clutched Alison's face in her hands and pulled her in for a deep, long kiss. "Take me back to your place."

She grabbed Alison's hand, and they flew through the bar from the private back room and out the door.

"Wait." Alison stopped her on the sidewalk. "Isn't it terribly rude of you to run out on your friends and that charming film director who clearly fancies you?"

"I guarantee you MJ's already forgotten about me and has made Anita forget about me, too."

"Oh. Thank God for MJ." Alison's smile outshone the streetlight they were standing under. She tugged on Kendra's arm, and they ran toward the subway entrance to Alison's uptown apartment.

The thought of making love to Alison till dawn ignited her more than anything else that had happened during that surreal, magical night.

CHAPTER TWENTY-THREE

The moment they entered Alison's tiny apartment on 127th Street, all the modesty she'd had about how pathetically small it was had vanished as soon as Kendra pushed her against the wall. Alison kicked the door shut and wound her arms around Kendra's neck, locking her in tight as they kissed wildly. She tasted the sweet bitterness of rye on Kendra's tongue as she explored her mouth. The throbbing between her legs was too urgent to ignore, so she took the reins and pulled Kendra toward her bedroom, never letting their lips disconnect, even for a second.

"I've missed you so much, Kendra." Alison was already panting in anticipation as she pulled Kendra's dress off her shoulders and began kissing her neck.

"I've missed you too, baby," Kendra whispered. She tilted her head back, apparently surrendering to Alison's dominance.

"Blimey, this dress is tight."

"I don't think you're going to get it off on your own."

Kendra dragged the dress down, letting it drop to her ankles once it cleared her hips. Her coral, lace, half-cup bra presented her full breasts like a marble sculpture.

She couldn't contain the arousal raging through her as she clawed at the back of the bra to unleash her beautiful, naked chest. She shoved Kendra down onto the bed and hopped on top of her, flinging the last stitch of her clothing from Kendra's body. Sitting up on top of her, she then ripped her own clothes off until they were both gloriously nude in the room illuminated by street lights outside her building.

When she lay on top of Kendra and their hot skin and wetness melded together, Kendra let out a whimper of anticipation. Alison couldn't wait to put her tongue down into Kendra and satisfy her ache, but she needed to look into her eyes and see that, after all this time, she still felt the same way.

She cradled Kendra's head in her hands and ran her lips sensually over hers. Kendra opened her eyes and looked up, seeming startled by the tenderness Alison added to their animalistic attraction to each other.

"I need you, Kendra," she whispered as sincerely as she'd ever uttered anything. She instantly felt Kendra's fingers slid inside and stroke her. She groaned against the pleasure, deciding now wasn't the proper time for a heart-to-heart.

"I need to taste you," Kendra replied. She pulled at Alison's torso until she slid up and lowered herself onto Kendra's face. Lost in her desire, she rocked back and forth in harmony with Kendra's tongue, clamping her hands on the headboard for control.

Kendra's sex was on fire as she listened to Alison's groans become louder and more unrestrained as her climax swept her away. She loved making Alison cum, loved how fully she submitted to her charge. But it wasn't about control. It had everything to do with the trust Alison had in her…in them.

She nudged a limp Alison onto her back and gently ran her fingertips over her skin as her breathing returned to normal. Once it had, Alison produced a silky scarf from her nightstand and draped it around Kendra's eyes. At first Kendra was taken aback at the swiftness of the move, but she laid her head back down on the pillow and submitted to whatever Alison had in mind.

Her physical senses now heightened, she felt Alison's tongue and lips roaming over her stomach and breasts as she anticipated how Alison planned to use her hands. As if reading her mind, she raised Kendra's wrists over her head and tied them with what felt like another silky scarf.

Kendra lay there, tantalizingly powerless to Alison's will. The blind anticipation was the most erotic thing she'd ever experienced. Here she was in her late forties, experiencing the pleasure of relinquishing complete control to another, someone she'd loved and desired and needed in her life.

She let out a giggle when Alison's hot lips startled her as they landed on hers.

"How do you feel?" Alison whispered directly into her ear.

"Curious," Kendra replied.

"Oh, yeah? What are you curious about, love?"

"When you're going to let me cum," Kendra said, writhing beneath her.

"So you're ready, are you?"

Kendra shivered as fingers glided over her wetness. "So ready." She licked her lips. "Please."

"Oooh, I love the begging. That's a nice touch."

Kendra giggled again in the darkness, then felt warm fingers slowly making their way inside her. Alison maneuvered them with expertise, filling Kendra with sensation. Kendra could barely contain herself as the speed of the thrusts increased and brought her to a deep, shuddering orgasm. She lay there as she radiated satisfaction.

Alison untethered her bindings and cuddled up next to her, molding herself into Kendra's side.

"That was incredible," Kendra said. "How did you learn to be so uninhibited?"

Alison lifted her head from Kendra's shoulder. "Dare I say before I met you, I was a good student?"

Kendra chuckled. "Once again, I find myself thanking the good teachers of the past." Then an appalling thought encroached. "So how many teachers have you had since we broke up?"

"None."

"None? Come on." Kendra scoffed, assuming Alison had saved her biggest lie for last.

"I swear to you, Kendra. I've had a few dates, but I just can't invest in anyone—emotionally, sexually, whatever. If I'm honest, I haven't been able to get over you. Not only are you insufferably desirable, but I'm madly in love with you."

"Still? It's been over a year and a half."

Alison propped up on her elbow. "Kendra, I never stopped loving you. I'd just learned to live without you. That's what I meant earlier when I said I needed you."

Kendra flushed. "Oh, I'm sorry. I thought you meant sexually."

"No, but I certainly wasn't about to stop you in the middle of what you were doing." Alison resumed her position and snuggled up again.

Kendra sighed. Was Alison about to suggest reconciliation? As much as the thought appealed to her, she bristled at the idea of a long-distance relationship. How could they make something as complicated as that work, being in such different places in their lives, both physically and mentally? This night together was incredible, but she couldn't help wondering if the all-consuming bliss was worth how it would feel leaving alone in the morning.

"You're suddenly quiet," Alison said. "Have I said the wrong thing?"

"Not at all." Kendra paused to formulate her thought. "I'm just trying to figure out where we go from here."

"To sleep, I would imagine."

"You know what I mean," Kendra replied.

"I do know." Alison's playful tone dissipated. "But I was hoping we could save that conversation for the morning. Do you have to rush home?"

"Uh-uh," Kendra uttered. "MJ's already said she's expecting me to be as hung over as she probably will be."

"Goodness. I hope I didn't ruin your celebration. She must be hating me right now."

"No, no. She knew how much I needed this night with you. If nothing else, it was the closure I needed."

Alison sat up, pulling the covers up with her. "Is that all this night is to you? Some sort of rite of passage so you can move ahead with a clean slate?"

"God, no, Alison." Kendra started getting frazzled. "I'm still in love with you, too, but sometimes that's not always enough. Your life is on a completely different trajectory from when I met you. That's a wonderful thing for you."

"Not if it forced me to choose only one wonderful thing. Kendra, I love you. I want us to have another go at it. Don't you?"

"Well, yes, but—"

"No. There are no 'buts' in this. You either love me enough to want to make it work or you don't."

Kendra's throat felt like it was about to close as she grew more flustered. This was not even remotely close to how this night was supposed to turn out. “Alison, I can’t move to New York.”

“Who’s bloody asking you to?” She flipped the covers off and grabbed a robe from behind her door. “I’m sleeping on the couch.” She stormed into the living room, shutting the bedroom door behind her.

Kendra exhaled in a groan and stared at the ceiling. She wasn’t cut out for this level of drama. Maybe she should just slink out of the apartment at sunrise and leave all this in her rearview mirror. Alison would probably be better off if she were free to pursue the life of adventure the City promised a young, beautiful, intelligent woman.

The scream of a fire engine siren reminded Kendra where she was and how easy it would be to walk away from this frantic place and return to the peace of her solitary life in Connecticut.

And leave another important relationship to languish in the recesses of her mind. No. She’d had enough of that, and Alison was the person she could turn the page with.

Energized with new purpose, she wrestled to get out from under the pile of covers. When she stood up, she realized she could either put her dress back on or march out into the living room totally naked. In either case, it would be hard for anyone to take her seriously as she pleaded her case. She threw on her underwear, reached into Alison’s dresser drawer, and pulled out the first thing she grasped.

“Alison, we have to talk this out,” she said, standing by the sofa where Alison was curled up. “I am not leaving this apartment until we’ve settled this matter once and for all.”

Alison looked up at her and burst into laughter.

“What’s so funny?” Kendra asked. She looked down at the T-shirt she’d selected in the dim light and found the answer. “‘Tell ’em to feck off. Vote Father Jack,’” she read aloud. “What the hell am I wearing?”

Alison continued giggling as she sat up and turned on a lamp, revealing the image of a disheveled old cleric. “Father Jack was a sitcom character on the telly in the UK. He was an old, drunken Irish priest.”

“Perfect. You and I are making just about as much sense as that right now.”

“That’s my favorite sleeping shirt.” Alison pulled her blanket snugly around her.

Kendra dropped down next to her. "We're arguing at three in the morning after having the most beautiful, intensely intimate experience together. Have we lost our minds?"

"I dunno. Perhaps we have." Alison twisted toward Kendra. "I just know that I'm crazy about you, and it occasionally makes me do crazy things. Seducing you on the biggest night of your life after not seeing you for over a year is about the craziest thing to date. I'm sorry if my turning up out of nowhere has stressed you out."

"Alison." Kendra took her hand and cupped it in both of hers. "If I hadn't wanted any of this, I could've said no at any point during the evening." She paused for a deep breath. "I want it all with you, but the challenges that lie ahead of us scare me. I don't know if I can handle it all, especially having a much younger girlfriend who has the world at her feet."

"Having the world at my feet won't mean anything if you aren't in it."

Kendra cringed at the tears pooling in Alison's eyes as she fought back her own. How could she walk away from a woman so willing to gamble on her? Even if the odds were against them, didn't Kendra owe it to Alison, to herself, to give it a sincere try? "So, are you saying you wanna give this commuter-relationship-thing a shot?"

"Absolutely." Alison pulled her in for a kiss, then wrapped her blanketed arms around her.

Kendra pressed her lips into Alison's hair and allowed the warmth of their commitment to quiet any temptation to worry about the future. Then the words "I love you" floated out in a whisper.

"God, I love you, too." Alison nuzzled closer and kissed Kendra's neck. "How about we go back to bed now?"

"Great idea. But I'm wearing this T-shirt to bed," Kendra replied as they got up and strolled toward the bedroom. "Maybe forever."

"You will not pilfer my Father Jack shirt," Alison replied. "I'm not above tearing it off you if I have to."

Kendra chuckled as they climbed back into bed, and soon she fell into a peaceful sleep in Alison's arms.

CHAPTER TWENTY-FOUR

Kendra spent the morning on her deck writing scenes for her fourth novel, a second-chance love story she was particularly motivated to write. After her third novel was well received, she exhaled all the insecurities and angst that came with writing after a successful, award-winning debut. MJ and Anita had been encouraging her to shift over to screenwriting since the film version of *The Winding Road* was moderately successful on an LGBTQ streaming service and use her real name.

It was a flattering suggestion, but Kendra wasn't ready to abandon the pseudonym she'd chosen to honor her mother. She also wasn't ready to commercialize her storytelling and have it hacked up to please producers, much to MJ's consternation.

After writing a particularly naughty sex scene to end her session, she put her laptop away, had some lunch, and attended to the chores she'd put off all weekend.

With Alison set to move in with her next weekend, Kendra needed to clear out closet space for her. She pulled out several plastic storage containers filled with who-knew-what and opened the one full of cards and letters gathered through the years. Digging around, she discovered a small pile of letters tied together with ribbon. Their worn edges and discoloration indicated their age. Assuming they were notes she and MJ had written each other in the age before computers, she pulled the ribbon open and unfolded the one on top.

But it wasn't a letter from MJ or any other friend. It was a letter to her father from her mother. She'd recognized that impeccable cursive writing from the numerous birthday and Christmas cards in which her mom had penned the most poignant words to her only daughter. She'd forgotten things like this existed because, when her father sold the family home, Kendra had grabbed whatever of her mother's personal effects she could and hidden them, as she couldn't bring herself to go through them.

Now some thirty years after her mom's passing, she began reading without reservation. The date was about two weeks before she died.

Dear Steven,

I can't believe this is how our love story ends, at least here on earth. I'm sorry I couldn't beat this. I fought so hard not to leave you and Kendra and Ryan. My heart breaks knowing I'll miss so much of their lives as they grow into adults, but I have complete faith that you'll guide them every step of the way. I still smile when I think of how ecstatic you were when Kendra was born and then Ryan. You're the best dad for our children I could've ever asked for. The only thing I hope for when I'm gone is that you all stay as close as you are now, no matter what the future brings. That would be the best way to honor my time here on earth with you. If there's any way I can watch over you all, you know I will.

Yours forever,
Meredith xoxoxo

Kendra wiped away her tears and read it again, minus the cloudy eyes. Her heart was heavy and felt anchored to the floor in her bedroom. Without even knowing it, she'd been ignoring her mother's final wish, the one and only thing she'd asked for. At that, she covered her face with her hands and wept. Loudly. Gutturally. If her sobs had the power to summon her mother's spirit, surely it was around her now.

After she finally cried herself into silence, she searched the stack of letters and read how her parents' love affair had remained constant throughout their twenty years together. After a swell and fall of anger at the universe for its random cruelty, she felt grateful that it had brought Alison back to her. They were starting their journey of forever this weekend, and she was determined to appreciate every moment they had together.

She picked up her phone and texted Ryan. No sooner had the message gone through when Alison FaceTimed her.

"Hey," Kendra said. "I was just thinking about you."

"I've been thinking of you all day," Alison said. "I just got home from the office. Editorial meetings." She shook her head in resignation.

"I can't wait to see you Friday," Kendra said and heard the melancholy in her voice.

"Are you okay, darling? You look like you were crying."

"Yeah. I'm fine. I just came across some old letters that belonged to my parents. They'd been tucked away for decades."

"Wow. And they made you cry? I'm sorry."

Kendra laughed lightly through a sniffle. "Don't be. I'm glad I found them as I was making room for you. It was kind of cathartic and enlightening."

"How so?"

"It's all signaling much-needed change. I was static for a long time, which wasn't serving me. So thank you for coming into my life."

"Aww, baby. Have you been drinking?"

Kendra giggled. "No. I have not, but I'll probably have a few glasses of wine with dinner."

"Are you sure you're okay? I can hop a train and come there tonight if you need me."

"You're so sweet. No. I'm fine, really. I'm actually busy getting the place ready for your arrival."

"I can hardly wait," Alison said. "I'm more suited to having iguanas for coworkers than people. Unless I have to take them out for walks on my lunch break each day, like I used to have to do for Carmen's dog."

"Only in the summer. They hate snow."

"What?"

Kendra chuckled at Alison's expression. "Kidding."

"I bloody well hope so," Alison said. "But I'd do it for you if it made you smile like that."

"You always make me smile. I'm so ready for a lifetime of big, daily Alison smiles after waking up to you each morning."

"Oh, the rest of the week is going to drag by."

"But it'll be so worth the wait."

"I know." Alison smiled and fell back onto her pillow. "I have to get ready and meet Carmen uptown for a farewell dinner, but I just want to lie here and stare at your face."

"Ugh. Don't do that." Kendra picked at her messy hair. "Go and have a good time, and don't forget to say good night to me later."

"Only if you promise to talk dirty to me."

"How about I read you the new sex scene I wrote today? It'll probably sound familiar."

"Oh, I'd like that. It's a date."

When Kendra saw the text bar from Ryan appear, she ended their call until later. She never thought she'd ever type this, but she suggested that he invite their father to join them for their next billiards date. Honoring her mother's memory by using her name as a pseudonym was a nice, symbolic gesture, but after reading that letter, she realized her mother had been waiting a long time for her to make peace with her father.

Hopefully, it was what he wanted, too.

❖

By Saturday night, Alison was settled into Kendra's condo. They'd worked through the day Saturday to organize things and get Alison's belongings put away in their new spaces. Then after an order of Chinese takeout and a bottle of wine, they went to bed to watch a movie and fell asleep halfway into it.

Kendra woke early the next morning, the little spoon tucked snugly in Alison's arms, and lay there listening to Alison breathe and the songs of birds waft in through the open windows. She closed her eyes and savored the serenity until Sergio jumped up with a loud meow to inform her that his food bowl was empty.

"Shh," she said as she scooped him in to be the even littler spoon.

"I see that bloke's an early riser like you," Alison said in a gravelly voice.

"Sorry we woke you. It's nearly impossible to teach a cat manners."

Alison giggled and reached her arm over Kendra to scratch Sergio's head. "You didn't wake me. I was already stirring before he hopped up."

Kendra turned over, and they smiled at each other from across their pillows. "Good morning," she said.

A radiant smile appeared on Alison's sleepy face. "Good morning."

"How did you sleep?"

"I can't remember when I've had a better night's rest. Certainly not at Carmen's when she'd have phone sex with her girlfriend fifteen feet away me."

"Ugh. Well, I can assure you nothing like that will be going on here…unless, of course, you're involved, too."

"What shall we do? Take out our cell phones and sit across the room from each other?"

Kendra chuckled. "That's a great idea. It'll be like a 3D Zoom meeting."

"Hmm. Let's keep that one in the queue," Alison said and kissed her tenderly on the lips. "I love you."

"I love you, too," Kendra whispered back.

Apparently, Sergio thought they'd had sufficient time to say good morning and began meowing rather insistently.

"Let's be sure to revisit this later." Kendra flipped the covers off and padded into the kitchen with Sergio rubbing against her ankles. After filling his bowl, she put on water for Alison's tea and dropped a pod of dark roast in the Keurig for herself. What should she make them for breakfast on their first morning as a live-in couple? It had been so long since she'd lived with anyone, that for a time she believed she'd never want to go there again. But having lost and won Alison back, the vision for the future she wanted became clear.

After breakfast, Kendra relaxed on the deck with her second cup of coffee while Alison tidied up the kitchen. She watched a robin poke at the wet grass and slurp up worms, contemplating how they should spend this gorgeous spring Sunday.

"What do you think, babe?" She called through the open sliders. "Kayaks or bikes?"

"Either sounds fab to me," Alison replied as she stepped out onto the deck. She handed Kendra her cell. "Your brother texted you."

"Thanks." Kendra read the text, and suddenly, the Disney-movie feel to her life for the last twenty-four hours evaporated with the morning dew.

In the text, Ryan informed her that her father had called him to cancel on their billiards night on Monday and that he would call her. She typed back "whatever" and sipped her coffee. "Fuck…you…" The phrase hissed out as she felt her temples pulse. She should've known better than to expect her father to inconvenience himself on her behalf. She should've known, but that didn't stop her from allowing a germ of hope, or was happiness a better word, to grow in her heart.

"What's wrong, love?"

"My father is blowing us off tomorrow night. Big surprise."

"I'm sorry. Is he okay?"

Kendra looked up at her concerned expression. Funny how the thought of whether he was okay hadn't even occurred to her. "He must be. Ryan said he was going to call me, I guess to explain. I ought to text him back to tell my father not to bother."

"Aren't you even a bit curious as to what he has to say?"

Kendra nodded reluctantly, more than *a bit*.

"Come on." Alison pulled her up from the chair. "In the meantime, let's go for that bike ride. It'll help clear out your head."

❖

After their morning bike ride along a scenic trail, Kendra showered and prepared a bag of microwave popcorn in anticipation of settling in on the sofa for an afternoon movie or two. Quiet Sundays were what life was all about. Alison had stepped out for a quick grocery run for the week, so when Kendra's cell starting ringing, she'd assumed Alison had a question about something at the store. She hurried into the living room to grab her phone on the coffee table, not at all expecting the number on the screen.

"Hello, Kendra? It's your father."

"Hey. How are you?"

"Oh, I'm fine. How are you doing?"

"Fine," she said, dragging out the word.

"Do you have a minute to talk?"

"Sure."

"Would you mind if I dropped by?"

"Okay. What time works for you?"

"How about now? I'm parked outside your unit."

Kendra glanced around to make sure the house was neat and organized, then rushed to the front door. She looked out the side window, and sure enough, his pickup truck was parked in front. "Sure."

When she opened the door he handed her a house plant. "Joyce said I should bring you a little something for your place."

"Thank you. That's very nice of you. Come in." She stepped aside, finding it weird that she'd lived in her townhouse for over eight years, and this was the first time her father had been in it other than the day Ryan asked him to help move her in. "Can I get you anything? Coffee? A beer? Leftover lo mein?"

"I'll take a beer," he said. "As long as it's not that sour junk your brother drinks."

"No sours allowed in this house. How about a lager?"

He nodded. She grabbed two bottles of beer from the fridge and led him out onto the deck, where they sat in uncomfortable silence side by side in chairs facing the small yard behind her unit. Kendra began fidgeting. Was he going to speak, or were they just going to stare out into the afternoon sky like an "American Gothic" painting? She cleared her throat to make sure she was still alive.

"So," he said, as if taking a stage cue. "I wanted to thank you for inviting me to play pool with you and your brother. Sounds like it'd be a hoot."

"Then why did you cancel?" Either it was her imagination or her voice had just sounded like a disappointed little girl's.

He finally turned and faced her. "I didn't so much cancel as I'd like to reschedule. I wanted to talk with just you first, to sort of clear the air before meeting up with Ryan."

"Okay." Kendra looked out at the yard again and went still.

"I uh, I don't know how to apologize for not being the father you needed…other than to say I'm sorry. I know it isn't enough, but it's all I've got."

"Are you dying or something?"

He chuckled. "No, no. Not yet anyway. It's just that I've been enjoying my relationship with my adult son so much that I thought why not try to double my pleasure by having a real relationship with my daughter, too."

Wanting desperately to keep an open mind to him, she fought off her decades-old impulse to lash out, first for his failings as a parent and then for his nonchalance. But this was what her mother had wanted all along. She had to try to make it work—for her.

"I mean I know we have our work cut out for us," he said when she didn't answer. "But if it's all right with you, I'd like to meet you where you are. Whatever you need, you know? I'll do what I can for you, Kendra."

"Thank you." Something was stirring in her, but she couldn't organize her thoughts to determine what it was.

"I mean it," he said. "You want to scream at me? Hit me? Go ahead. Whatever it takes, I…"

When his voice trailed off, she turned to him again. His eyes looked glassy, as if genuine emotion had made its way up to them for the first time in years. He looked so old. She just needed to study his face for a moment. Finally, she said, "Would you walk me down the aisle if I asked Alison to marry me?"

"You're getting married?" His eyes flashed with glints of surprise and disapproval that instantly faded.

Kendra tempered her knee-jerk reaction of frustration with him. "Not yet, but yeah. It's in my future."

"You'd really want me to?"

She thought she detected sincerity in his question, and it made her smile. "I'll be honest with you. If Mom were here, I'd want her to."

He chuckled. "If Mom were here, neither one of us would have a say in the matter."

She embraced the moment of tenderness and laughed, too. It felt good. "But since she's not, you'd be okay filling in for her?"

"I'd be more than okay. It would be an honor." He reached for her hand, then pulled back, seeming unsure if he had the right to. "When is the big day?"

"Not for a while, but I'm glad to know I can check off that box."

"She seems like a nice girl, uh, woman," he said. "From what Ryan tells me. I'm happy for you. And I know your mother would be, too."

Kendra's eyes watered. Although she'd constantly thought about her mother, talking about her again with her father brought her a sense of peace, as though her connection to her mom was somehow made stronger sharing her memory with the only other person on earth who'd known and loved her as deeply as she did.

"You have to meet her. If you can hang around, she should be home from the store any minute."

"Sure. I have time."

❖

When Alison came back from the supermarket, she'd assumed the pickup truck parked out front belonged to Kendra's brother. But once she got inside and saw that Kendra was out on the deck with a man whose voice she didn't recognize, she smiled. Instead of going out and interrupting their conversation, which sounded more like reminiscing than a serious exchange, she stood by the open sliders to listen.

Kendra's voice sounded lighter and her laughter a little freer. Something was happening to her, and as badly as Alison wanted to witness and be part of it, she hung back and put the groceries away as quietly as she could.

"Hey, babe," Kendra said as they came inside. "I'm so glad you're home. My dad was just leaving. Dad, this is Alison."

"Steve Blake," he said, extending his hand. "Pleasure to meet you."

"It's nice to finally meet you," Alison replied. "I've heard so much about you."

"Don't believe any of it," he said with a chuckle.

When Kendra grinned at his quip, Alison saw where she'd gotten her dazzling smile. "Well, I don't want to interrupt your visit, so I could go—"

"No. You're fine," Kendra said. "We're all having dinner together over at Ryan's this week."

"Yeah. We'll have more time to talk then," he said, glancing awkwardly between them. "Great to meet you, Alison."

They said their good-byes as they walked him to the front door.

"Dad."

He turned around, and Kendra surprised them all by giving him a quick, tentative hug. After Alison did the same, he left.

"Well, that was quite a surprise," Alison said as they headed toward the living-room sofa and plopped down together. "You should've seen my face when I walked in and heard his voice."

"You should've seen mine when he called and said he was outside."

"It seemed like it went well."

"It did." Kendra raised her legs onto the coffee table and crossed them. "It's definitely a start."

Alison slipped down and snuggled against her. "I'm so happy for you. It must feel like the weight of the world is off you."

"It feels good to know I've honored my mother's final wish. That's brought me more peace than you can imagine."

"And it should only get better from here."

"Yeah," Kendra said and casually added, "Now I have someone to walk me down the aisle if you ever decide you want to marry me."

Alison popped her head up. "It's not at all a question of 'if.'"

They exchanged tender kisses, then settled in for a Sunday-afternoon movie.

About the Author

Jean Copeland is an award-winning, multi-genre lesfic author, blogger, and educator from Connecticut. She enjoys collaborating with her author friends, and when not writing novels, she's dashing off political blogs on her Wordpress page, chatting with the women on *The Weekly Wine Down* podcast, or sampling a plethora of Connecticut-made alcoholic beverages. *Poison Pen* is her eighth novel.

Books Available From Bold Strokes Books

Flight SQA016 by Amanda Radley. Fastidious airline passenger Olivia Lewis is used to things being a certain way. When her routine is changed by a new, attractive member of the staff, sparks fly. (978-1-63679-045-9)

Home Is Where The Heart Is by Jenny Frame. Can Archie make the countryside her home and give Ash the fairytale romance she desires? Or will the countryside and small village life all be too much for her? (978-1-63555-922-4)

Moving Forward by PJ Trebelhorn. The last person Shelby Ryan expects to be attracted to Iris Calhoun, the sister of the man who killed her wife four years and three thousand miles ago. (978-1-63555-953-8)

Poison Pen by Jean Copeland. Debut author Kendra Blake is finally living her best life until a nasty book review and exposed secrets threaten her promising new romance with aspiring journalist Alison Chatterley. (978-1-63555-849-4)

Seasons for Change by KC Richardson. Love, laughter, and trust develop for Shawn and Morgan throughout the changing seasons of Lake Tahoe. (978-1-63555-882-1)

Summer Lovin' by Julie Cannon. Three different women, three exotic locations, one unforgettable summer. What do you think will happen? (978-1-63555-920-0)

Unbridled by D. Jackson Leigh. A visit to a local stable turns into more than riding lessons between a novel writer and an equestrian with a taste for power play. (978-1-63555-847-0)

VIP by Jackie D. In a town where relationships are forged and shattered by perception, sometimes even love can't change who you really are. (978-1-63555-908-8)

Yearning by Gun Brooke. The sleepy town of Dennamore has an irresistible pull on those who've moved away. The mystery Darian Benson and Samantha Pike uncover will change them forever, but the love they find along the way just might be the key to saving themselves. (978-1-63555-757-2)

A Turn of Fate by Ronica Black. Will Nev and Kinsley finally face their painful past and relent to their powerful, forbidden attraction? Or will facing their past be too much to fight through? (978-1-63555-930-9)

Desires After Dark by MJ Williamz. When her human lover falls deathly ill, Alex, a vampire, must decide which is worse, letting her go or condemning her to everlasting life. (978-1-63555-940-8)

Her Consigliere by Carsen Taite. FBI agent Royal Scott swore an oath to uphold the law, and criminal defense attorney Siobhan Collins pledged her loyalty to the only family she's ever known, but will their love be stronger than the bonds they've vowed to others, or will their competing allegiances tear them apart? (978-1-63555-924-8)

In Our Words: Queer Stories from Black, Indigenous, and People of Color Writers. Stories Selected by Anne Shade and Edited by Victoria Villaseñor. Comprising both the renowned and emerging voices of Black, Indigenous, and People of Color authors, this thoughtfully curated collection of short stories explores the intersection of racial and queer identity. (978-1-63555-936-1)

Measure of Devotion by CF Frizzell. Disguised as her late twin brother, Catherine Samson enters the Civil War to defend the Constitution as a Union soldier, never expecting her life to be altered by a Gettysburg farmer's daughter. (978-1-63555-951-4)

Not Guilty by Brit Ryder. Claire Weaver and Emery Pearson's day jobs clash, even as their desire for each other burns, and a discreet sex-only arrangement is the only option. (978-1-63555-896-8)

Opposites Attract: Butch/Femme Romances by Meghan O'Brien, Aurora Rey & Angie Williams. Sometimes opposites really do attract. Fall in love with these butch/femme romance novellas. (978-1-63555-784-8)

Under Her Influence by Amanda Radley. On their path to #truelove, will Beth and Jemma discover that reality is even better than illusion? (978-1-63555-963-7)

Swift Vengeance by Jean Copeland, Jackie D & Erin Zak. A journalist becomes the subject of her own investigation when sudden strange, violent visions summon her to a summer retreat and into the arms of a killer's possible next victim. (978-1-63555-880-7)

Wasteland by Kristin Keppler & Allisa Bahney. Danielle Clark is fighting against the National Armed Forces and finds peace as a scavenger, until the NAF general's daughter, Katelyn Turner, shows up on her doorstep and brings the fight right back to her. (978-1-63555-935-4)

When In Doubt by VK Powell. Police officer Jeri Wylder thinks she committed a crime in the line of duty but can't remember, until details emerge pointing to a cover-up by those close to her. (978-1-63555-955-2)

A Woman to Treasure by Ali Vali. An ancient scroll isn't the only treasure Levi Montbard finds as she starts her hunt for the truth—all she has to do is prove to Yasmine Hassani that there's more to her than an adventurous soul. (978-1-63555-890-6)

Before. After. Always. by Morgan Lee Miller. Still reeling from her tragic past, Eliza Walsh has sworn off taking risks, until Blake Navarro turns her world right-side up, making her question if falling in love again is worth it. (978-1-63555-845-6)

Bet the Farm by Fiona Riley. Lauren Calloway's luxury real estate sale of the century comes to a screeching halt when dairy farm heiress, and one-night stand, Thea Boudreaux calls her bluff. (978-1-63555-731-2)

Cowgirl by Nance Sparks. The last thing Aren expects is to fall for Carol. Sharing her home is one thing, but sharing her heart means sharing the demons in her past and risking everything to keep Carol safe. (978-1-63555-877-7)

Give In to Me by Elle Spencer. Gabriela Talbot never expected to sleep with her favorite author—certainly not after the scathing review she'd given Whitney Ainsworth's latest book. (978-1-63555-910-1)

Hidden Dreams by Shelley Thrasher. A lethal virus and its resulting vision send Texan Barbara Allan and her lovely guide, Dara, on a journey up Cambodia's Mekong River in search of Barbara's mother's mystifying past. (978-1-63555-856-2)

In the Spotlight by Lesley Davis. For actresses Cole Calder and Eris Whyte, their chance at love runs out fast when a fan's adoration turns to obsession. (978-1-63555-926-2)

Origins by Jen Jensen. Jamis Bachman is pulled into a dangerous mystery that becomes personal when she learns the truth of her origins as a ghost hunter. (978-1-63555-837-1)

Unrivaled by Radclyffe. Zoey Cohen will never accept second place in matters of the heart, even when her rival is a career, and Declan Black has nothing left to give of herself or her heart. (978-1-63679-013-8)

A Fae Tale by Genevieve McCluer. Dovana comes to terms with her changing feelings for her lifelong best friend and fae, Roze. (978-1-63555-918-7)

Accidental Desperados by Lee Lynch. Life is clobbering Berry, Jaudon, and their long romance. The arrival of directionless baby dyke MJ doesn't help. Can they find their passion again—and keep it? (978-1-63555-482-3)

Always Believe by Aimée. Greyson Walsden is pursuing ordination as an Anglican priest. Angela Arlingham doesn't believe in God. Do they follow their vocation or their hearts? (978-1-63555-912-5)

Courage by Jesse J. Thoma. No matter how often Natasha Parsons and Tommy Finch clash on the job, an undeniable attraction simmers just beneath the surface. Can they find the courage to change so love has room to grow? (978-1-63555-802-9)

I Am Chris by R Kent. There's one saving grace to losing everything and moving away. Nobody knows her as Chrissy Taylor. Now Chris can live who he truly is. (978-1-63555-904-0)